THE
INVISIBLE MOON

J. ROBERT DIFULGO

D1087721

THE INVISIBLE MOON

iUniverse books may be ordered through booksellers or by contacting:

iUniverse
1663 Liberty Drive
Bloomington, IN 47403
www.iuniverse.com
1-800-Authors (1-800-288-4677)

Because of the dynamic nature of the Internet, any web addresses or links contained in this book may have changed since publication and may no longer be valid. The views expressed in this work are solely those of the author and do not necessarily reflect the views of the publisher, and the publisher hereby disclaims any responsibility for them.

Any people depicted in stock imagery provided by Thinkstock are models, and such images are being used for illustrative purposes only. Certain stock imagery © Thinkstock.

ISBN: 978-1-5320-3427-5 (sc)
ISBN: 978-1-5320-4907-1 (hc)
ISBN: 978-1-5320-3428-2 (e)

Library of Congress Control Number: 2018902014

Print information available on the last page.

iUniverse rev. date: 09/11/2018

For my mother, Helen,
and
Anne

In memoriam

Glenn J. Sevier

(1945–2010)

THE DREAM, GEORGETOWN, DC, AUGUST 1991

In the quiet blackness of a late-summer night, Bryan was swirling in the eye of a hurricane. This once-infrequent dream was now becoming repetitive. He swirled like a top, his body soaring higher, until the clouds dispersed and the spiraling came to a sudden halt. Indistinguishable images assembled with the strange sense of unseen familiarity. Scrambled voices sounded in a variety of pitch and tone, and painful discordant sounds echoed over and over as the images began to define themselves. All his senses seemed to be stimulated. Bryan sprang from his bed, stood in the dark room, and just screamed.

When will it end? God, when will I be released from this damn dream? It makes no sense. What the hell is going on in my mind? Tears welled up in his eyes. A sudden agony of shivering took possession of his whole frame, and he shook with an almost childlike abandon. The perspiration chilled his body as he stood trembling. He returned to bed, eyes wide open and frozen.

What is it that I need to remember? What have I forgotten? The harder he tried to make sense of it all, the more difficult it became to unlock the clues. Just as the new moon could not illuminate his room, neither could it shed any light on his predicament. He reached to turn on the lamp by the bed, which was the only relief from past ghosts. As he rested his head on the pillow, cool tears ran down his face. It was another night when artificial light would be the only relief from his mental demons. His vast sense of helplessness terrified him and made his mind feel like a chaotic whirlwind. He felt himself being crushed and swept off his feet in a dreadful avalanche.

Tonight is so different. I don't understand the change in the dream. I've never heard voices before. I don't understand. I don't understand. He repeated these words until his eyes closed and he drifted off to sleep.

As the August sunrise softly lit the room, the sudden sound of music from the clock radio awakened him, and he arose from the bed feeling as though life had been drained from his body. He forced himself to conduct his morning rituals.

Bryan stood about five foot eight with a husky frame. His terra-cotta-colored hair had resulted in the nickname "Carrottop," much to his dislike. He had seductive brown eyes that seemed to laugh when he smiled. He was a man of letters and was a professor of history at the university.

He zoned out on the thirty-minute drive from Georgetown to Fairfax City, Virginia, to his appointment with his psychiatrist. He only acknowledged the light traffic due to the vacation month. As he drove, the altered pattern of the dream continued to haunt him. He tried to identify the voices but with little success.

He walked quickly to the town house offices, checked in with the receptionist, and sat down in the waiting room and leafed through a couple of magazines.

Bryan had been suffering from post-traumatic stress disorder for over twenty years and had been having counseling intermittently with various specialists, none of whom had been able to alleviate the psychological pain he was experiencing. Today was a day when he needed to talk.

"Dr. Ruocco, the doctor will see you now."

"Thank you," said Bryan.

As he entered the room, he waited for no greeting. "I had the dream again," he said in an anxious, troubled voice.

"Hello, Bryan," said Dr. Kay, a short, bald man. He was about sixty years old and had a scratchy voice. "Come in and sit down over here. Now tell me, was it the same?"

"Almost, but this time with hues of scarlet, and then the spinning stopped. Strange—this was the first time I heard voices, but I could not make them out."

"How has it made you feel? Any different from previous times?"

"I feel tired, almost lifeless and devoid of emotion. I feel like the walking dead. I get upset over the smallest problems and agitated by the minutest things. When I thought my tenure was not going to be granted, I lost the will to fight. I almost felt that I was being tossed to the winds of fate. There is no fight left in me. I have days when I'm productive, but then there are those when I cannot even muster the energy to get out of bed."

"Does your dream seem to be related to these swings in behavior?"

"I just can't remember."

"I believe you are aware of the true meaning of all these dreams, but some event is hidden so well within your mind that only the freedom of unrestricted sleep allows it to escape. We have already discussed whether there are any missing pieces in your past or any incidents in your family history or military service that warrant such a blackout, like military sexual trauma perhaps. I have also explained that post-traumatic stress disorder usually occurs following the experience of or witnessing of life-threatening events, such as military combat. In some cases the brain carves a survival pattern too deep to erase on its own, and its automatic reactions to stress only worsen over time."

The doctor's words hit a nerve, and Bryan paused. "I just can't remember."

"Bryan, it has been many years since you were first diagnosed, and I can see from your records that you have consulted several other doctors before me. Yet you seem to have had little or no progress in your treatment. I'm concerned that your symptoms have lasted this long and not developed in the conventional way. However, your symptoms are severe enough to significantly impair your daily life. Therefore, I suggest that I make an appointment for you to see a specialist colleague of mine, Professor Gurstein, who is from the Veterans' Center. A different kind of talk therapy may prove to be useful, enabling you to come to terms with the trauma you have suffered. We can then successfully integrate the experiences in a way that does not further damage the psyche. What do you think?"

"Yes, I agree. Thank you for the suggestion. I just want this nightmare to end. I'm so overwhelmed and emotionally numb."

"Right, let's recap so that I can forward your case history. You are experiencing flashbacks, nightmares or dreams, and emotional distress when something reminds you of a previous trauma that is unknown to you at present. You also seem to be having avoidance symptoms, which include avoiding thinking of the event or reminders of the event. All perfectly natural. I could give you medication, which would reduce the anxiety, depression, and insomnia, but no particular drug has emerged as a definitive treatment for PTSD. However, I know you are averse to any sort of antidepressant. There are other medications that are often used to treat depression and anxiety. They can be used alone but are more effective when paired with talk therapy."

"More should be done to prevent the syndrome in the first place," Bryan said.

"I agree. All this is a herculean task for the VA," Dr. Kay said. "Now, Bryan, as we conclude our session, is there anything else you would like to review?"

"Not at present. I'm totally exhausted, and I have to get back to the university."

"Goodbye, Dr. Ruocco. You should hear from Professor Gurstein within a couple of weeks, but if there are any further problems meanwhile, please call me."

"Thank you. Goodbye, Doctor."

Bryan's drive to the university was routine. As he drove, he replayed the voices from the dream in his head. Suddenly blinking car brake lights interrupted his reflections. The abrupt red lights flashed and flickered, spraying vivid redness across his windshield that seemed to drip like blood. He closed his eyes and braked while shaking his head slightly. *God, now I'm hallucinating!* When he opened his eyes, the road ahead was normal, and his racing heartbeat had subsided. The traffic had come to a complete standstill.

Bryan had been sitting in his car for more than twenty minutes when other drivers started leaving their cars, making their way toward a gathering crowd of people. His inquisitiveness drew him out as well, and he followed the others. As he approached the large crowd, he saw that there had been a tragic car accident. The cacophony of sirens and the harsh *thwap-thwap* of a helicopter, like a beating heart, deafened him. The black shadow of the descending helicopter passed over him, causing vibrations on the ground beneath him. The pounding grew louder as the helicopter continued its descent. As he watched, the white-and-red medevac appeared to flash a camouflaged green.

The circular slipstream created by the helicopter ruffled his clothes and blew his hair. All at once fear engulfed him; perspiration coated his trembling body while his heart hammered in his chest. He turned and quickly ran back to his car, wondering why this felt so familiar, like déjà vu. *I want to remember, but I just cannot. I have to get out of here.*

Once inside his car, he slammed the door and switched on his cassette of Rachmaninoff's Second Piano Concerto, filling the car with the thundering sound of the last movement. As he listened, he started to drift and became subdued. Eventually the beeping and bellowing of vehicles jerked him to attention, and he started the car.

While he drove, he sang, talked, and used every technique he knew to dismiss the thoughts the car accident had triggered. Only at the entrance to the sparsely populated campus of the university was his consciousness fully restored.

A shrill voice greeted him inside. "Good morning, Dr. Ruocco." A dark-haired, middle-aged woman handed him a pen and some forms.

"Good morning, Amy," he replied.

"I have your revised class list and need your signature for student waiver forms."

Bryan signed the forms, gathered his paperwork, and headed toward his office.

"Before you leave, Dr. Ruocco, I had two calls just before you arrived—one from Sandy and the other from a Mr. Radnor

Richardson. He asked if he could meet with you sometime today at your convenience."

Bryan looked up from his paperwork, his hands tightening around the papers, crinkling them. "What name did you say?"

Amy picked up the message to recall. "Radnor Richardson, from a congressional Vietnam veterans' organization. He said that you served with him."

"Radnor, yes, of course," Bryan said in a calm and relaxed tone, hiding the emotional earthquake taking place. *Radnor … My God, it's been twenty-three years. Whatever could he want?* He remembered Radnor as being of Northern European descent and average height with light eyes and dirty-blond hair.

"Did he leave a number?"

"Yes, I put it with the other phone messages."

Bryan took his calls, avoiding any eye contact with his secretary. "Thank you. I'll be in my office completing some transfer requests."

"Yes, Dr. Ruocco. But Mr. Richardson seemed quite adamant about hearing from you …"

"Of course. Thank you," he said with a smile as he went into his office, closing the door behind him with a push from his shoulder.

Strange, thought Amy, looking up from her desk work, *usually he never closes the door.*

Bryan walked over to his desk, placed the papers down, and went to the window. His eyes were drawn to the campus activities below his second-floor window. A group of students were having a small barbecue, and the waft of cooking meat filled the air. With the mouthwatering thought of a hamburger and an overwhelming need to get out of his office, Bryan made his way down the stairs and onto the grounds, still pondering the phone call from Radnor.

His thoughts were interrupted by a voice calling from behind him. It was Nicholas, one of his graduate student assistants.

"Hey, Dr. R, how are you?"

"Hi, Nico. I'm good, thanks. I couldn't resist the enticing aroma from the barbecue, so I thought I would grab a hamburger from you guys."

"Yeah, sure! Lettuce and tomato?"

"Thanks. What are you doing here? I wasn't expecting you until next week. Have you finished the research project already?"

"Almost, but I'm here to meet some of the freshmen for their orientation. I was just explaining the tradition of the annual hayride."

Last year the hayride had been held in November, and neither the cool temperature nor the wind deterred students from sitting on hay bales on a flatbed trailer for the tour of the college barns and labs. Sandy and Bryan had cooked hot dogs and burgers before getting on the hayride. As Bryan recalled the event and the texture of the straw, his palms began to sweat, and his hands began to tremble. He could feel the straw in his mind—the deceptively silky appearance that, in reality, was dry and brittle when touched. Chameleonlike, but a change in consistency not hue. The sensation was foremost in his thoughts and felt, once again, almost like déjà vu, but why?

"Dr. R, are you okay? Here, let me take your plate. Sit down, and I'll get you some water."

"Thanks. I'm okay." Bryan sneezed.

"Bless you. You must be getting sick."

"No, it's just allergy to the ragweed," he replied and continued sneezing. Suddenly his nose began to bleed. As the blood and saline ran down the back of his throat, an uncomfortable sensation consumed him, and an obnoxious taste lingered in his mouth. He wanted to throw up. He wanted to purge himself of the taste, which was both familiar and alien to him, though he could not understand why. He became frustrated by his inability to remember. It was all too much.

"Dr. R? Dr. R! I thought you were going to pass out."

"Sorry, Nicholas. Yes, thank you, I'm fine. I'll just go back to my office. I'm expecting a visitor anyway."

Distracted from his thoughts, Bryan made his way back to his office, trying to stem the flow of blood. He returned to the window. The smoke twirled to the tops of the trees, escaping through the branches. He felt almost hypnotized as his eyes scaled the rising smoke. The present seemed to disappear and was replaced with images from his past.

7

THE BARBECUE,
WALLINGFORD, PENNSYLVANIA,
AUGUST 1965

It was a hot and humid August afternoon, and Bryan's family was gathering at home in the backyard for a farewell barbecue. Bryan sat leafing through his history books on the causes of World War II.

"Dad could use a little help," his mother said, interrupting his thoughts as she placed a red-and-white-checkerboard cloth on the picnic table. "The family will be arriving shortly, and he's having a time of it trying to start the grill."

Bryan's mom was a small Italian American woman about five foot two with black hair in a bouffant style typical of the mid-1960s look.

"No problem, just let me finish this paragraph. Mom, did you know—"

"Bryan, not right now," she said as she looked up from her task, eyes glowing with restrained tears. "You'll upset me. I think that you should be going to college, not to war."

"Mother, don't start! I may not get a ship in the Pacific fleet. I may be stationed in Norfolk or Philly. Who's to say? Don't worry!" He hugged her and then dashed off.

"Dad, I'm here to give you a hand, or make Mom think that's what I'm doing!"

Bryan's dad, also of Italian descent, was short with dark hair and a receding hairline. His physique could pass for that of a jockey.

Seeming dazed, his father said, "I can't believe this is happening. It seems like yesterday that I left your mother to go into the service. Son, I'm proud of you and know that you believe in what you are about to do. The sad part is your innocence will be lost to the harsh world, which is even worse in war. I need you to help me be as brave as you." He held Bryan close.

"Dad, it will be fine. Everything will work out. I'll make you proud. I love you. This will only make us closer than we already are."

His father turned from him and went toward the house. It was apparent to Bryan that his dad was distraught. *What's wrong with them? I don't understand them. Things will be okay,* Bryan thought as he turned the white-fringed briquettes to accelerate the fire.

The late-summer evening brought more heat and humidity as Bryan's family assembled to bid him farewell. The needs of the guests gave Bryan's parents relief from the emotional trauma that had consumed them earlier. Bryan paced anxiously, glancing at the gate, awaiting his high school sweetheart, Michelle, as he chatted with his relatives.

"Bryan, I'm glad you're going to help stop that plague of commies in Vietnam," Uncle Chuck said. "We haven't put them in their place since World War II."

"Sure, Uncle Chuck, as if I'm going to take them on single-handed, just me! But I do think the Communists need to be halted. We can't allow what happened in Cuba to continue. Also, Hitler went unchecked, and you saw what happened in Europe."

Uncle Chuck was a World War II vet who had taken part in the D-day Normandy landings.

"If it's not war, it's politics," interrupted Michelle with a hug and a kiss. Michelle was of Irish American descent and medium height with strawberry-blonde hair and blue eyes.

"Sorry for being late, but I was packing for college," she panted, out of breath. "It's so hard for me to believe that you're not going, Bryan. All those plans picking colleges and getting accepted. If only you had heard a few days before that draft notice."

As she spoke, she combed her fingers through Bryan's wavy, terra-cotta-colored hair. "Oh, how I shall miss my sweet Carrottop."

"Stop with that Carrottop garbage," he muttered as he pulled her close to his body. "Are we all set for tonight?" he whispered. "I've got my mom's car for the night, and we'll leave for the shore after the barbecue. I can't wait." Michelle interrupted, "How I love you. God, I don't know how I will make it without you."

"Why does everyone act as if I'm going into the marines? It's the navy, with ships and a guaranteed bed every night. I'm not going to be a leatherneck or foot soldier, just a sailor, fighting behind the lines. A real hero—ha ha!"

Her warm, soft skin excited him. At that second of her embrace, an abrupt realization struck him. The world that he loved was about to vanish. A cold chill filled his body. "Michelle, hold me close."

"Enough of that!" Bryan's dad interrupted. "We have guests, and I would love a hug from my favorite girl. Where have four years gone? I remember when Bryan took you to that freshman dance. You were such a cute girl and Bryan's first date. What a lovely young woman you have turned into."

"First date? Nonsense! She was one of many I had to pick from." Bryan smiled.

"Bryan, I've kept you long enough. We'll get together later." She kissed him on his cheek. What was it about this eighteen-year-old guy that still held a mystique for her after four years? He was sensitive, generous, always thoughtful, and had a great sense of humor. Also, he was handsome with his terra-cotta hair, seductive brown eyes, and inviting smile accentuated by dimples. On the other hand, she knew that he could be arrogant, with a touch of pretentiousness, and self-absorbed at times. He was not short of self-esteem!

"So what do you think about Johnson sending more American troops to South Vietnam?" asked Bryan's cousin Vince.

"I think Johnson has no other choice since the Viet Cong attacked the American Green Beret camp near Pleiku last February," Bryan said. "We lost eight men, and 109 were wounded."

"But don't you think it's strange that American intelligence had no idea but later found a detailed map on one of the dead Vietnamese? This leads me to believe that the locals may not want us there."

"Do you really believe that the Vietnamese people don't want the greatest country on their side? If we help them, they're bound to win. So bomb the North to hell," said Bryan, red in the face with blind patriotic fervor.

The discussion was getting louder, and personal, and Bryan's dad stepped in. "This is when I wish my son was more like other teens and had no idea what was going on in the world," he interrupted and offered Vince a hot dog or a burger.

Bryan turned and mumbled, "How will they ever win with that kind of attitude?"

The evening rapidly came to an end as the mosquitoes began their nightly feast. The guests began to leave, and Bryan and Michelle helped his parents clean up.

"Bryan, I'm sure that you and Michelle would like to get started for the shore. Your dad and I will finish up." His mother kissed him on the forehead.

Bryan's dad walked them to the car. He hugged them both and whispered, "Remember, tonight can affect both your futures. Use sense and have a wonderful last night at home."

"We will," Bryan called out the car window as they departed for the hour's journey to the New Jersey shore.

THE SHORE,
MARGATE, NEW JERSEY,
AUGUST 1965

Margate was the traditional post-prom destination for high school students. A city in Atlantic County, New Jersey, Margate was home to Lucy, the famous six-story elephant made of wood. This piece of novelty architecture was the oldest roadside tourist attraction in America designated as a historical monument and had become the symbol of Margate. At last the silhouette of the elephant came into view.

The breeze from the open car window blew Michelle's hair. Bryan watched her rest as passing headlights illuminated her. She slept peacefully as they continued their journey. Bryan inhaled the smell of the salt air as they approached the ocean. The lights from the distant beach town reflected against the night sky like a strand of pearls.

"Michelle, sweetheart, we're here," Bryan said as he pulled the car to a stop in the driveway.

"We're here already?" She stretched and leafed through her purse for a comb, which she began running through her hair. "The beach house may be a little musty. We haven't been here since the fourth."

Bryan watched Michelle as she moved her head from side to side while continuing to comb her hair. Slowly he moved close enough to embrace and kiss her. Within a few minutes they were in the house.

"The first thing we need to do tomorrow is buy groceries," Michelle said.

"Let's not worry about that tonight. I can only think about you." He gently unbuttoned her blouse, kissed her lips and neck, and nudged her blouse open wider with his nose, exposing her warm chest.

As his passionate lips reached Michelle's breasts, she said, "Bryan, I love you. This evening will be special for us." As she spoke, she pulled his shirttail from his jeans and tickled his smooth neck.

In the house they left a trail of clothing as they made their way to the bedroom, unaware of their surroundings and the world itself.

The next morning, Bryan woke to soft-sounding waves. The sun's brightness from the French doors was hypnotic and defined the interior of the bedroom. He rose from the bed, studied Michelle's sleeping form, and, without disturbing her, walked through the doors to the deck. The orange morning sun appeared just over the ocean's horizon.

The previous night's happenings raced through his mind, similar to a rerun movie. While he felt content and his masculine pride overshadowed his emotions, there was a lingering feeling of something lacking in the experience. It hadn't been quite all that he'd thought it would be. *Where was that emotional ecstasy?* His thoughts were broken by Michelle's voice.

"So when were you going to wake me?" she asked as she kissed him and wrapped her arms around him.

"I hated to wake you, as you looked so peaceful. I didn't mind sitting here alone, enjoying this beautiful view of the sunrise over the Atlantic."

"It sure is lovely, but I'm quite hungry, and I'm sure that you will want to eat later, so enjoy while I go to the grocery store."

"I'll come with you."

"No, I want to go alone so that I can recall our wonderful night."

Her real reason became apparent when Bryan noticed the glow in her eyes and sad expression on her face as she turned quickly.

"Michelle! Michelle!" he called as he sprang from his seat. She dashed into the house, reached for her purse, and headed for the door without stopping. A moment later Bryan heard the car rapidly accelerate away. Her quick exit indicated to Bryan that she needed to deal with the issue in her own fashion. The reality and uncertainty of his future surfaced within him for the first time. The world that he knew was going to change, and this thought frightened and yet excited him. Would he be able to make a change to the world with his small contribution?

He stripped, put on his swim trunks, and headed toward the ocean. He dashed across the hot, burning sand and dived into the warm, salty water. The world above became silent. As he came to the surface and raised his head above the water, he began swimming, steering toward the endless horizon of the ocean. Shore sounds were replaced by the lapping of the waves. Bryan paused, treading water. The ocean's overpowering might seemed to surround him. He felt helpless and alone, and a sudden fear of the unknown instinctively drew him back to the shore. Seagulls cried and rolling waves greeted him as he headed for the house, soaked and chilled.

Michelle greeted him with a large, thick, yellow towel. "Where have you been all these hours? I've been worried." She wrapped him in the towel, drew him close, and kissed his lips, which were moist with salt water.

"I've been swimming and thinking." Bryan hesitated. "Thinking about us and our future."

"Well, so have I. Forgive me for running off. A thousand things have been running through my head. Before you leave for boot camp, I think we need to talk about us."

"Sure, but I don't understand what the problem is. You're my girl, and we'll go through this together."

"Bryan, this is not some Greek tragedy. I can't be expected to wait until you return from the service. It's not fair to either of us. You made the choice, and I'm forced to live with your decision? Well, I don't believe I can do it." She ran her hand through his hair.

"This hurts me … And why now? You've known for months. Surely we can reach some kind of compromise?"

Is this the first hint of a relationship about to unravel? Bryan thought as he sat staring at the deck with his head bent, squeezing his knees.

Michelle placed her arms around his neck. "I think the love I have for you is tearing me apart, and I truly wish I could do what you want, but I can't."

He looked at her, his expression like that of a small boy's, and said, "I will agree, but only because I have no choice. But I will prove to you that our love will last the test of time. You may see other guys, but I will remain faithful."

She embraced him, his head resting close to her breasts. They both sat in silence. Nothing more could be said.

WALLINGFORD, PENNSYLVANIA, FALL OF 1965

L
arge piles of maple and sweet gum leaves dotted the lawn as Bryan and his parents drove up to the house.

"Dad, stop here for just a minute. Let me look at the house. I've seen this view in my dreams many nights. I learned that sometimes the price for a dream is homesickness."

As he looked at the stone colonial home, he could hardly believe that he had really returned.

"I don't think Michelle will find you very handsome with that bald head," his mother said as she pulled off his navy cap. "You look dreadful!"

"It will grow back," he said with his eyes fixed on his surroundings. He had an appreciation for his home and parents like never before.

"Go on, Dad. I'm anxious to find out when Michelle will be home."

His dad parked the car and went to the trunk to get Bryan's seabag. Before they went inside, Bryan hugged his father. "Dad, I've missed you and the things we do together so much. Did you make plans? You know that I will be home for a month."

"I sure did. We'll get some tennis in tomorrow and catch a few football games. I almost had to sell my soul to get those tickets at work!

I also got tickets for the Philadelphia Orchestra and a few plays, and your mom and I saved a few movies we would like to see. I hear *The Cincinnati Kid* is a great film. It stars Edward G. Robinson and Steve McQueen."

They made their way into the house. Bryan's dad was huffing as he dropped Bryan's seabag in his room. "What in the world do you have in this seabag? Well, I'll let you get cleaned up for dinner and give you time to make some phone calls. You don't know how happy I am to see you, Son. I've missed you."

Bryan stretched out on his bed, flipped on the clock radio, and listened to his favorite classical music station, finding it hard to believe that he was really home. As he lay on the chenille spread, pulling at the fabric balls with his fingertips and staring at the milk-white ceiling, his mind drifted to his first night in boot camp at Great Lakes, Illinois.

The number of new recruits had far exceeded the space available at the training center, so they'd been forced to spend their first night in a drill hall. Bryan had tried to close his eyes and fall asleep, but the repeated mental picture of this sea of men around him and strange sounds of coughing, snoring, and subdued crying had kept him awake. The black drill hall had frightened him. He'd eventually dozed off, dreaming that he'd awakened at home. His actual surroundings had caused him discomfort and homesickness, but Bryan had quickly dismissed these feelings as weak and immature. He'd vowed that he wouldn't become fearful of what was to be. Finally, between the mental and physical fatigue of his overextended day and night and his unfamiliar environment, he'd fallen into a deep and almost death-like slumber. Hours later, he'd woken to a shocking blaze of lights and deafening shouting. It had seemed as though he'd slept for only a few minutes. How tired he had felt.

Bryan's thoughts were interrupted by a soft and gentle voice. "Bryan, Bryan, are you ready for dinner?"

"Mom? Is it time for dinner already?" He yawned.

"Already? It's close to eight! Your dad and I thought you should rest, but you've been sleeping for several hours now, so we thought we ought to get you up."

"Has Michelle called?"

"Not as yet, but I'm sure you will hear from her soon. I'll let you get cleaned up for dinner."

The normal dining setting greeted him. The table was set informally with the everyday dishware and heavy cotton napkins. Bryan sat down, placed his napkin on his lap, and surveyed the room and contents. "Woo! This is the first time I've eaten like this in two months. I had forgotten, or never realized, how pleasant all this was. Eating off tin plates makes one appreciate home."

"Bryan, unfortunately we're the exception, not the rule. You will find how different our lifestyle is from others', but it makes them no less valued than you," his father reminded him.

"Dad, I realize all that. Going to college would have sheltered me more from the real world to which you are referring. This opportunity for me to meet people from all walks of life will surely be invaluable."

Two hours passed as Bryan and his father discussed society and the ills of the world. It was their favorite pastime and a mental exercise that took them through dessert to their after-dinner beverages. After dinner they continued their conversation in the living room and began to feel uneasy when they realized they had unintentionally left out Bryan's mother.

"Dad, let me give Mom a hand with the dishes," Bryan said, jumping up from the wing chair and hurrying into the kitchen.

As Bryan left the room, his father pulled himself from his leather chair and reached for the poker to stoke the fire. As he stared into the fire, his face became heated, and tears blurred his vision.

The next morning the ringing of the phone awakened Bryan from a deep sleep. "Hello," he said in a groggy voice.

"Hi, sailor! How about a tennis date?"

"Michelle! It's you. I thought you would have called last night."

"I would have, but I couldn't get off campus. I had some last-minute things to do for the organizations I'm thinking of joining."

"Oh," he said with a yawn.

"You're still asleep! Let's meet at the club courts around nine thirty and hit a little. Then we can have breakfast. I can't wait to see you."

"That sounds great. Looking forward to seeing you. I've missed you. Love you."

"Love you too, sweet Bryan."

SAN DIEGO, CALIFORNIA, NOVEMBER 1965

Landscaped in lush Mediterranean foliage with tall, stately date palms, the naval base had a hint of Spanish colonial design with red-tiled roofs and adobe and beige-stucco buildings. The wooden-arched porches were replicated throughout the base.

When Bryan left the barracks for breakfast, the warm San Diego day took him by surprise. The semiarid climate made it feel more like September than November.

"Hey, Ruocco, I hear we will be getting our ship orders after zero nine hundred," a friend called as he ran to catch up with Bryan.

"Yeah, right, we've heard that for the last two weeks. I don't think we're ever going to leave. I hate those working party assignments. We're always cleaning bathrooms."

"You mean heads. No, this is from a yeoman who works in navy office personnel here on base."

"I hope so. I'm ready to get settled on my ship. Living out of a seabag is a pain in the butt."

After breakfast, Bryan and selected others were instructed to pack and pick up their orders. Bryan read through his bulky, inch-thick clump of papers. He was to report to the USS *Delaware* (*APA-28*).

"I thought state names were given to battleships?" he asked the officer passing out the orders.

"No. This is not a battleship; it's an amphibious personnel attack ship. They're named after state counties and are specifically designed to transport invasion forces ashore. The soldiers climb down netting on the sides of the ships into tenders," the officer replied brusquely.

"Well, how about that! Named after my home county!"

Bryan was filled with both excitement and reluctance as he prepared to report to his ship. He was on the threshold of an unknown destiny.

Bryan made his farewells and took a cab to the pier where the ship was berthed. The driver took his seabag from the trunk and stood it upright. Bryan paid the driver and swung the heavy bag over his right shoulder, balancing the weight as he walked to the ship.

Cranes on massive train wheels creaked while lifting goods to the ships. Sporadic steam hissing from released pressure valves combined with the sharp odor of diesel fuel to give off a repugnant scent that was alien to Bryan. Seagulls screeched, swooped, and descended toward containers of trash. As he moved along the pier, he noted the white-painted identification numbers on the bow of each ship. He spotted "PA-28" on a ship that was designed for maritime and freighter use. Bryan's eyes followed the contour of the massive gray bow. He then climbed the Z-shaped metal steps, which echoed as he made his descent to the ship's quarterdeck. Half out of breath and struggling to balance his seabag, he stepped on deck.

"Permission to come aboard. Reporting for duty." He saluted the American flag and then the officer of the deck.

"Welcome aboard, seaman. Boatswain's mate, please take this seaman to the ship's office for processing."

"Aye, aye, sir."

Within forty-five minutes, the yeoman from the office took Bryan to the sleeping quarters in the supply and operations compartments at the rear of the ship. Bryan thought the yeoman's work clothes were surprisingly unsoiled and pressed. Due to the work duties of the crew, the area was quiet.

"Pick any locker, store your things, and I'll see you topside when you're through. Oh, pick any bunk without sheets."

"What's your name?"

"Radnor Richardson, seaman third class."

As Bryan finished unpacking, another seaman descended the ladder with a seabag. He turned his head to listen to similar instructions.

"At last I'm here," the seaman sighed as he dropped his seabag.

"I'll be out of your way in a few minutes. I'm almost through," Bryan said.

"No problem," the other seaman said, unraveling a name tag for his locker. "Take your time. I have lots of it—like three years!" He tilted his head slightly as he spoke

The seaman was of Nordic descent, well built, and about six feet tall with golden-brown hair and deep-bluish eyes. Immediately Bryan noticed his friendly smile.

"I'm new on board too; my name is Bryan Ruocco."

"Where are you from?"

"Pennsylvania, just outside of Philadelphia." Bryan stretched out his arm to shake hands.

The other seaman shook Bryan's hand. Then, as he placed his name tag on his locker, he said, "As you can see, the name is Greg Seaton."

"Do I detect a southern accent?" Bryan asked.

"Funny, I thought you had the accent! But your observation is correct. I'm from Virginia, not too far from Thomas Jefferson's home—just a Blue Ridge mountain boy. I'm going to be working as a signalman in the operations department. How about you?"

"I'm going to be working in supply as a storekeeper. Well, I best get moving. I need to report to the supply office to meet with my division officer and get my work assignment," Bryan explained, darting toward the compartment exit.

"I'll catch you later at lunch."

"Great!" Bryan replied.

Months passed. Both Bryan and Greg had become familiar with the ship's in-port routine. Up at 0600 Monday through Friday with the workday concluding at 1600. Out in the evening and gone for the weekends.

As the boatswain's pipe signaled the end of the workday, Bryan continued to check the stock inventory.

"Are you going to be much longer?" Tag, his supervisor, asked.

"I'm just about through," he replied without looking up.

"How about locking up? I want to get ashore and go to the beach," he said, handing Bryan the supply keys.

After working for a bit longer, Bryan was interrupted.

"Hey, buddy, are you going to the beach?"

"Hi, Greg. Boy, you're in your blues and ready to run!" He stepped back and took a breather.

"Why don't you come to the beach with Richardson and me? He knows of a great go-go bar downtown and a hot college party. Maybe we could meet some girls?"

"Not in those clothes!"

"No, of course not. I'm changing into civvies at the locker club. So what do you say? Join us."

"Sure, but I need a little time to complete these orders before we leave for Asia."

"That's at least two months from now."

"Before you know it, Christmas will be here, and the whole supply department will be on leave. Guess who'll be left. Me! Storekeeper apprentice with all the work and no one to help."

"Not so gung ho—I may puke," Greg said as he rolled his eyes and tossed his white cap at Bryan.

"Okay, but I want to eat something before they close the mess hall."

"I'm going to shove off. We'll meet you at the Old Dixie Bar in a few hours."

The cool night and light fog chilled Bryan as he exited the bus for downtown San Diego. The main thoroughfare was Broadway, lined with go-go bars, tattoo parlors, and locker clubs—establishments that catered to both sailors and marines. Flashing, brilliant-colored lights attracted the eyes of the most unaware and innocent.

Bryan darted to his locker club to change from his military clothes into his civvies and hurried to meet his friends. The only telltale sign of his military status was his neatly trimmed hair. He raced down Broadway and was just about out of breath when he found the bar. Puffing and gasping for air, he entered the smoke-filled bar. Leaning against and sitting at the bar were both his friends, drinking large, cold mugs of beer and smoking cigarettes. Watching their heads sway and listening to their raucous laughter, Bryan knew they had been drinking for some time.

"Hey, Carrottop, we'd almost given up on you," Radnor yelled over the piercing rock music.

"Buddy, I'm glad you made it," Greg said as he embraced Bryan. "A beer for my friend, bartender."

"I'm not crazy about beer—maybe a mixed drink."

"You don't like draft beer?" they echoed together.

"I didn't realize there was a difference," he responded defensively.

"Try it, and we'll make a believer out of you," said Radnor.

Bryan took the large mug and began drinking. The cold, soothing taste was delectable. He savored the beer as if it was a fine French wine; his dry mouth and overheated body enhanced his thirst.

"I think he likes it," Radnor said with a laugh.

"Wow, that was great! I never knew."

"That's what life is all about—new experiences!" Greg said as he held up his mug in a toast. Bryan and Radnor followed his lead and lifted their mugs in unison.

"Hear, hear!"

"Talking about new experiences, I hear that the ship will be leaving for West Pac in February," Bryan said. "You know what that means?"

"'Nam!" interjected Radnor. "I wonder why the hell we're going there."

"I sure can't wait to get out of San Diego and see something of real value," Bryan said, rubbing his eyes, which burned from the cigarette smoke. "So what's the problem with going to 'Nam? We need to stop pussyfooting around with the Communists. You sound like Robert Kennedy; you agree that we should be against the war?"

"I heard that conference on the news. It sounded to me that he was only protecting our right to challenge government policy," Greg said.

"How are we ever going to win with this halfhearted attempt?" Bryan asked, shaking his head. "McNamara believes that simply to stabilize the situation he needs about 175,000 American troops, followed by another 100,000. With those numbers he hopes to 'halt the losing trend' by the end of the year, undertake an offensive of indefinite duration in 1966, and round up remaining enemy forces during the following year."

"Rad, now you've got him going. He's really into politics and the war. He always has his head in the paper. Give it up!"

"You're right," Radnor said. "Let's talk about women. That's one thing we all agree on. Enjoy them, because in a few months, no more round-eyed women. Let's shove off to the party."

The three men caught a bus to Mission Valley, a section of the town dating from 1769. The locals called the area Old Town. The beautiful, white-bleached church on the hill, the first of twenty-one Californian missions founded by the Franciscan Junipero Serra, radiated with light.

"Bryan, I see you are impressed by this part of town," Radnor said.

Bryan was staring out the window, totally absorbed in the view, taking little interest in their conversation. "Boy, I sure have had the wrong opinion of San Diego," he said.

"That's why you need to get off ship and see more than downtown," Greg said.

"This is our stop," Radnor alerted.

They made their way to an apartment complex that had easy access to public transport and the main highway. As they approached, familiar party sounds could be heard in the hall. Upon their entrance, a pretty girl of around nineteen or twenty, with long straight brown hair and large cocoa eyes, began her introductions. Her quick embrace and affectionate kiss confirmed that this lovely woman was Radnor's wife, Marian. Until now, Bryan had only known her name.

"Marian, these are my buddies Greg and Bryan."

"Nice to meet both of you. I've heard a lot about you. Rad, you should have told me these guys were so good-looking," she teased while shaking his arm. "It won't be hard to fix them up."

"Fix them up, right! Goldilocks and Carrottop, good-looking?" Radnor pulled back, laughing in disbelief.

"Carly! Diane!" Marian waved her hand across the room. "I want you to meet Rad's friends."

Following the introductions, the couples separated.

"Diane, Marian told me you go to the University of San Diego," Bryan said. "What's your major?"

"I'm not sure yet. Maybe radio, TV, or journalism. I haven't made up my mind. Why did you join the navy?" Diane asked. "I would think one would avoid the service with a war on. Why didn't you go to college?"

Bryan was uncomfortable answering personal questions, but he didn't have to, because Diane never waited for a reply. He surveyed the room. Radnor and Marian seemed to be in an endless embrace. *It must be nice,* Bryan mused inwardly and wishfully.

Greg, dressed in an off-white turtleneck sweater and corduroy slacks, sat on a chair drinking a bottle of beer, and Carly sat on the floor with her arm locked around his calf. She turned and looked at him while she stirred her drink in a clockwise direction.

"How soon do you leave for Asia?" she asked.

Greg touched her nose and whispered in a soft, heavy voice, "Our ship is leaving in February. We'll have enough time to get to know each other, if that's okay with you?"

"I would like that a lot."

From the large grin on his face, Greg was enjoying her attention. As he looked into her blue eyes, he was drawn to her. He wanted her. Physical desire stirred in him. He combed his hands through her long, blonde hair, and with each brush of the soft strands, excitement filled him. He pulled her head close to his and kissed her warm lips with his burning pair, igniting her sensual needs. Both left for an adjacent bedroom.

Hours passed, and the party's excitement and guests dwindled. Bryan sat in the kitchen as Radnor and Marian cleaned and picked up after their guests.

"So, Bryan, what do you think of Diane?" Marian asked.

"She seems real nice, but I'm still committed to Michelle, my girl back home. We'll probably marry when I get out of the navy. She'll be visiting when we get back next fall."

"That will be great. We would like to meet her. Rad, she could stay here—what do you think?"

"We have room. No problem with me," he answered as he washed dishes.

"Since Greg is bunking with Carly, you could stay here for the weekend if you don't want to go back to the ship," Marian said. "We have a pullout."

"If you're sure that won't be a problem, it would be wonderful to sleep here. I haven't slept off ship since I left home."

Once in bed, Bryan's thoughts turned to Michelle and their last summer at the beach. Hearing the soft footsteps of one of his friends, he slowly opened his eyes. There was a burst of blinding light from the kitchen, and he quickly pulled the covers over his head.

"Sorry, buddy," Greg apologized in a hushed voice. "I thought I knew where the fridge was. I need some orange juice."

Bryan pushed the covers to his waist as Greg moved toward the couch. He sat on the floor, pulled his legs together, and placed the juice on his knees.

"I really think Carly is something. God, she makes me feel so good both in and out."

"I know what kind of in and out you're talking about," Bryan laughed.

"No, Bryan. Get serious. I really think she is special. You don't think so?"

"Is it really important what I think?"

"It is to me."

"Why?"

"You're a good friend, and I value your opinion."

"Greg, I don't know what you want me to say. I don't know the girl, and we've only known each other for a few months. This is all kind of peculiar to me."

"Fuck off, Bryan," he said defensively.

"I don't understand. Don't be angry with me," Bryan pleaded. "I'm tired. Why don't we get some sleep before we wake the others?"

"Okay, I guess you're right." Greg sprang to his feet, took the bedcovers, threw them round Bryan's face, and tugged at his nose. "It's okay, buddy."

In the dark, Bryan wondered why Greg needed his opinion so badly, as he always seemed to be the epitome of self-confidence. Bryan was flattered that Greg was seeking his approval and regretted his cool reaction.

On Monday, Bryan, Greg, and Radnor had to report back to the ship by 0700.

"Let's get moving, guys, before we hit traffic," Radnor commanded early that morning.

"Rad, I'll drive you all to the base today. I need the car," Marian said.

Within forty-five minutes they had reached the base and the ship's berth. Radnor and Marian seemed to want to be alone, so Bryan and Greg headed down the pier toward the ship while Radnor stayed behind to kiss Marian.

"When we get back in the fall, why don't we rent a place on the beach?" Greg suggested. "That's the only way to go."

"That sounds great to me. Having a place on the beach would be neat. Greg, sorry about how I acted last night."

"Hey, don't trouble yourself. I was drunk and probably didn't make much sense, and between you and me, I don't remember."

While they talked, they reached the ship's quarterdeck.

"Those two deck apes have the watch," Bryan said. "I can't stand either of them. Polk is always making passes at me, and Filipo just smiles and licks his lips. Those are two sick faggots. I've never hated two people as much as them."

"You really do hate them, the way you're name-calling. Don't let them bug you. They are harmless, I'm sure."

"Well, look who's coming aboard," Polk said. He made kissing sounds as Bryan passed. "Hey, Seaton, are you going to share the sea pussy with us on those long weeks out at sea?"

"I don't think your mouth or your butt is big enough to take the two of us. If so, come and see me," Greg replied and discreetly pinched Polk's rear.

"You think you're a smart fucker. I'll get you for that."

"Oh, I'm scared," laughed Greg as they continued to make their way on board.

"You are unbelievable, how you turned the whole thing around," Bryan said. "That was skilled thinking."

"Learn from me and don't let them get to you."

6

SAN DIEGO, CALIFORNIA, FEBRUARY 1966

At breakfast, Bryan grabbed a roll, scooped up a fried egg, made a sandwich, and then dashed topside, spilling coffee on his way. He sat at the ship's bow, waiting to watch the sunrise over the San Ysidro Mountains. Today was special. The ship was scheduled to get under way for Asia. This would be his last day in the contiguous United States for some time. He was excited and anxious, as this was his first time leaving the mainland. It was so hard to believe that he was now going to see everything he had read about. Pearl Harbor in a week and Japan in two. All of Asia lay ahead to be discovered and explored. He felt like Columbus or Magellan and gasped with fervor.

The rising of the sun had taken on a new and special meaning to Bryan. It now symbolized home and everything that he loved. It was east, and the brightness was home, parents, and all those things that dwelled there. It was as if all those pleasures caused the brilliance. At times he missed them all, especially his dad. Sadly, he realized he could never do and see all these wonders in the confines of home, though.

He took out the letters folded in his top pocket and reread them. One was a letter from Michelle, updating him on college and their high school friends. She seemed to enjoy college and the interest her peers showed in current US conditions. His letter packet from home always contained letters from both his parents. He read over both and noted what he needed to answer. His dad was concerned about Senator Mike Mansfield's fact-finding tour of Vietnam, the gloomy picture of the war, its expansion, and now the renewed bombing of the North. He was terribly saddened by the loss of over two hundred men in the Battle of la Drang Valley last November, saying, "The North Vietnamese loss has maybe given our political leaders a false sense of victory." Bryan then read the morning paper.

Hours passed, and the ship was getting under way. All hands were instructed to man the rail, a custom in which the ship's crew lined the rails from bow to stern. From the shore they looked like Cracker Jack cutouts. This activity lasted until the ship exited the harbor.

At sea, shipboard routine began with the boatswain's pipe at 0500, a call for reveille, and the sudden burst of shocking light. Breakfast at 0655. Work till noon, lunch, then work again until 1600. Daily movie call at 1830. This was the highlight of the day—a time when everyone could escape the boredom of ship life and forget those particular people and places missed. The thrill was in the zealous magic allowing them to flee for a few hours—the celluloid escape. Every night the movie was rumored to be a James Bond thriller, but it never was. Taps at 2100 ended the day, at which point the ship's lower sleeping spaces filled with blackness like the inside of a great whale.

Bryan's eyes popped open at reveille. The ship was approaching Hawaii, the first port since San Diego. A week at sea had passed at last. He'd hardly been able to sleep that past night. It was like the excitement of Christmas morning.

"Rad and I were thinking about renting a car and getting a hotel room on the beach," Greg said, dropping only his head and his hands down from the top rack to look over at Bryan below. "We both figured you would know what sights there are to see, and in the evening we could hit the nightspots. What do think?"

"That sounds great. We can talk about it at breakfast and work the rest out on the beach. I want to get moving so I can take pictures of our entrance into Pearl Harbor," Bryan said while dressing quickly, never once looking up.

"*These boots are made for walkin'*," Radnor sang with the radio as he strolled toward Bryan. "So are you coming with us?"

"Sure am!" He disappeared among the other shipmates.

"Where in the world is he off to? I never saw anybody so anxious to get on with liberty," Radnor said in a puzzled voice.

"Get ready for a history lesson. He'll be pointing out all the sights at Pearl Harbor! Ruocco is a walking history textbook," Greg laughed.

Morning light had stretched across the eastern sky, reflecting off the calm Pacific. Bryan stood on the starboard quarterdeck, keeping himself clear of deckhands preparing to make port. As the ship slipped through the Kaiwi Channel, hugging the coast of Oahu, the recognizable feature of Diamond Head towered over the island. The mountain range was shaped like an alligator drifting through the peaceful water. The excitement mounted as the city of Honolulu stretched at the base of the mountain with its sides like paws. The ship glided through the glassy, still harbor water. History began to unfold for Bryan—Hickam Air Force Base, Ford Island, and the motionless USS *Arizona* Memorial, a contemporary white structure stretched across the rusted battleship. Between the clicks of his camera a sense of strange calm and disbelief overtook him. Realizing the time, he raced down to breakfast.

"I can't believe you guys are sitting around stuffing your faces," he said, shaking his head as he placed his tiny plate of food on the table. "There is so much to see topside."

"We wanted to save the best for last," Greg said. "You can give us a rundown after muster. I sure would be interested, right, Rad?"

"Sure," he answered with a mouth filled with steak and eggs.

"I want to take the shuttle to the *Arizona* before we leave base," Bryan said. "What do you all think?"

"Okay by me," Greg said.

"Fine."

"Is that all you're eating?" Greg asked Bryan. He stretched his arms and then patted his stomach. "This is the calmest the ship has been in a week. You're not seasick, are you?"

"I'm fine. Just not very hungry." He looked up. "Oh boy, we got trouble. Polk and Filipo are on their way over here."

"So where are all you girls off to? Going to get a little ass on Hotel Street? Sorry, wrong place," Polk laughed. "That's not where guys go to meet men." Polk leaned over behind Greg, supporting himself with the top of the chair, and whispered, "Would you like me to tell you, Greg, baby?"

"And how would you know?" Greg asked mockingly. Within a few seconds Greg had taken hold of Polk's neck and flung him to the floor. He stood over Polk with his foot lodged on his neck. "You fucking creep. You ever get near me, I swear I'll kill your sorry ass." With a free hand he took a banana from the table and stuffed it in Polk's mouth. "This is the closest you'll get to my dick, so enjoy!"

Bryan was in shock, at both the incident and Greg's quick response. He stood motionless, unable to comprehend this anger, violence, and strength, which Greg had never before alluded to or hinted at. How well he disguised himself. He was like a genie in a bottle!

"Greg, get off him before the master-at-arms throws both of you in the brig," pleaded Radnor. "We've made plans, Greg. Let him go. He's choking."

"Greg, stop! You're going to kill him!" Bryan shrieked. The fear in Bryan's voice seemed to snap Greg out of his temporary madness. He stopped, stood erect and silent, and then quickly left the mess hall. With the arrival of the master-at-arms, the crowd dispersed. The conflict had ended. Bryan and Radnor soon followed; Polk was left wiping his face, humiliated.

"I'll get him back for this," Polk muttered. "I'll fix that fag."

"I think he is going to be a little harder to take care of," Filipo said, "but there is always Ruocco. That pussy looked like he enjoyed the fight." He put his arm round Polk's shoulders and whispered, "I've got a plan to fix them all."

The ship's crew was called to muster. Bryan reported his division's locality on the port side of the ship. He surveyed the harbor, where his eyes were drawn to the battleship *Arizona* that lay just across the harbor to the northwest, paying little attention to his division officer and the morning announcements. Both ships simultaneously hoisted their union flags, and the action triggered a mental account for Bryan. The attack at 0755 on December 7, 1941, had taken place during this routine ship activity. Bryan visualized battleship row, *the Nevada, Arizona, Tennessee, West Virginia, Maryland, and Oklahoma.* From the northwest, the first wave of planes had flown over the Koolau mountain range. The sky had been dotted with planes dropping torpedoes and bombs. The harbor had filled with smoke, fire, and explosions. Then had come the direct hit on the *Arizona.*

Just then, Greg interrupted his thoughts. "What are you thinking about? Are you ready?"

"Look there's the *Arizona,*" Bryan replied excitedly. "Can you believe this? We're really here!"

"I know it's the *Arizona.* Are you ready for weekend liberty?"

Bryan's mind was instantly restored to the present. "Sure, okay. By the way, how are you doing after that fight?"

"Fine. Come on; let's go!" Greg replied, changing the subject. "I just want to get to the beach and have some fun. Rad is waiting on the quarterdeck."

DA NANG, VIETNAM, JULY 1966

With the first light of dawn the ship pulled into Da Nang Bay. A gray haze encircled the base of the jagged, green-blue mountains that surrounded the city and harbor. Da Nang was a major port for the deposit of war freight in the struggle against the Communists. Close to two hundred thousand tons of cargo arrived a month. Here resided both the US Air Force and the Naval Support Activity.

Da Nang was the second most populated city in South Vietnam, surpassed only by Saigon. The war had doubled its population thanks to the surplus of jobs and wave of Americans.

"So what's there to do here other than possibly getting killed?" Greg asked facetiously.

"I read in the Special Services brochure that there is a shrine with a pagoda carved from living rock in one of the caves in the Marble Mountains, which is the sole attraction in Da Nang, but I'm not sure whether we should go there," Bryan replied. Then he garbled something about the Vietcong (VC) that Greg did not understand. "Another fascinating place is the old capital of Vietnam, Hue—a miniature of the Forbidden City in China."

"How far is it?" Greg asked.

"Just a couple of hours. We won't get liberty today. We got a lot of stores to unload. You remember those supplies we picked up in Okinawa? Well, this is their last stop. The scuttlebutt is we'll be pulling out each night and returning in the morning. There's some concern about the VC swimming out and blowing up the ship."

"This sounds like a real fun spot!"

The ship's crew worked the entire day unloading supplies or continuing in-port routine. As Bryan checked and released stores to the crane operators, he felt as if he would lose his mind between the hoisting crane noise beating in his ears and the never-ending removal of war material from the cargo holes. Barges floated alongside the ship, and no sooner were they filled than another would appear. There seemed to be no end to this repetitive job. He kept looking at his watch, anxiously waiting for lunch.

When Bryan returned from lunch, several marine officers and three blindfolded and gagged Vietnamese were arriving on deck. The Vietnamese were chained hand and foot with a long chain linking their hands and feet together. He watched them carefully. Who were these men? Were they VC or North Vietnamese soldiers? They soon disappeared below deck to the ship's brig. He gave it little thought and continued his work. Hours passed, and the three marines returned and proceeded to secure the area of the ship with rope. A few of his shipmates noticed the goings-on and started to talk.

"Boy! Not here twenty-four hours and we have POWs on board!"

"What's going on?" Bryan asked.

"We got us some North Vietnamese officers, and our ship is where they will be interrogated. The roped area is off limits to ship's crew."

Bryan felt strange and was filled with disbelief. Just a year ago he had been home, and all this had been on TV. Was he really here in the middle of a war? It was all so hard to comprehend.

After breakfast the next morning Bryan made his way topside to begin another day of cargo transfer. He took his clipboard and began verifying the stock ledger. Stooped and counting the boxes, he was distracted by the sound of rattling chains. Bryan froze. A POW was approaching him. He wanted to turn, but fear stopped him. Why was the man coming toward him?

"Yank! Don't turn around," came a twittering voice from behind him.

"Why are you talking to me?" A chill ran through him.

"There's not much for me to do, and why not? I'm curious: Do you have any idea why you are in Vietnam?"

"I'm not allowed to talk to you."

"Why? Does your government fear you'll learn some truth?"

"You're a Communist. What other truth is there to know?"

"I wonder, who is the more brainwashed between the two of us?"

A marine officer said something in Vietnamese. He must have told the prisoner to keep moving, as the man quickly continued his walk. Bryan was puzzled as to why the marine hadn't spoken in English. As the prisoner walked across the deck, Bryan caught a glimpse of his back. The man stood a little over five feet, with silky, india-ink hair. His loose, black clothing did not fit, and "POW" ran across his shirt in large letters. Bryan was dazed by the encounter but soon returned to his work.

"Bryan," interrupted Radnor, "guess what I heard. The ship is going to throw a barbecue tomorrow on China Beach. Liberty at last! Greg and I were wondering if you're going? We missed you at mess."

"Sure, I have a lot of things to see. Are you joining Greg and me when we go to Hue? We're making arrangements through Special Services. It may be an overnighter."

"Let me check it out with my division officer. I don't believe the both of us could get off, but it sounds great."

The next morning Bryan arrived on deck around the same time, in the hope of encountering the POW again. Within a few minutes of his arrival the prisoner was on deck for his routine morning exercise.

Bryan took the same position as the previous day behind the large cargo boxes, so as not to be noticed by the marine guard. All night he had thought about his short conversation with the POW. He wanted to take advantage of the exchange of thoughts between them, realizing that this chance opportunity might never occur again. He told no one—not even his best friends.

"I see you have returned, yank."

"If you insist on calling me yank, then I'll refer to you as commie."

"That's fine since we're enemies. And why is that the case? Do you know, yank?"

"We're enemies because you will not allow the South to determine its own system of government."

"In 1956 President Ngo Dinh Diem refused to hold elections as he had promised in the Geneva Agreements. He realized the people would vote him out and side with us. Did you not learn that in school?" Then the man quickly dashed off.

Bryan had no idea what the POW was talking about. Who was President Ngo Dinh Diem? Why were the elections never held? He remembered what his world history teacher had said about Napoleon: "To conquer your enemy, you must know him." He and most Americans knew nothing of the Vietnamese people. They had the military might and the arrogance to think they didn't needed to know anything of the Vietnamese. At that moment he promised himself he would make sense of this society.

He dashed below deck to get a letter off to his dad. In his letter he asked for books that dealt with Vietnamese history, as a search in the ship's library had proved fruitless.

"Liberty, liberty call. Are you ready to hit the beach?" Radnor asked. "First we can go into town and then to the ship's party this afternoon. Greg is on deck waiting for the next shuttle."

"Just a minute—I want to put a stamp on these letters."

"Why, when we can mail them free?"

"I don't tell my parents when we are in a war zone. By the time they get these letters, we'll most likely be in Hong Kong. Why should they worry?"

The port of Da Nang had limited deepwater piers, so the three of them, along with the rest of the crew, had to take one of the ship's landing crafts to reach the city.

"Did you know we have POWs on board?" Bryan asked.

"Yeah, I was talking to the marine guard, and he told me that when they are through with them, they will take them 'for the drop,'" Greg said.

"What do you mean?" Bryan asked.

"They take them for a helicopter ride over the bay, shoot them in the back of the head, then drop them in the water."

"No! I can't believe that. You've got to be joking! America has resorted to that? No! That's not us," Bryan replied incredulously.

"This isn't a declared war, so I guess there are no rules of war to follow," Greg said nonchalantly.

"That doesn't make it right."

"Is there anything right about this war?" Radnor asked. "Who knows the truth?"

"Did you know one of them speaks English?" Bryan asked, having been surprised by this fact himself.

"You've spoken to one of them?" Radnor asked with a look of shock.

Bryan looked around to see if anyone was listening. "Well, sort of."

"I wouldn't. You could get into a lot of trouble," Radnor warned.

"Well, I wouldn't have either, but it just happened, and I was fascinated. I just can't get over the fact that he's going to be killed."

"Listen, buddy, we're here, and it's either us or them," Greg said.

Bryan had now come into actual contact with the enemy. The encounter had given the war a face. The war was no longer conceptual—it had become a physical existence. Inadvertently, the seeds of creed and morality had been sown.

"We're here! Get over it! Time to disembark!" Greg interrupted as Bryan continued to muse and mumble about the imminent execution.

Da Nang was not a place for one who wanted to rest. The city was merciless to the senses of smell and hearing. The traffic of trucks, jeeps, and an assortment of motor vehicles filled one's nose and lungs with dust and fuel exhaust fumes. The atmosphere was both subdued and uncomfortable. There was a sense that things were not as they seemed. A veil of disguise seemed to permeate the place and its residents. Was the smile given by the merchant or young girl carrying goods in a green basket genuine? Who was foe or friend? This feeling followed them as they made their way through the city, through the powdery, soil-covered streets cluttered with vendors selling an assortment of wares from vegetables to cold drinks to trinkets. The city had no visible plan or layout. Buildings appeared at random—white stucco structures with orange or light-gray roofs.

Men and women carried goods on carts, bicycles, or their shoulders like human scales. The language exchange among the people was high-pitched and almost songlike. Most wore black slacks with white blouses and conical straw hats. Every city activity seemed to ignore the war and portray a world that had found harmony in the madness.

"This bar looks like a great place to get a beer and cool off. They've got Tiger draft," said Radnor.

"With a welcome sign like that, how could we resist?" Greg said. He then read the sign aloud:

US HERO OF COM 7TH FLEET,
SO SORRY TO HAVE TROUBLED YOU AT
VIET-NAM.
PLEASE STAY LOVELINESS OF AN EARTHLY
PARADISE AS LONG AS YOU LIKE THIS EVENING.
WE GIVE SERVICE TO YOU IN ANYTHING,
WHATEVER YOU WANT.
SEE IS BELIEVING. MANY BEAUTIES WAITING
FOR YOU.
COME IN. STRIPTEASE COME FROM TOKYO.
SHOW ON EVERY HOUR.
CLUB OWNER JOE TRAN WELCOME YOU!

"Now, how could we go wrong with a guy named Joe Tran? Any place

The Invisible Moon

would be better than this heat and humidity. It must be ninety plus," Greg complained as he wiped the moisture from the back of his neck.

"These people put together sentences better than half the crew, and it's not their language," Bryan said. "I see why they let us go on liberty in our work clothes. I don't think my whites could handle all this dust," he added, brushing his jeans with his hand.

The three sat at a table and ordered beer. Within a few minutes four or five girls flocked around them like locusts, hugging them and sitting on their laps.

"You like Lan?" one of them said. "Buy me a drink so I can sit with you."

Bryan's face turned red as she stroked his crotch.

"No drink for Lan. I'm a married man," said Radnor.

"I won't tell your wife. I want to keep you in practice so when you get back to the States you have not forgotten how to fuck."

"I'll take the best-looking one on that promise!" Greg shouted.

"Count me out," Bryan said. "I can wait until I get home. I'm getting married at Christmas. I can see me getting clap."

Within a short time the girls had left the men, with the exception of Lan. Greg was buying drinks for her, and so she stuck to him.

"So, Lan, how about telling a cabdriver and a tour guide that we want to go to the Marble Mountains?" Bryan asked.

"That's not far from the city, only about six miles from us," she replied. "But be sure you leave before dark, as Viet Cong sniper fire could kill you. It is very dangerous, although it's still beautiful with its great Buddha."

"Oh great! I'm killed viewing Buddha and shooting my camera. So that's what you were gabbling about," Greg said and slapped Bryan on the back of the head. Then he turned to Lan. "You're quite cute, Lan. How about you and I get together later?"

"That will be fine. I don't think I will be going anywhere soon."

Within an hour they arrived at Non Nuoc village at the foot of the Marble Mountains. The village had been inhabited by stone carvers since the fifteenth century and was a short walk from China Beach.

"These mountains are awesome," Greg said. "What's the story, Bryan?"

"Legend has it that the turtle god hatched a divine egg and the shells, which cracked into five pieces, became the five mountains named after the five ritual elements. The most important is Thuy Son."

Housed within the center of the irregular mountain was an oriental structure reputed to be the home of a great Buddha. A warrior figure painted in bright red, green, and gold stood guard. Buddhist pilgrims, tourists, and worshipers filled the sacred ground.

"This is something to see," Radnor said as he looked on with amazement.

"Interesting!" Greg added.

The men watched the worshippers while keeping alert to time and the need to return to the city.

Greg moved to the other side of the entrance to the cave and called to Bryan and Radnor, "A great view of the guys at the barbecue from here. We should be down there eating!"

"Right, we need to get moving. We'll miss the ship's beach party, and this place gives me the creeps," Radnor said in obvious discomfort.

"Yes, you must leave before dark, or VC snipers could kill you," agreed the cabdriver. "It is very dangerous."

"Yes, let's go back now. I'm starving. I could go for a few hamburgers or chicken legs," Greg said.

Within a few minutes they returned to the cab and were off to the ship's picnic.

HUE, VIETNAM,
JULY 1966

S pecial Services, a naval tour agency, arranged for Bryan and
Greg to travel to Hue by train to meet up with a local guide for
a cultural tour of the city.

"Are you sure this is where we're supposed to meet the tour rep?"
Greg asked.

"We have to go through the Noon Gate by the four cannons,"
Bryan said, his head buried in a guidebook. "This is interesting. Back
in 1601 the city was built on a hill shaped like a dragon. Legend has it
that a lady predicted a king would build a pagoda. This pagoda would
lure the forces from heaven, and energies would be found in the veins
of the dragon."

"Very nice, but please answer my question."

"Yeah, yeah, this is the place. Relax. We still have a few minutes
yet. Listen and let me finish. After her prediction she disappeared into
the heavens. Lord Nguyen Hoang built a pagoda on the hill and called
it Thien Mu. Translated it means 'Heavenly Lady.'"

"Thien Mu. I'll have to remember that." Greg repeated the name
to himself several times.

"We can't visit there today, as it is west of the city."

"Anyway, that is all very interesting, but what about the city itself? You're the historian. Now's your chance to educate me! Seriously, please continue reading. I'm genuinely interested."

Bryan continued reading: "The citadel city of Phu Xuan was built on the site of present-day Hue in 1687, and in 1744 it was the capital of the southern part of Vietnam, which was under the rule of the Nguyen lords. The Tay Son rebels occupied the city until 1802, when it fell to Nguyen Anh, the tenth lord, who renamed the city Hue. He proclaimed himself Emperor Gia Long, thus founding the Nguyen dynasty, which ruled the country—at least in name—until 1945. He established the court and government at Hue. Traditionally the city, located along the banks of the Perfume River, has been one of the country's cultural, religious, and educational centers."

Suddenly a man behind them said, "Good morning, gentlemen. My name is Long. Please follow me to where your English-speaking guide is waiting for you."

They walked toward the citadel across the arid moat, overgrown with vegetation, and approached the Noon Gate, or the Ngo Mon Gate.

"Please wait one moment," Long said.

"I'm not going anywhere," Greg replied as he looked around. "Wow!" he exclaimed. "Look at that flagpole. How high is that?"

Bryan referred to his guidebook. "That's called Cot Co, the King's Knight, and is the country's tallest flagpole at thirty-seven meters in height."

Greg was then distracted as Long returned with a young woman who looked to be about twenty years old. From a distance it was difficult to tell whether she was Vietnamese or European, but there was something different about her.

"That must be our guide," Greg said, directing Bryan's attention to the slender woman. "I can't figure out her nationality."

Bryan turned to look. "Woo, she is beautiful. I'd guess she's Eurasian."

"Whatever she is, she is most outstanding."

The blend of her features seemed to exemplify the best of two worlds, producing a human form that was exceptional and ravishing.

Taken by her exotic harmony of beauty, both men were speechless. They walked to meet her as she approached them. Her long, straight, black-brown hair moved like silk fluttering in the wind. Shades of red reflected the sunlight. She wore a traditional ao dai, a long, golden-yellow gown slit to the waist and worn over white trousers. She walked with elegance and sophistication.

"Gentlemen, welcome to the ancient capital city of Hue. Let me introduce myself. I'm Tuyet. Long explained that you are in need of an English guide. I would be happy to assist you both. We don't have many American visitors, and I would enjoy practicing my English. What are your names?"

"I'm Bryan," he said quickly, filled with excitement and curiosity. He took her small hand and gently shook it. How soft and warm it was.

"Hi. I'm Greg. A pleasure to meet you." His tone was reserved and prudent as he also took her hand.

"Where are you from?" she asked, stretching her arm to lead and direct their tour.

"I'm from Pennsylvania near Philadelphia; Greg's from Virginia."

Greg didn't mind Bryan answering for him. He was taken with Tuyet's loveliness and wanted only to enjoy the feast that filled his eyes. She stimulated him like no woman he had ever met. A yearning and hunger built within his excited body. He wanted her. He imagined running his fingers across the soft, smooth skin of her face. Primeval feelings consumed and aroused him.

"I don't want to be offensive, but are you Eurasian?" Greg asked.

"I'm not offended at all. I'm part Vietnamese, French, and Chinese, and my surname is DuMont."

"Bryan thought you were Eurasian," Greg explained. "Are you a tour guide by profession?"

"Oh no." She smiled naturally, enhancing her lovely facial features. "I'm a political science and history student at Hue University, but with the war and the constant disruption of classes, I may be forced to complete my studies at the Sorbonne in Paris—the city of my father."

"Wow," Bryan said. "Hue University is well known as a prestigious training and research institution for the whole of Vietnam."

"Yes, you are right," Tuyet said. "Hue University has had a history of more than two centuries, beginning with the establishment of the Imperial Academy."

Bryan looked at Greg as if to say, *This one's from money.*

"By giving tours voluntarily I satisfy a portion of the requirements for my degree. Now let's start our tour of the citadel.

"The principal gate to the Imperial Closure is the Ngo Mon Gate—the Noon Gate. This central passageway, with its yellow doors and the bridge across the lotus pond, was reserved for the emperor. Everyone else had to use the gates to either side or the path around the lotus pond. Look on top of the gate. That is Ngu Phung, or the Belvedere of the Five Phoenixes, and is the place where Emperor Bao Dai ended the Nguyen dynasty on August 30, 1945, when he abdicated to a delegation of Ho Chi Minh's Provisional Revolutionary Government. Now I want to show you the Forbidden Purple City. This was reserved for the personal use of the emperor."

"Was anyone else permitted to enter the compound?" asked Bryan.

"Only the eunuchs, because they would have no temptation to molest the royal concubines!"

The citadel's atmosphere was pure Vietnamese. Apart from groups of American servicemen, not a foreigner could be seen. Even the war seemed elsewhere as people strolled through the citadel's innermost enclosure, the Forbidden City.

"That was a marvelous, informative, and enlightening tour, Tuyet. Thank you," Bryan said. "Now, can you suggest a place for us to eat, and would you please join us for a light lunch before continuing?"

Tuyet hesitated, wondering whether accepting the invitation would be appropriate, as they had only just met, and whether the invitation was also extended by Greg, who then said, "Yes, do join us. That's a great idea. It is the least we can do to show how much we have appreciated this wonderful tour."

"Then I would be delighted to join you both, and thank you. I can suggest the Ban Khoai Thoung Tu, which is a few blocks from the flagpole. It serves a Hue specialty called *banh khoai*—a crepe with bean sprouts, shrimp, and meat inside."

"That sounds delicious. I'm real hungry!" Greg said approvingly.

After lunch they continued their tour of the citadel, crossed over the Trung Dao Bridge, and visited the Thai Hoa Palace (the Palace of Supreme Peace), which was used for the emperor's official receptions and was also where ranks of mandarins would pay him homage as he sat on his elevated throne.

"I'm so sorry there is no time to show you the famous Thien Mu Pagoda."

The familiar words drew Greg's attention. "Ah, the Heavenly Lady."

"We'll be back again, I'm sure," Bryan interjected. "Is there any way we can contact you to take us on another tour?" he asked as Greg kicked him, encouraging him to elicit more information about her.

"You can reach me at the university and leave a message—or this is my university address," Tuyet replied, hastily writing on a scrap of paper from her purse.

"Thank you. I hope we'll meet you again."

As they left her, Greg sighed, "What a wonderful day!"

"If I didn't know any better, I'd think you were in lust again."

"Thien Mu, Thien Mu," Greg repeated, smiling to himself, as they made their way back to Da Nang.

9

THE AFFAIR,
JULY 1966

"How long is the train ride back to Hue?" Greg asked as he paced up and down in the train station.

"Just a few hours."

"I can't believe Tuyet never wrote back to you after our wonderful tour."

"No, she must have dropped off the face of the earth. We're on our own today," Bryan said.

"What, no Thien Mu?"

"What a job getting those overnighters! I've made reservations at the Hotel Saigon Morin by the Perfume River."

Within a few hours they arrived in the city and caught a cab to the hotel.

"I'll get the keys so that we can check out the room and change into our civvies," Bryan said.

The hotel had a 1920s style and strong French architectural influence. As they walked to their room, they admired the bonsai plants placed on small mahogany tables along the corridor. After a quick change they made their way to the lobby to meet their tour guide.

"I have a surprise for you," Bryan said teasingly. "Look who our guide is!"

"*You creep!* Thien Mu, my Thien Mu!"

"No, it's Tuyet," Bryan corrected him.

"She's more beautiful than I remembered," Greg whispered.

"Xian, chao," Bryan greeted her excitedly.

"And hello to you too! Are you ready? Our boat is waiting to take us to the Thien Mu Pagoda. I'll tell you about it on the way."

They passed under the bridge and saw the citadel. On seeing the flagpole, Greg exclaimed, "Ah, Cot Co," remembering his last visit.

"I shall tell you about Thien Mu. It is an icon of my country. According to legend, Thien Mu—Heavenly Lady—appeared and told the people that a lord would come to build a pagoda for the country's prosperity. On hearing this, Nguyen Hoang ordered a pagoda to be constructed. Beautiful, isn't it? It has been destroyed and rebuilt several times over the centuries, and it was a hotbed of antigovernment protest a few years ago …"

Bryan, Greg, and Tuyet returned to the hotel for coffee, and as Bryan approached the receptionist, he was handed a message: "Stores unaccounted for. Return to ship ASAP. Tag."

"Damn!"

"What is it?" Greg asked.

"I've got to go back to the f'ing ship."

"Okay, but let's have a coffee, say goodbye, and then we'll get our stuff."

After Tuyet had excused herself, Bryan said, "No, no—you may as well keep the room. There's no need for you to return. Have dinner and enjoy yourself."

Bryan darted off to pack his things and left Greg standing at the reception desk by himself. Tuyet returned and asked, "Where's Bryan?"

"He had to return to the ship, but he suggested that I stay on, as the room is already booked. Anyway, I'd like to remain in the city for the night rather than go back … I'm sure that there is more of the city to see."

"Well, if you would like, we could take a tour of the city by night and take a ride on a *xich lo* or a *tuk-tuk*," Tuyet suggested in her soft-spoken voice. "It's wonderful to see the citadel illuminated. It is so beautiful."

"That would be wonderful, but do you have any other plans?"

"No, Greg, I don't have any other plans, and I would enjoy showing you more of my city."

"That would make me very happy," Greg responded.

Bryan appeared with his duffel bag. "I'm off," he said to Greg. "I'll see you tomorrow. You are going to stay, aren't you?"

"Yes, I am."

Bryan embraced Tuyet, thanked her for the tour, and summoned Greg over. "You'd better be good. You represent your country!"

"Okay, I'll be good, but like Mae West says, 'When I'm bad, I'm better!' Now get out of here! Seriously, I'm real sorry you have to go back, buddy. Hey, your cab is here. See you back on the ship."

Greg turned to their guide. "Tuyet, will you please join me for dinner tonight—say eight thirty?"

"I would love to, but first I must return to the university."

During dinner Greg was absorbed in her conversation. Whenever she asked him a question, he was fairly monosyllabic, as he was enraptured by her voice and her very essence.

"My family's home is in Saigon, not far from our rubber tree plantation near Cu Chi. With all the VC activity and American intervention there, they don't go very often. In fact, my father is thinking of selling the plantation and returning to Paris if the war situation does not abate. My parents have a French colonial–style villa overlooking the ocean, not far from Da Nang."

"Oh, that's not too far from our base."

After dinner, they took a *tuk-tuk* toward the citadel and stopped for a few moments at the four cannons; Greg reminisced that this was where they had first met.

It was a warm, humid night with the rumbling of an imminent thunderstorm. As they reached the hotel, Greg took her hand and asked, "Would you like to take the *tuk-tuk* back to the university, or would you like to join me for a coffee? I don't really want the night to end so soon."

Tuyet bent her head and said softly, "Neither do I."

They went to the bar on the third floor, took a table by the window overlooking the river and the Truong Thien Bridge, and ordered coffee and cognac.

Greg reached his hands across the table and took hers. "My Thien Mu," he said.

Tuyet smiled. "My handsome Greg with a beautiful smile."

Silently they rose from the table. Greg put his arm round her waist, and she clasped his hand as they made their way to his room. He poured another glass of cognac, and as she took it from him, his hands encircled hers. A warm thrill shot through his body like a bolt of lightning on a summer night. Greg watched her every movement and was enthralled by her delicate hands around the glass. His hands lingered for a moment, and then, as their eyes met, she withdrew.

"Greg, we cannot complicate our lives any more than they are already."

"Why not just embrace the moment?" he said softly, brushing her long, silky, ebony hair from her face. He gently but firmly drew her head toward him, and, in spite of her efforts to retain her distance, their lips met. It was everything he had imagined. Her moist lips stimulated him. His heart raced, and his body tingled. He slid his hand inside her ao dai and began to unfasten it, tracing the contour of the snaps up from her waist to her delicate neck. His hands were like a soft autumn breeze that blows the leaves from the branches, sending them fluttering to the earth, and the blue silk ao dai gently fell to the floor. He cupped her warm, firm breasts with his strong hands, and a flash of fire consumed her petite body as he whispered, "My Thien Mu."

She pressed her hands against his throbbing chest in a faint effort to resist but then cautiously drew him toward her, and they surrendered to one another's love.

10

THE VILLA,
AUGUST 1966

Tuyet's parents owned a French colonial–style villa in the Son Tra district, about two miles from Da Nang on My Khe Beach, overlooking the romantic landscape of the sea and the Marble Mountains. It was a low, ochre building with a Chinese roof, red and white tiles, and green shutters open to the tropical air. Over the doorway was a round piece of wood with the yin-yang symbol in the middle surrounded by a spiral design. These *mat cua*, or "watchful eyes," were supposed to protect the residents of the house from harm.

In Vietnamese tradition, the living room contained dark furniture, deeply carved with the French fleur-de-lis. The dark red of the velvet curtains had faded a little with the sun. Two altars held incense burners and offerings of fruit and flowers to Tuyet's ancestors, to the spirits of great men of the past, and to Buddha.

"What religion are you?" Greg asked, looking around.

"If I had to give it a name, I would call myself a Confucianist, but labels are misleading. Most Vietnamese believe one should behave correctly toward one's parents, teachers, rulers, everyone. Taoism teaches us how to stay in harmony with nature and with the spirits—one's future and one's happiness depends on keeping the spirits of one's ancestors happy. And Buddhism teaches us compassion, self-denial, and universal love. Buddhism flourished here in Vietnam centuries ago but then withered. Now, as a moral force and a force for nationalism, it flowers again. Now, would you like some tea while I prepare dinner?"

"Thank you. That would be nice," Greg replied.

The porcelain pot from which she served him tea was decorated exquisitely. It showed a bearded sage, for longevity; a woman bearing a peach, for prosperity; a child, for many descendants; a dish with a duck, for good food; and a deer, for good luck and riches. The happiest sign of all was a red bat. Greg knew that red was a lucky color but was curious about the bat. When he asked, Tuyet explained, "The bat sleeps with his head down and his feet high. He is truly relaxed; he has no worries at all. Eat red bat meat and see what it will do for you!"

"I think I'll give that specialty a miss," he chuckled.

Tuyet served a different specialty for dinner—fried river fish, so tiny that they looked like french fries, and venison steak. Ice cream followed for dessert.

"That was a wonderful dinner, Tuyet. May I help you clean up?"

"It's not necessary."

Greg watched her every movement, then got up and walked around the villa, drawn to the light from the west room, which turned out to be a bedroom. A large window opened onto a small patio, providing a view of the setting sun. He stood silently and gazed at the palm trees and the tropical vegetation outside.

Tuyet came up behind him. "This is one of the three bedrooms in the villa. There are two more upstairs." She moved and stood in front of him and slowly glided her hands down from his face, caressing his neck, until she reached the buttons on his shirt. She unfastened the top one, dropped her hands to his, and led him to the bed.

11

USS *DELAWARE*, AT SEA, LATE AUGUST/SEPTEMBER 1966

B ryan made his way to the mess hall, which was a rectangular space with a low ceiling and fixed tables with rotating seats of four to accommodate a complement of almost five hundred enlisted sailors. Bryan gave his order to the server: "I'll take some eggs, but not with the hard scale on them. Thanks." He saw Greg was already eating and walked over to join him. "Hey, buddy, when did you get back? So how was your evening? How did everything turn out?"

"It was a nice evening," Greg replied quietly.

"Yeah? And? And what?" Bryan asked. "Why do I get the sense that you are holding back?"

"If I told you, you wouldn't believe me, so what's the point?"

"What wouldn't I believe?"

"That I think she's special."

"And who's saying this—you or your groin?"

"I told you that you wouldn't understand," Greg snapped, springing up to leave.

"Catch you at the movie tonight?"

"Sorry, not tonight. I've made other plans. Catch you later."

As Greg left the mess, Bryan was confused and wondered what plans Greg had.

In a new mission, code-named Operation Attleboro, the US 196th Light Infantry Brigade and twenty-two thousand South Vietnamese troops began aggressive search-and-destroy sweeps through Tay Ninh Province. Almost immediately, they discovered huge caches of supplies belonging to the National Liberation Front's Ninth Division, but there was no head-to-head conflict.

The ship concluded its military objective in Vietnam and departed to another port of call for rest and relaxation for the crew.

The compartment was eerily quiet, as most of the crew had gone to see the movie at the mess. Bryan and Greg had already seen it, so they had stayed behind. Bryan was instructing Greg in the art of chess.

"Keep the queen here so that you don't jeopardize your opportunity to move the two knights."

There was a sudden sound of feet and clanking of the ladder as six guys approached. Greg looked up as Bryan continued to give instructions.

"You're not listening to me," Bryan said.

"Is the movie over?" Greg asked.

"They're running the second feature, and it was boring," Garland replied.

"Yeah. It was boring. What are you two doing?" Polk asked.

"Trying to learn chess," Greg answered.

"Guess what we have stashed in the number one hole," McLaughlin said.

"What?"

"If you can break away from your friend and your game of chess, we have some pot. We know you're into it."

Greg looked up.

"I thought you had given it up," Bryan said. "It will mess with your mind."

"Yeah, but it helps me deal with things."

"Are you coming, then?" McLaughlin asked impatiently.

Ignoring Bryan, Greg replied, "Yeah, I'll come."

Greg left with McLaughlin and two other seamen, leaving Bryan in the compartment with Polk, Filipo, and Garland.

"So show us how to play chess," Polk said.

"You need to have a brain first," Bryan replied arrogantly.

"He needs to be brought down to size. Agree, guys?"

"I bet he'd make a good fuck!" Filipo said.

Bryan began to feel uncomfortable and wanted to leave. He picked up his chess set, but Polk kicked it out of his hand. The others continued to antagonize him.

Meanwhile, at the number one hole, Greg, McLaughlin, and the two other seamen were passing around the pipe.

"This is good weed," Greg enthused.

"You seem to be really into it," one of the seamen said.

"I take it once in a while when I need it."

"So what's the story with your friend?" McLaughlin asked.

"What do you mean?"

"He thinks he's better than everyone else."

"You don't know him. He's just in the wrong situation—a square peg in a round hole. He should be an officer. He doesn't belong with our kind."

"You've got brains. Why are you different? You were at Annapolis, weren't you? Does he look down on you and act in the same way with you?"

"No, of course not. As I said, you really don't know him. He really is okay."

"He sure doesn't show it. He has his head up his ass—always reading and ignoring us. Here, have some more weed. Take another hit."

"Gosh, this is real good," Greg said.

All four began to laugh as Greg repeated, "He's my buddy."

"Yeah, he's your buddy! Okay, but he still needs to be brought down to size."

Greg was on a high, but something about the conversation was giving him an inexplicable feeling that diminished his ecstasy. Why were they asking him all these questions? The others began to look at their watches and at one another.

"The movie has another hour or so to run. Do you think that will be enough time?" one of the seamen asked.

"Shut up!" McLaughlin said.

"What are you talking about?" asked Greg.

"Have another hit, buddy."

Greg's head began to spin. "This is unbelievable."

"Almost with us, eh, Greg?"

"Yeah. Yeah," Greg slurred.

"We're all going to get a treat tonight," the seaman who'd spoken before said.

"I told you to shut up!" McLaughlin reiterated.

"What's going on? What treat?" Greg asked.

"You're getting high, and someone's getting laid," the seaman said.

Greg sprang up, but the two seamen pushed him down.

"Just relax and enjoy yourself," the seaman said. "He's in safe hands."

"Safe hands?" Greg questioned.

"Have another hit!" McLaughlin said. "Your friend is getting what he deserves. He's about to be a little sea pussy." They all laughed. "We're going to break his cherry!"

Greg tried to get up, but his head was spinning. As he put the pieces together and realized that his friend might be in trouble, he felt torn between the pleasure of the high and the need to help his friend.

Greg leaped to his feet and pushed two of them apart. One tried to grab him, but he made his way out of the loft, clasping at the chains to pull himself up the ladder to return to the compartment. His head was reeling, and he couldn't move or walk fast enough. He missed his step and fell down. In physical pain, his eyes glazing over, he cried, "I've got to get back. I've got to get back."

Running through his head was the poignant melody of the slow movement of Mozart's Piano Concerto no. 23, a piece that Bryan had so often played to him. Over and over again the same section replayed as he ran. The melody was first introduced by the solo piano, and then, when taken up by the full orchestra, it turned into an aching, yearning, haunting, impassioned composition. The music emulated the agony and anxiety that he was now feeling. It was almost surreal. He had never known the name of the piece, but, even in his disorientation, he identified that it was inextricably linked to Bryan.

What usually took ten minutes seemed to take forever, as he had to make his way under the mess hall because of the movie, along the corridor past the library, then up again to the main deck before reaching the aft compartment. The closer he got, the more the horror pieced together in his mind. Profuse tears ran down his cheeks at the thought of his friend being desecrated. At that moment he realized that Bryan was more than just a friend to him. "I'm going to lose you! I'm going to lose you," he cried as he ran. "I've got to help you. If I don't, I'm going to lose you. Those bastards are going to take you away from me."

Greg realized that this far-reaching event was going to have serious ramifications for both him and Bryan. *Why is this tearing me apart?* he wondered as he desperately tried to return to assist his friend. *Why is everything in jeopardy? What have I not acknowledged until today? I never thought that I would feel like this again.*

While Greg was off smoking, Bryan bent down to pick up the scattered pieces of the chess set Polk had kicked. It was dark, only scattered red lightbulbs lighting the area. Bryan slid into his bunk, a little light-headed from a few pills that he had taken earlier to help calm his seasickness. The ship's movement was easier to take lying down.

The muffled voices of a few sailors playing cards in the passageway prevented him from immediate sleep. Bryan looked around. Three feet above him was a bunk; a bulkhead encased his right side and ran behind his head, while a three-foot locker was on his left side. Slowly his eyes closed as he created endings in his mind to the movie the crew was seeing.

The familiar sounds of his shipmates Polk, Filipo, and Garland readying for bed awakened him. Judging from the noise, laughing, and foolishness, it appeared that they had been drinking again in the number one hole. This customary event caused him little concern, and again he dozed off.

The approach of soft footsteps drawing near caused Bryan's eyes to spring open. Three silhouettes moved toward him, their bodies growing larger and larger until they eclipsed one another, obscuring and diminishing the light. These black, faceless figures drew closer until his sleeping berth was void of illumination.

"How about some sea pussy?" Filipo asked the others.

"Just the thing to take care of three weeks out at sea."

"You guys need to hit your racks," Bryan said, not amused and showing little concern.

"He thinks we're joking," Filipo said as he peered into Bryan's bunk.

"I'll check and see if anyone is coming," Polk said, grasping the hanging chains that held the sleeping racks secure.

Bryan's heart started to race, its throbbing vibration bouncing and echoing in his ears. Bryan closed his eyes, hoping that this possible vile act of desecration was not going to occur, that he was just the brunt of a bad joke.

"Ruocco, how about a little?" whispered Filipo.

Reality set in. Filipo's face dropped in front of Bryan's, and Bryan sprang and recoiled in a futile attempt to escape. What had been a womb of protection was now an inescapable trap.

Filipo flung himself on Bryan. Poised on all fours in a savage and wild posture, he resembled a beast braced to devour its prey. Bryan pushed at Filipo's shoulders with both hands, but Filipo's massive weight made his arms buckle in pain. In desperation, he punched Filipo in the face. Suddenly a blow to Bryan's chin whipped his head to the side, dazing him. He began to yell.

"Shut him the hell up!" screamed Polk.

Filipo wrapped his hand over Bryan's mouth with the pressure of a vise.

"If you keep yelling, we'll all get kicked out, you fucking fool," Filipo hissed.

The horror of this compromising situation quieted Bryan's passion to yell for help. He began to punch without direction, resulting in a severe beating from his attackers.

Garland ripped at his T-shirt while the others pulled his boxer shorts to his ankles. Bryan's face became swollen and throbbed with pain. His head felt as if it had come loose from all the punching. He became dazed and disoriented. A pair of large hands grabbed his hair and turned his head while other hands rotated his limp and almost lifeless body onto his stomach.

He screamed into the moist and saturated pillow one last time. "Please don't! God, please don't!"

"Don't resist. This is all we want."

Bryan was sick and started to vomit as he was forced to submit to the three men's sexual desires for penetration. He became void of thought as he lay facedown, motionless. Tears rolled down his cheeks, mixing with blood and perspiration.

The shock of his ordeal and the disbelief at what was occurring caused him to return home mentally. He called, "Dad! Oh, Dad!" and for a few seconds he found some degree of comfort.

Within less than an hour, the terror had ended, and then he was forced to deal with the desecration, which filled him both mentally and physically. He lay like a corpse. The wounded lower portion of his body rumbled and contracted like an earthquake. He pulled his pain-ridden body from his bunk and made his way to the bathroom. He removed his remaining clothing and entered the shower. The steaming water seemed to burn the pollution from his body. He leaned against the wall and slowly slid to the floor in the corner. The steam thickened, filling the shower with a scorching heat that engulfed him and cleansed him.

Bryan lifted his head at the sound of voices and rattling footsteps ascending the ladder to the sleeping berth. "If only the movie had ended a few minutes earlier, just a few minutes earlier," he muttered to himself.

"Damn, this head is hot. Who left the shower on?" Radnor asked as he approached the steaming stall. As he pulled open the shower curtain to turn off the water, he saw Bryan crouched in a fetal position in the corner with his head in his hands.

"Oh my God, Bryan, what happened to you? Who beat you? What

the hell are those marks on your neck? Bryan, what the hell is going on? Please tell me."

"Just a few minutes earlier," Bryan mumbled.

Greg finally arrived to find the bathroom filled with other shipmates, talking and whispering among themselves. "Move, move, let me through. What's going on? Oh my God, it happened!" he cried out as he saw Bryan shivering and moaning. "I'm too late. God, I'm too late."

"Bryan, please tell us what happened here." Radnor leaned over to Greg and whispered, "Some guys were talking about rape."

"You're fucking nuts, Rad. He's been beaten up," Greg replied in denial. "We'll find out what the hell is going on. Why don't you go to sick bay and get some ice for his swelling?"

"Let's take him to sick bay," Radnor suggested.

"No, I don't want to go," Bryan groaned.

"Let's take him to his rack," Greg said as he helped Radnor wrap Bryan in a woolen blanket and remove him from the shower.

"No, I don't want to go into that trap. No! No, not there!" Bryan screamed.

Still shouting and seeming to lose any sense of reality, he pushed both of them as if he had forgotten they were friends.

"Okay, okay, you don't have to go," Greg reassured him.

"Calm down; it's okay. Greg and I are here," Radnor said.

"Greg, they'll come back. You guys, please stay," Bryan begged.

"Greg, put him in Horn's old top bunk across from you, at least for tonight, until he can get a grip on things."

"Good idea. Okay, buddy, you can stay up top with us." With the help of his friends, Bryan made the climb to the fourth bunk, which overlooked the entire sleeping compartment. He tried to make sense of the night's insane events.

The weight and rattling of someone climbing toward him put Bryan on alert. Greg's head rose over the side of the bunk.

"Here's some ice. It will help the swelling. Bryan, whatever it is, let's talk. What did they do? How far did they go? I want to hear it from you. You're my best friend, and I'll understand." While he spoke, he reached over and patted Bryan's shoulder. Bryan withdrew quickly from his touch.

"Perhaps tomorrow? Maybe we'll talk tomorrow." He turned and pulled the blanket over his head. "Thank you," he said, the words muffled under the blanket.

The swaying and gentle movement of the ship awakened Greg before reveille. He glanced over to Bryan's bunk to check on him and was surprised that he wasn't there. *I guess he went to the head*, he thought. A good twenty minutes passed, and still there was no sign of Bryan. Greg was filled with concern as to whether Bryan was thinking clearly and wondered where he could be. With these disturbing thoughts he began searching for Bryan, checking the compartment, the passageway, and then the ship's fantail. As he walked onto the deck, the black ocean with tips of white waves drew his attention. *God, I hope he didn't.* A cold rush chilled his body. The night sky was clear with dazzling stars as never seen on land. He inhaled the clean salt air as his concern mounted. Then he heard the muffled sound of a familiar piece of classical music, and his tension was relieved. Bryan frequently played that same scratched record when he was reading or writing letters. It was either Bach's Air on a G String or Fauré's Pavane—Greg could never tell the difference.

Greg made his way to the tack room. There, sitting on one of the pairs of bits and rocking the chain quad rail with arms stretched, was Bryan, staring at the sea's horizon.

"Would you like some company?" Greg asked as he extended himself over the rail, his eyes fixed on the same view.

"Look how bright Venus is. It looks like a ship's mast light making its way over the ocean's horizon. When I miss home or feel like shit, I come out here to watch the sunrise. Somehow seeing this routine event makes me feel that things aren't so strange or unreal and that home is not so distant. I guess it's the only constant thing I have with this ever-changing life of mine."

"I think I understand about changes," Greg said. "I've had a lot of changes in my life that caused me and others a lot of pain."

"In most cases I feel I've had little control over most of my changes," Bryan responded.

"Like what happened last night?" Greg asked.

Bryan froze. He didn't want to be reminded. Unbeknown to him he was in the midst of a psychological phenomenon in which his traumatized subconscious was causing his conscious mind to forget the incident as time passed—a chrysalis of the psyche.

"So what changes are you talking about?" Bryan asked.

"You're really interested, aren't you?" Greg said, looking at him with a smile.

"Sure I am," Bryan said, grateful for the opportunity to remove himself from the focal point. He turned his head toward Greg and studied him with fascination.

"I was kicked out of the Naval Academy for breaking the rules. I had an unauthorized overnight visitor."

"Naval Academy? I had no idea. You could have been an officer. This is a real surprise."

"Aren't you curious about the details? You seem more concerned about my possible commission," Greg said, laughing and tossing his head.

"So what's the big deal? You were horny and got caught getting a little tail. I hope she was worth it."

"It was all worth it. My life changed after that night. I learned about myself and who I really am, but at a price. Soon after the incident my father cut off my funds and demanded I return home. I did a disappearing act for a few months—typical behavior for me. You know how good I am at taking orders! So I enlisted to piss off my father and find a way to support myself. By the time he found out, it was too late for him to do anything. My father now considers me dead."

"That's unreal. I'm sure that he will come around in time."

"You don't know my dad. One doesn't disobey him, the quintessential Virginian gentleman. Between his political power in Charlottesville and his Capitol Hill connections, people jump for him, including his family. Now that I have disgraced him, I'm as good as gone. If it wasn't for my sister, I wouldn't have any family left."

"That's why at mail call you only receive letters from her? I've always wondered about that. I guess you and she are close?"

"We sure are. Laurice and I are just a year apart. I'm her little brother. We share a lot." Greg paused and then said, "How did we drift from you to me? I'm really concerned about you."

"I know you are, but what's the point of it all? It happened, and now it's over."

"But you need to say what happened and put it behind you."

"Why the hell are you so concerned that I tell you? I don't understand," Bryan snapped in an agitated tone, turning his head once more toward the ocean's horizon. Greg continued to look at Bryan and noticed his eyes glazing over with tears.

"I'm so ashamed and embarrassed. How can I live with myself or face the others?" He turned to Greg. "Tell me how I deal with the fact that I was raped by Filipo, Polk, and Garland. Tell me how. And while we're on the subject, where in the hell were you when I needed you?" he asked angrily.

"I tried. I really tried," he said remorsefully.

Bryan grabbed Greg's shoulders and shook him while screaming and crying. "This is not how it is supposed to be. How can I deal with something I never even conceived as possible? Neither you nor anyone else has the answers. I have to deal with it in my own way and the only way I know how."

"Those sick fucking bastards!" Greg's eyes and forehead tightened, his face flaring with anger. "God, I wish I could do something to them."

Suddenly Bryan turned and jumped to his feet, swaying forward and backward as he grasped the chain rail, his back to Greg. It appeared to Greg he might jump.

"No, buddy. No!" Greg flung his arms around Bryan's upper chest and clutched him. "It's okay. I'm going to stick by you. Buddy, it's okay." Bryan dropped his head and cried profusely as Greg continued to comfort him.

"Bryan, look, the sun is rising. Last night's horror is going to be behind you. Just as you said, it will no longer exist."

Bryan lifted his head. The majestic sunlight stretched over the once-black ocean. Now the brilliant dawn sparkled and reflected across the water like gems.

"I think I'm okay now. I don't know how to thank you for seeing me through this hell. I'll never forget it."

Greg released him. "You're okay?"

"I'm ... better."

They turned and walked toward the superstructure.

"Greg, I wasn't going to jump. I thought I was going to puke."

"Now you tell me. You sure had me going. Why didn't you stop me?"

"What," he asked with a grin, "and have you lose the opportunity to be the big hero?"

Laughing and joking, they sealed their bond with an arm upon each other's shoulders.

SAN DIEGO, CALIFORNIA, DECEMBER 1966

After an evening of nightclubbing, Bryan and Greg arrived at the hotel. They checked in and were directed to take the elevator to the third floor.

"This looks to be the right way—thirty-two, thirty-four, thirty-six …" At the door of room 38, he put the key, which was attached to a hexagonal, black, plastic key chain that identified the hotel, into the lock. "I'll open the door. You're a little looped."

"Nice room, but I thought it had two beds," Greg said when they got inside.

"We can always change rooms."

"No, I'm too tired. I just want to get cleaned up and hit the hay. My flight leaves early in the morning."

"I've put in a wake-up call for you at zero six hundred."

"Good. Thanks. I need the bathroom!"

"The booze is making a quick exit tonight, isn't it?" Bryan laughed.

Within a few minutes Greg had showered and was ready for bed.

"That was fast," Bryan said. "I think I'll take a quick shower now. I hope you haven't used all the towels."

When Bryan came out of the shower, Greg appeared to be asleep already. Bryan gently got into bed. As he put his head on the pillow, Greg turned and opened his eyes. "I'm not sleeping. I noticed that picture on the wall and just started thinking."

"About what?" Bryan asked.

"About Tuyet, my Thien Mu," Greg replied. "You know, I've had about twelve letters from her already," he said, waving his forefinger at Bryan and smiling in his inimitable style. "Recently, the smallest event will trigger the memory of her, just like that picture of the pagoda on a hill. That period of our lives seems almost fictitious now, as though we have slipped into another dimension. I shall always think about her standing on the sand-covered pier, waving at us, my eyes fixed on her. That will remain with me forever. Our lives go on while she remains untouched by the movement of time. The shuttle rumbled and moved cautiously to the open harbor. She stood and waved, holding her straw hat against her slender left leg. The wind was blowing her long, black hair to one side. She was wearing that long, yellow gown, slit to the waist. You remember, the one she wore when we first met her?"

"I remember," Bryan said. "It ruffled like a flag, and her white trousers blew in the breeze, contouring the side of her delicate figure."

"Yes, but she looked lovely in spite of nature's inconsideration," continued Greg. "The taste of her soft, moist, plum-red lips still lingers within me. You will be surprised, I'm sure, but I felt a tearing of our physical and emotional bonds. I felt powerless to alter the events taking place, and with each foot of distance, the pain sliced a little deeper. I wondered how I would resume my past life as though she never existed. It seemed impossible. I watched her until she became just a dark object on the pier and I was unable to distinguish her from all the rest. But she had gone only from my sight."

"Yes, I'm surprised. This is a side of you I haven't seen before. It doesn't sound like you at all. My God, you really do love her, don't you?"

After a few moments' hesitation, Greg said, "Yes, buddy. This is it—the real deal."

"I'm glad about that, as I wouldn't want you to hurt her. I have a real affinity with her too, you know. I sort of like this sensitive side of you and am glad that you shared it with me. But let's save further confessions for the morning, bud. We need to get some sleep. Zero six hundred will soon be here!"

Greg turned to Bryan and said jokingly, "Don't worry; I'll always have a place for you."

Bryan raised his eyebrows, wondering if these were just empty words. "First of all, who's worried?" he retorted. "As always, the booze is talking again. Those gin gimlets really do a number on you. Go to sleep."

As Greg turned over and settled down, his arm flopped around Bryan's shoulder. "Get off!" Bryan said. "Move over and let's go to sleep."

It was as if Bryan had only just closed his eyes when the wake-up call heralded 0600. Greg was already up, packed, and almost ready to leave.

Bryan drew back the drapes and thought, *This is the first time I have seen serious rain since I left home.*

"Hey, Greg, it's pouring with rain," he said out loud.

"It sure is," Greg agreed nonchalantly. "I'd better go, buddy. The cab will be here in a minute. See you after the first of the year. Have a merry Christmas and a happy New Year," he said, giving Bryan a big hug. "Give your family my love."

"Will do. Have a good one yourself."

"I'll be in touch to let you know how things go back in Charlottesville. It's the first time I'll be home since I was kicked out of Annapolis, so you know what that'll mean. Laurice won't even be there for support, as she is spending Christmas with her future in-laws. So long!"

Bryan closed the door behind Greg and then went over to the window. The dawn was unusually gloomy because of the heavy rain clouds. He waved as Greg climbed into the cab and watched it drive off. Suddenly he was filled with a most peculiar and inexplicable feeling of emptiness—a kind of rumbling emotional undercurrent. *I guess it's like saying goodbye to the brother you never had,* he thought. The thought quickly dissipated with the anticipation and excitement of going home to see Michelle and his family and friends.

SAN DIEGO, CALIFORNIA,
JANUARY 1967

Bryan checked the classifieds page in the paper for available apartments to rent as Greg drove around town.

"Boy, this car handles well," Greg said. "This is the first time I've leased a Volkswagen. Any luck with other available apartments? The last three have been dumps."

"What do you expect on a sailor's income?" Bryan asked. "Ah, here's one on Twenty-Third and Broadway near Balboa Park that's affordable. It says it's furnished with two bedrooms, kitchen, and large living room in a quiet location."

"Sounds good. Let's go. Which way?"

"Just go right up Broadway, up the hill, and make a left on Twenty-Third."

"This is nice with these date palms, eucalyptus trees, and all."

"1056, 1054, 1052. Here it is."

"This one with two stories?" Greg asked.

"Yeah, that's it. Let's park."

"Does it say whether the apartment is upstairs or downstairs?"

"No. I guess we'll have to ask."

They knocked at the door and were greeted by an elderly woman who was neatly dressed with her hair tied up in a bun and spectacles hanging round her neck. She appeared to be very refined.

"Yes, gentlemen? Can I help you?"

"Yes," Bryan replied. "We're interested in seeing the apartment you have for rent."

The woman put on her glasses and looked them up and down. "I was hoping to rent to a married couple. This is a quiet, respectable neighborhood, and you sailors are noted for your inebriated and boisterous behavior."

Bryan was rather taken back by her preconceived, generalized opinion of sailors and instantly retorted, "Ma'am, I agree with you that some sailors can be quite rowdy and ornery, but I assure you we're not."

"And I promise you, ma'am, that we would be extremely well behaved," assured Greg as he leaned toward her, giving her his winning, endearing smile.

"You're from the South, aren't you?" she said, warming to his smooth southern accent.

"Yes, ma'am. I'm from Charlottesville, Virginia."

"What a coincidence. I have a cousin who lives in Virginia. Well!" She paused for a moment. "Let me get the key, and I'll show you the apartment. Come with me."

They walked through a short, narrow alleyway, and there, hidden behind the two-story house, was a single-story, perfectly square, west-facing house with a single tall date palm in the front.

"This is cool," Greg said.

The door of the apartment opened into a vast living room that had four sizable windows at the far end with a pleasant view overlooking the descending rooftops. The two bedrooms and bathroom were to the rear of the living room, and the kitchen was to the right.

"This would be a great place to live," Greg said to Bryan as they came out of the apartment.

"I agree. Excuse me, ma'am, where do these steps lead?"

"To a roof terrace. Go and take a look. I'll wait for you back at the house."

Bryan excitedly dashed up the steps. "Oh wow! I can see all of San Diego, the bay, Point Loma, and even the Pacific. Greg, come up here and check this out."

"This is real neat." The sound of a low-flying jet suddenly interrupted him as it descended into Lindbergh Field. "Oh boy! This apartment is under the flight path! If that jet was any lower, I could catch it!"

They made their way down the steps and returned to the house.

"So what do you two young men think?"

"We'll take it," Bryan announced firmly.

"Good. I think I can trust you. Now, I shall need a month's deposit in advance, and I will draw up the contract. By the way, the rent includes all utilities, and as a special favor, I will also include laundry. So when would you like to move in?"

"As soon as possible," Bryan said enthusiastically.

"And for how long would you like the lease?"

"Probably about a year, but we don't have our ship's orders yet."

"I know. I understand. You know what we used to say during World War II—loose lips sink ships."

THE WEDDING, CHARLOTTESVILLE, VIRGINIA, APRIL 1967

Laurice picked up Bryan and Greg from the Charlottesville airport at noon. Her physical appearance was as Bryan had imagined. She stood about five foot six with features similar to Greg's, including the warm smile.

"I'm so happy to see you, Greg," said Laurice, greeting him affectionately. Turning toward Bryan, she said, "You must be Bryan. I've heard so much about you. Welcome to Charlottesville. Greg, it is so wonderful that you are here. I've been so concerned about you. It's hard to believe that I haven't seen you for over two years, since you left the Naval Academy and had that terrible argument with Dad."

"Is he still so damn bullheaded?" asked Greg.

"Don't start already! It looks as if you're going to hit heads, and anyway, this is really an inappropriate conversation to be having in front of our guest. We shouldn't air our dirty laundry."

"Bryan is aware of the situation," Greg said.

"So you two have known each other since you boarded the ship? Where are you from in Pennsylvania?" asked Laurice.

"Just outside of Philadelphia—a place called Wallingford," Bryan said. "How long have you lived here?"

"Our family has been here for generations. We can trace our roots to the early settlement of Charlottesville. In fact, a relative of ours was part of the Lewis and Clark expedition."

"Bryan is a scholarly historian," interjected Greg. "Don't worry, Bryan; we'll give you a tour this week and take you to the university and show you where the Lewis and Clark expedition began." They continued to chat during the short journey to the family home.

"So your father is in politics, right?" Bryan asked.

"Yes, he is a member of the Virginia House of Delegates," Laurice replied.

"That's right," Greg said. "That's what fueled the fire of our big fight. The newspapers had a field day with the Annapolis incident. I embarrassed him yet again. You'd think he would have gotten used to it. What's the difference between that and getting suspended from high school for smoking and drinking in the boys' room? He thought he would send me to the Virginia Military Academy to straighten me out! Ha!"

"Boy, you must have been really incorrigible and out of hand!" Bryan said.

"Is he like that on the ship?" asked Laurice.

"No, I think he's calmed down now."

"Oh, I love the way you speak, Bryan. Every word, every syllable is pronounced and enunciated!" Laurice said.

They approached the long driveway, and Bryan's attention was drawn to the magnificent Greek Revival house with white columns, a line of rocking chairs under the portico on the porch, and a crescent row of magnolia trees lining the drive. The spring air was filled with nature's fragrance—the fresh, lemony scent of the magnolias. As they got out of the car, Bryan said delightedly, "This is just the image I have always had of the South."

Greg's mother, a petite and genteel woman immaculately dressed in pastels, came out to greet them. When she saw Greg, she paused and greeted him warmly in her southern Tidewater accent. "Gregory!

I can't believe you are here. Let me look at you. It's been so long since you were home."

"Hi, Mom. It's good to be here," he said, kissing her on the cheek. "Where's Dad?"

"He's finalizing the details for the wedding. He should be out soon." She called to the chauffeur, "Oh, Constable, would you get their luggage, please?"

"Yes, ma'am."

"Mom, this is Bryan."

"Welcome, Bryan. It is a pleasure to meet you at last."

"And you, Mrs. Seaton."

As Bryan was being introduced, he became aware of a figure, whom he assumed to be Greg's father, standing rigid on the veranda, his eyes almost glaring. He appeared to be in his late forties, with a receding hairline, and was dressed in that stereotypical attire of white, conjuring up the thought of a southern planter from the nineteenth century. Without either greeting or looking at Greg, he said coldly, "I hope you are not going to be an embarrassment at this wedding."

"I'm not here to fight or argue, sir. This is my sister's wedding, and I certainly wouldn't embarrass her."

"Please, Drew, you promised there would be no ugliness," Greg's mother interjected quickly. "Let's all go into the house and have an aperitif before lunch. We have so much to talk about, and I want to hear all your news." Turning to the cook, who had appeared on the porch, she said, "Darlene, please prepare lunch in the West Room for one thirty."

"Yes, ma'am."

After freshening up, Bryan and Greg proceeded to the Georgian dining room, which was decorated in eighteenth-century style, and sat down at the table. The atmosphere became more and more strained during the meal as Greg's father gave Bryan a summary of all the infractions of Greg's entire life. Bryan began to feel uneasy, and to try to alleviate the tension, he opened up a conversation with Greg's father and enthusiastically and eruditely discussed government, politics, the present political climate, and social history.

"I would never have imagined that my son would be associated with someone so scholarly and knowledgeable. He finds it all so irrelevant. If it's not focused on Greg, it's trivia."

Greg quietly restrained himself from responding to his father's continuous badgering and attempts to bait him into confrontation. Bryan glanced across the table at Greg. He had surmised that Greg's father was unforgiving and cold, their relationship so unlike the relationship he had with his own father. With the conclusion of lunch, Bryan excused himself from the table. He and Greg spent the rest of the day in and around Charlottesville, where Greg reminisced about the good times as well as the bad. He showed Bryan the historic B&B in the heart of Charlottesville that had been built by Thomas Jefferson's master craftsman, James Dinsmore. Greg had spent the night there once following an argument with his father. He also showed Bryan the Boar's Head Country Resort—with its spa, fitness rooms, swimming pool, and adjacent golf course—where he used to relax and recharge.

As Greg was reluctant to dine with his family that evening for fear of another possible altercation with his father, he persuaded Bryan to drive north of Charlottesville to the Silver Thatch Inn, an old log cabin building constructed by Hessian prisoners during the Revolutionary War. The cuisine featured a modern American menu of grilled meats and entrees served with healthy and eclectic sauces. After a peaceful evening and several liquors, they returned home.

"Wake up, sleepyhead!" Greg remarked as Bryan entered the kitchen. Greg was leaning back on the counter with a glass of orange juice in his hand. "No tour, no history today! We'll play a round of golf this morning, have a light lunch, then perhaps some swimming this afternoon. We could also take in a bit of canoeing with an outfitter on the James River while on the thirty-one-mile Walton's Mountain Museum loop, if you are up for it."

"Okay. That sounds good. So where do we start?"

"The Boar's Head Country Resort. Then later we'll hit a few bars downtown. We'll eat out again tonight. I'm tired of trying to deal with my father talking about my past, night after night. Do you want any breakfast?"

"Not really. Orange juice and coffee would be good. I'll take some of your juice."

"You wouldn't want this. I'll get you some fresh."

"Why? What's wrong with this?"

"Nothing. Relax while I get you a fresh glass."

Bryan was curious and took the glass from the counter. He took a sip and exclaimed, "This isn't orange juice. It's got vodka in it. You're drinking a screwdriver! Greg, you only drink when you have a problem. Hey, buddy, do you want to talk about it?"

"No, not really. I just need a little reinforcement for Anthony's bachelor party and Laurice's wedding, not forgetting the patience to deal with my father! I'm okay. Really! Forget it. Let's go and enjoy our day."

The next day, after breakfast, Greg and Bryan made their way to the little white church and settled into a pew. Bryan noticed Greg massaging his temples and whispered, "You must have one heck of a hangover."

"Pretty bad."

Greg's attention was drawn to the back of the church as the organist struck up the wedding march, signaling the arrival of his beloved sister. He turned around and watched his father escort Laurice up the aisle. She looked radiant. As the service proceeded, Bryan was conscious of Greg fidgeting; he seemed to be anxious for the events to conclude.

After the photos and the usual rice throwing, everyone made their way to their cars to go to the reception. As Bryan and Greg approached their car, Greg's father turned to Greg and said, "You can't even walk straight. You need to sober up before I see you at the reception. The press is here, and I don't want any more embarrassment from you that might jeopardize my career."

"I've had enough of all this. All week I've put up with your cynical and derogatory remarks," Greg said, tearing the bow tie from his neck.

"So no, I won't embarrass you. I won't even come to the reception. I'll leave right now and go back to California, and then maybe you'll be happy."

As the bridal car began to leave the church for the wedding breakfast, Greg headed over and signaled to the driver to stop. Laurice rolled down the window. "What is it, Greg? What's the matter? What's going on?"

"Laurice, Anthony, I'm so sorry, but I just cannot take any more of his sarcasm. Doesn't he ever let up? I cannot go through with all this. I have to leave now."

Laurice reached out and took his hand, noticing that his eyes were glazed over. "I must admit that you have been very tolerant this week, and I understand how you feel. He has been very unreasonable. Go now. We can meet up when we return from Puerto Rico—just the four of us. Say goodbye to Bryan for us. He's a great guy, and I know that he will take care of you."

"Thanks, Laurice. Bye." Greg kissed her and turned away quickly as the car drove off.

Bryan walked over to him, shocked at the turn of events.

"I'm sorry I had to cut your vacation short, but I really cannot take any more," Greg muttered.

"I think I understand. I was leaving early tomorrow morning anyway, to go and visit my parents for a few days before taking my flight to New Orleans."

"No, no, you can still stay here. My parents would be receptive, and I know my father would welcome someone 'scholarly and knowledgeable,'" he added cynically.

"Thanks, but I can't do that. I couldn't be here by myself. I'd feel awkward not being a member of the family."

"Well, I'm going to head back to San Diego."

"Why? You can't go back like this. I have a better idea. Since you have the time, why don't we both go straight to New Orleans?" suggested Bryan.

"Really? You wouldn't mind if I joined you?" Not waiting for an answer to his somewhat rhetorical question, he hastily added, "Right, let me get out of this monkey suit."

"You look more like a penguin to me!" laughed Bryan.

NEW ORLEANS, LOUISIANA, APRIL 1967

As the cabin became illuminated at the end of the flight from Richmond, the stewardess announced that the plane would be landing in New Orleans in ten minutes. Bryan glanced out of the window. "Hey, Greg, take a look at this view! I now see why they refer to New Orleans as the 'Crescent City.'"

"I'm looking forward to seeing it from the ground!"

"That wasn't such a bad flight."

"Not bad at all," Greg replied.

They made their way out of the airport terminal, and Bryan hailed a cab. "Are you okay?" he asked his friend.

"I'm fine. I just hated to leave the way I did. I didn't even say goodbye to my mom. My dad can be such a bastard. I'll call my mom when we've checked in at the hotel."

The trip to the Vieux Carré—the French Quarter—was a quick twenty-minute ride from the airport. Bryan was focused on his surroundings and looking at everything, from the trees draped in Spanish moss to the fan palms and the buildings painted in an array of pastel colors. When he glanced over to the other side of the cab, Greg was leaning his head back and staring at the roof of the cab.

"Are you sure you're okay?"

"Yeah, yeah. I'm fine," he said as he reached over, patted Bryan on the shoulder, and smiled.

"Here you are at your hotel," the cabdriver announced.

The hotel was designed in French Colonial style with a large, white Palladian window and an array of flags flying from each column.

When Bryan checked in, the receptionist said, "Mr. Ruocco, we received your wire requesting the change from a single to a double. Here's your key, and the elevator is on your left."

"Thank you," Bryan said. He then turned to Greg and suggested, "Let's take a break, and then we can check out the town and have lunch. What do you think?"

"Sounds good to me, but I'm also looking forward to that hurricane drink you promised me at Pat O'Brien's."

The day was warm and sunny as the men made their way through the narrow streets. When they reached Bourbon Street, the sounds of jazz could be heard from various establishments. They stopped briefly outside the Famous Door, the birthplace of Dixieland jazz, then walked to the Blue Angel, one of New Orleans's most famous nightspots, which was open from ten in the morning. Walking on a little farther, Greg shouted, "There's my stop! Pat O'Brien's."

"Well, let's go in and get a table!"

The old carriageway entrance was delightful, with its old slate flooring and crossed muskets.

"What are those for?" Greg asked.

"The muskets represent every country that once raised its flag over the city."

"This is great, a garden courtyard!"

The courtyard was surrounded with pink stucco. Large wisteria vines covered the building, seeming to embrace and envelop it as if there were a relationship between them. Black wrought iron tables and chairs filled the yard, and there was a large fountain with a fire emerging from the center. Ornate, black lampposts from the eighteenth century illuminated the area.

"So hurricanes are the specialty drink of this place, then?" Greg asked.

"That's right. They were created during World War II when whiskey was in low supply."

"What on earth is in them?"

"Let's see." Bryan read the drinks menu. "Hurricane rum or a good dark rum, a special hurricane mix, and crushed ice, garnished with a slice of orange and a cherry."

"Sounds potent! Let's order." Greg called over the waiter. "We'll have two of your famous hurricanes, please." As the waiter walked off, he pulled a pack of cigarettes from his shirt. "Want one?"

"Sure, why not?"

"This is marvelous," Greg said.

"You seem to be feeling better."

After a long pause he replied, "Oh, well, I guess I am better."

"I'm glad. We only have forty-eight hours to see the city, and then we're off to San Diego and back to hell," Bryan said.

As Bryan spoke, the waiter brought their drinks. The glasses were shaped like hurricane lamps, with an hourglass shape and pedestal base. Bryan reached for a frosty glass and took the straw in his mouth. "Wow, this is remarkable!"

"With all that booze we'd better not drink them too fast. They'll go right to our heads! So what's the plan for today?" asked Greg.

Bryan took out his guidebook. "Well, I thought we could have lunch at the Court of Two Sisters, hit Jackson Square, then go to the French Market for coffee and beignets at Café du Monde. We should visit the Garden District and have dinner in the Quarter. It would be good to go back to Bourbon Street late tonight for booze and jazz. So what do you think?" he said excitedly without taking a breath.

"Sure, sounds like a great plan," Greg said, shaking his head with a smile. "Why haven't you fitted in some time for a little tail?"

"I thought I would leave that up to you. That's your area of expertise," Bryan replied, shaking his head and rolling his eyes.

The spring day was perfect—sunny and warm with low humidity. The city seemed to seduce the two young men, with the sights of the French Quarter and its pink and blue buildings garnished with wrought iron–like vegetation. The buildings reminded them of birthday cakes decorated with icing. With each turn of a corner came other visual surprises accompanied by jazz sounds. The atmosphere was a Mardi Gras in miniature.

"This place is really cool. I'm so glad you invited me," Greg said.

"I'm delighted you joined me. It would have been a little lonely doing it by myself."

"Oh, lonely," Greg said, slowly putting an arm around Bryan's shoulders and pulling him close.

"Stop fooling around," Bryan said as he gently pushed Greg away. "Look, Café du Monde. We're here. Now for the café au lait and beignets."

"There's a table! Quick, let's grab it," Greg said, pointing.

They sat in an overcrowded and loud section, with little room to pull a chair out. People scrambled to secure tables, descending like vultures on their prey.

"Wow, this sure is a popular place," Greg said as he looked around.

"Two coffees and a large serving of beignets, please," Bryan ordered.

"Bryan, may I ask you a personal question?" Greg looked into Bryan's eyes.

"Well, I guess," Bryan replied, looking down at the table and toying with his napkin.

"How long will you keep pushing people away from you? Look at me, damn you!"

"What are you talking about?" Bryan looked at him with an annoyed expression.

"I really want to be close to you and help you put that ship incident behind us. It keeps us so distant otherwise."

"I've told you a thousand times! I don't want to ever discuss that." Bryan's eyes began to fill with tears.

Greg reached over and clasped Bryan's hand tenderly. "You don't know, do you?"

"Know what?"

"That I love you."

A few seconds passed, and Greg continued to hold Bryan's hands between his. Greg thought it was strange that his friend was not pulling away. The two men just stared at each other in silence.

Gradually and cautiously, Bryan withdrew his hand from Greg's clasp. He appeared to be in a state of confusion and disbelief. He gazed at Greg.

Greg took a deep breath, wondering, *What is he thinking about? What will he say?* A few moments flashed by.

"Love in a queer way?" Bryan asked with a tone and facial expression of disgust.

"No! No! I mean a love between two friends or brothers. A deep love," he said defensively.

"Great, our beignets are here," Bryan said, indicating that this topic was concluded.

The afternoon continued with visits to Jackson Square with its imposing equestrian statue of "Old Hickory"—Andrew Jackson. Bordering the square were some of the most historically significant buildings in the city: the eighteenth-century Cathedral of Saint Louis as well as the Cabildo and Presbytère, which originally served as government buildings but were now museums. On either side of the square stood the red brick Pontalba Buildings, believed to be the first apartment buildings in America.

"Let's take a quick look at the Garden District," suggested Bryan. "If you're not too tired, that is?"

"No, I'm okay. What's there?"

"It was founded in the 1850s by successful entrepreneurs—the nouveau riche of that time—who built large, elegant mansions in different architectural styles."

After walking around the district, Greg said, "I don't know about you, but I'm beat. I'd like to return to the hotel and rest a little before we go for dinner."

"Great idea. I would like to rest a bit as well."

"So what is the plan for this evening?"

"We have reservations at the Court of Two Sisters, and then I thought we could hit the bars on Bourbon Street. What do you think?"

"It all sounds great," Greg said in approval.

Within half an hour they had returned to the hotel. Bryan threw himself on the bed. He took off his sunglasses and put them on the table. When he turned around, Greg was sitting at the end of his bed.

"I don't think you understood what I was talking about earlier."

"Greg, I'm really beat."

"Fine! Don't discuss it then," Greg said in anger and irritation. "I'm going to take a shower." He sprung up, unbuttoned his shirt, and tossed it on his bed in an agitated manner.

Without saying another word they rested, changed for dinner, and made their way to the restaurant. They passed through the picturesque, old-world courtyard with its original gaslights and flowing fountains. The maître d' led them to their table in one of the three different-styled dining rooms.

"I hope this table is suitable, sirs."

"This is neat. It's like being in someone's private residence," Greg said as he surveyed the room. "Not at all like a restaurant."

After a few drinks Greg calmed down, and they ordered their meal. Greg chose a more conservative dish, while Bryan was anxious to try the local creole food.

"No starter for me, but I'll take the charbroiled tenderloin of beef, rare," Greg said.

"I'd like the creole seafood gumbo and the corn-fried Allemands catfish with the jumbo lump crabmeat. We'd also like two of your special dinner salads. Thank you."

The next day, neither of them mentioned the previous day's incident, although Bryan thought that Greg seemed rather disgruntled at breakfast.

"So what do you want to do today?" Greg asked.

"I'd like to visit the Museum of Art and take a walk in City Park. The Kress collection of Renaissance paintings is on exhibit. Also, I think you would enjoy seeing Degas's Portrait of Estelle, which he painted when he lived here in New Orleans for a brief period."

"Right, let's go," Greg responded coldly. The excitement of the visit to the museum put Greg's apparent apathy out of his mind.

They crossed the huge City Park, which was surrounded by moss-covered live oaks, and approached the museum. Inside the museum was like a small but precious jewelry box. They walked through to the Hyams collection of nineteenth-century art. Just as Bryan noticed that Greg did not seem to be very receptive to the exhibit, Greg turned to Bryan and said, "I'm going to hit the Quarter. I've had enough."

"What's this? Stupor time?"

"I'm just thirsty," Greg retorted. "I'll see you later."

Bryan continued to be enthralled with the exhibit, and his insatiable appetite for art dismissed any thought of Greg from his mind.

It was approaching midafternoon, and Bryan thought that he would take a cab back to where the atmosphere was most concentrated—Vieux Carré. He walked past the sidewalk artists, who specialized in recreating the city's picturesque landmarks on paper, and returned to the hotel.

By the time he had freshened up and changed for dinner, there was still no sign of Greg. As it was their last night in New Orleans, Bryan decided that if Greg was hitting the bars, then he would do his own thing. He went to the enchanting Louis XVI restaurant, which was famous for its French, creole, and fish cuisine, and then took a walk down to the levy to watch the Mississippi.

He became almost hypnotized by the flow of the river and was drawn into its power and mystique. *Strange how the Mississippi divides the land into two and so does the Nile,* he contemplated. He reflected on his home in the East, where the sun rose—the side of the living and his comfortable and predictable life. Then he thought of his home in the West, where the sun set—the side of the passing and the unknown life where he was dealing with emotional growth and frightened of the future. Comparing the two sides of the river with his two worlds, he made his way back to the hotel.

Soon after he had returned and begun to pack, Greg staggered in, still holding a glass in his hand.

"I'm glad to see you're here to make the flight home," Bryan said sharply.

"Curious to know where I've been?" Greg smiled tauntingly.

"I don't need to ask," he retorted sarcastically.

"So I've been drinking and got myself a piece of ass. You're pissed with me, aren't you?"

Bryan responded with a silent look of indifference. "We've a plane to catch in an hour," he said, changing the subject.

"I got you this time, didn't I?"

"I don't want this conversation. Just drop it, and let's get moving."

They checked in, boarded the plane, and found their seats. Bryan ordered a champagne cocktail, and Greg ordered a gin.

"Bryan," Greg began.

"Yen nau! Shut up! I want to take advantage of this four-hour flight to try to gain a working knowledge of Vietnamese for when I see Tuyet next time. You do remember her, don't you?" Bryan asked sarcastically.

"I try not to remember her. It hurts too much. I sometimes think that is why I get involved with others, just so that I can forget the pain for a while."

"You give your love so freely. How diminished it must be," Bryan responded unsympathetically.

"That's a cold and cruel thing to say."

Bryan buried his head in his Vietnamese grammar book and, after a while, glanced at Greg unnoticed. Greg had shown such emotion at just the mention of Tuyet's name that Bryan suspected he was now lost in contemplation of her.

THE APARTMENT, SAN DIEGO, CALIFORNIA, MAY 1967

Bryan turned on the light to see the time. It was 2:57 in the morning. He got up and went to get a drink of water. As he passed Greg's room, he vaguely noticed that the door was open and Greg was not home yet.

I guess it's going to be another one of those nights again, thought Bryan. *He'll be in a real stupor when he returns.* He went back to his room and fell asleep.

Suddenly, loud crashing and banging awakened him.

"Can I come in?" Greg slurred.

"You're drunk. Go to bed and sleep it off."

"No, I'm not," Greg said with his inimitable smile.

Bryan pulled the covers over his head. "Turn the light off and go to bed," he said impatiently.

"No, I need to talk with you."

"Can't it wait until morning?"

"No. I might not have enough courage," Greg garbled, trying to pull the covers off Bryan.

As Bryan sat up and tried to replace his covers, Greg enveloped him. At that, Bryan shrieked and sprang out of bed. "Don't touch me. I don't want to be touched," he yelled angrily. "What do you want to talk about that is so important right now?"

"Why are you so sensitive?" Greg asked, taken back by Bryan's overt rejection.

"What is it that you need to tell me? Just get it over with and get to bed."

"I need you to forgive me," Greg pleaded.

"Forgive you for what? What have you done?"

"I need your forgiveness because I wish that I could have prevented the events of that night. The booze isn't helping me anymore. I have to get this off my chest. That night plays over and over in my mind. What could I have done differently that could have changed the outcome? If only I had gotten there in time. I keep trying to make revisions in my mind, but the outcome is always the same. The only way that I can end this constant hell I have been living with is your forgiveness. I'm at the point where I cannot punish myself any longer."

"What happened, happened. How could you have prevented it? Why is all this suddenly so important to you now? I have told you a thousand times that I don't want to discuss this. The subject is closed."

"Please, just hear me out. Polk, McLaughlin, and the others wanted me out of the compartment and played on my weakness. It was only after they got me high that I figured out what was going on and what they were up to. I tried to get myself to the compartment, but in my stupor, I couldn't find my way. I was so totally disoriented. I tried—oh, how I tried—to get there in time."

"You son of a bitch! You mean your own selfish pleasure prevented you? How could I ever forgive you? It's your damn pursuit of your own personal pleasures that has always dictated your whole life. Getting thrown out of Annapolis because you had to have a little tail. And then there's Tuyet. Don't you think I know that she succumbed to you? And what part does Carly play in all this? Don't you think I know you've been with her too?"

"You can be quite heartless. You, like everyone else, think that I'm insensitive, carefree, and pleasure seeking, but all that pursuit is to fill my insatiable void and longing for love."

"What possible pleasure is it that you would get in the pursuit of me? Was I to become another item in your repertoire of gratification?" Bryan asked as that familiar emotion he had been trying to suppress for months bubbled up. He felt used and hurt inside. And angry. Trying to dispel the feeling, he said, "Greg, you're so drunk. You are saying things that are out of character. Go the hell to bed."

"Please, Bryan—"

"Not now, Greg. I can't take any more."

"I guess that's all there is to say, then. That's it. Don't ever say that I didn't try to explain."

OCEAN BEACH,
CALIFORNIA,
MAY 1967

B ryan and Greg left the ship together to go into town at 1600.
"We're not going straight home tonight," announced Greg.
"Carly has invited us to dinner."

"Oh? Diane isn't going to be there, is she? I'll have to spend the whole night fighting her off if she is," laughed Bryan.

"Here we go again. You're here; Michelle is back east doing I don't know what. Why don't you take advantage of the opportunity?"

"You know, I don't like it when you talk like this. It really angers me. You know I'm committed to Michelle."

"I don't know. I just don't get it."

"And neither do I," Bryan said abruptly. "Here we are, off to Carly's house. So have you forgotten Tuyet already? What's the story here? Do you really think that being with Carly makes it more bearable to be without Tuyet?"

"I'm tired of your moralizing, and I need a drink. We have plenty of time, so I suggest we stop at Quiig's Bar on Santa Monica Avenue and enjoy the splendid view of the Pacific. Maybe that will improve your mood."

"No thanks. I need some space. I'll check out the tide pools south of the pier and take a walk along the oceanfront. I'd also like to take the opportunity to check out the Cabrillo National Monument. I've heard that it is a great place to take a break and enjoy the monument's spectacular views, historical buildings, and exhibits. I'll meet you at Carly's in a couple of hours."

"Whatever," Greg replied nonchalantly.

Ocean Beach—OB to locals—was a hippie, liberal, middle-class beach community that loved dogs and wasn't terribly fond of big business; the boardwalk north of Newport Avenue was a great way to take in the local flavor.

Bryan and Greg met up at Carly's at the appointed hour. As Carly opened the door, her sister's baby tried to run out, but Carly grabbed her.

"Oh my God! Is this why we're here?" Bryan asked in jest.

"Carly, how nice to see you again," Greg said in a sensual tone. He drew her face toward his and kissed her tenderly.

Carly's long, blonde hair moved as rhythmically as delicate branches of a willow, and her sky-blue eyes glistened from Greg's very presence. Her face glowed as she greeted Greg. "Come in, come in. Dinner is almost ready. Greg, please get a drink for yourself and Bryan while I put Elizabeth to bed."

They made their way to the dining room through hanging beads and the permeating smell of patchouli oil from the scented candles. The living room was furnished like a collection from a secondhand shop.

During dinner, the conversation was between Greg and Carly, which made Bryan feel uncomfortable, as if he was in the way. He couldn't participate in the conversation anyway, as they were reminiscing about times and places exclusive to them. He quickly became bored. They were like starry-eyed lovers fixed only on one another. Carly was rather like a plant drawn to the rays of the sun.

"You know, I don't really know why I was invited here," he said eventually, half questioning, half making a statement.

"Ahhhh! If he's not the center of attention, he feels left out," Greg said sarcastically.

"No, I don't think so. I just think that you are both being rather rude to me."

"No, no, Bryan," Carly said, leaning over and hugging him. "I'm glad that you came."

Bryan moved away from her embrace, and within a few moments the attention was focused on Greg again, as Carly hung on to his every word.

When Carly went into the kitchen to refill the glasses, Greg leaned over to Bryan and, with a smug and satisfied look, whispered behind his hand, "I don't think I'll be coming home tonight."

Bryan stood up and excused himself from the room. "I think I'll catch the eleven o'clock bus back to downtown. I'm tired all of a sudden."

"Are you sure that you have to leave so soon?" Carly asked as he grabbed his coat and made his way toward the door.

Bryan thought that it was an appropriate question to ask but totally insincere, and therefore he ignored it. "Good night, Carly, and thank you for dinner. Good night, Greg," he called from the door.

"Good night, Bryan," Greg muttered, not even bothering to get up from his chair.

As Bryan left the beach house, the cool sea air chilled him and permeated his body. An absence, a loss, a cursory pain seemed to overrun him. He could not comprehend the strange feeling of loneliness and absence. He could not associate these sentiments with anything or anybody. There was no point of reference. His thoughts were interrupted as his bus arrived. He found a seat, hugged himself, and stared out the window into the darkness throughout his journey. In his mind the opening of "Cherish" by the Association played over in his head: *Cherish is the word I use to describe all the feelings that I have for you hiding here inside ...*

SAN DIEGO, CALIFORNIA, JUNE 1967

B ryan left the ship early and made his way back to the apartment. He walked through the narrow alleyway, opened his mailbox, and stuffed the mail under his arm while he searched for his key. He leafed through the mail—a letter from his parents, a couple of bills, a letter from Michelle, but nothing for Greg. He was excited about Michelle's letter and, as he hadn't heard from her for a while, decided to save it until last. He freshened up, changed into his comfy clothes, and headed up to the roof, where he could relax with a drink, breathe in the cool Pacific air, watch the evening sky, and enjoy reading her letter.

My dearest Bryan,

How does one begin? As you are one of the closest and dearest individuals in my life, I feel that it is now time to allow both of us to pursue our lives unhampered by our relationship. I feel that indirectly we're both stifling ourselves, and I sense that I have a purpose and things I must do, as I'm sure is true of you.

I do not want to have to justify myself as to what I may or may not want to do, nor do I want to be accountable to anyone other than myself.

I feel that our present relationship is inhibiting and holding us back from our true passions and direction in life and if we continue as we are, it could cause us both pain and frustration in the near future. I also sense that there are pieces missing in our relationship in order to sustain it.

It is difficult for me to ask you to sever the ties that we have, but I have no alternative.

However, I'm truly certain that, in time, we shall be better for it. I hope you will understand.

Once exclusively yours,
Michelle

Bryan forced himself to read the letter again and again. *How could I have known that this would be the last letter I would receive from Michelle?* Heaviness filled him. *Is it really over? Will I ever see her again? I just don't understand.* He shook his head and tightened his lips. His hands gripped and crinkled the letter as he buried his head in the words. Emptiness filled his whole being as he lay back on the recliner and gazed at the sky while trying to come to terms with the contents. His mind went back to the relationship they had had all those years—his first love, his first intimate experience. Everything that they had shared replayed in his mind. It was hard to believe that she was gone. He took a deep breath and sighed and moaned like a wounded animal.

His thoughts were interrupted by Greg's return from work on the ship. He could hear Greg in the apartment below and as he made his way up to the roof.

"Hey, bud! Any mail for me?"

Bryan turned and looked at him. "No, nothing from Tuyet."

"Are you okay, Bryan?"

"It's happened."

"What's happened?"

"She's left me. She wrote me a Dear John letter today." Greg stooped down, and Bryan handed him the letter. "Read it."

"Are you sure you want me to?"

"Yes. Go ahead. Read it. Verify this nightmare."

Greg took the letter and read. "Wow. This is pretty bad. How are you going to deal with this one?"

"Do I have any choice?" Bryan asked.

"Is there anything I can do?"

"Like what?" Bryan said, not really expecting an answer.

Greg reached over and hugged him. Bryan did not withdraw from him or reject his gesture, which Greg thought peculiar. At first Bryan felt comfortable with the embrace, but then his comfort level dissipated. The embrace became fear inducing and almost repugnant to him, and he abruptly sprang to his feet.

"What's wrong?" Greg asked with astonishment as his friend recoiled. "What did I do?"

"Nothing. Nothing. I just want to be left alone."

"Are you sure you don't want company?"

"No, please just leave me alone. I'm going to lie down for a while."

Greg returned to the apartment, got himself a beer, and began preparing a light dinner. Later, when Bryan didn't appear for dinner, Greg knocked on his bedroom door.

"Bryan, are you coming for something to eat?"

"No thanks, I don't want to eat."

"May I come in?"

"Yes," Bryan replied quietly.

Greg stood over the bed and asked, "Are you sure there's nothing I can do? Shall I stay here for a while and talk? Let me help you through this."

"There's always Greg to help me through. What would I do without Greg?" Bryan asked facetiously.

"Is it a problem that I'm here for you?" Greg retorted.

"Yeah, in some ways it is. I don't want to become dependent on you."

"Your rejection of help is not going to provoke me, because although you won't admit it, I know you need me to be here. And, before you say it, taking another college class is not going to be the solution to this crisis."

"But maybe another hit from the bottle would be? Do you really think that you can take on my issues when you have a juggling act going on with Tuyet and Carly?" Bryan taunted.

"These hits below the belt are not going to work," Greg said, abruptly raising his hand in the air to indicate his wish to prevent any further verbal altercation. "This is getting ugly and cruel. I'm leaving before one of us says something we might regret."

As Greg turned to walk away, Bryan stretched out his arm toward him. "I'm sorry that I don't seem grateful for your concern," he said, realizing that he had been rather brusque and callous in his response. "One of the pillars of my life that kept my world together has crumbled. I'm just very confused." He paused and then said mildly, "There's nothing you can do. I just need some time, Greg. Greg?"

Without turning or responding, Greg walked away, and Bryan's only consolation was the semblance of a shadow cast on the wall.

SAN DIEGO, CALIFORNIA, AUGUST 1967

The months passed, and as Bryan continued to try to deal with his breakup with Michelle, the rift between him and Greg widened. Greg began to spend less and less time at the apartment and more time with Carly at Ocean Beach. What had once been just weekend visits became weeklong visits. Bryan tried to distance himself from Greg while trying to deal with the realization that he needed Greg more than he cared to admit. He enrolled in extra classes at San Diego State University and became more obsessed with Vietnamese history. He knew that Greg would eventually move out, and it was as if he was preparing himself to cover up any feeling that he would miss him. That day came sooner than expected.

"Well, I guess you are really going. Do you have everything?"

"Yeah. It's best. Just one more box, and then I'll be off."

Greg reached out to embrace him and gave him that now all-too-familiar smile, but Bryan pulled back and stood rigid, his eyes tightened, still angered by Greg's self-absorption.

"I really disgust you, don't I?" Greg asked. "Will you ever not relive that night?"

"That was your choice. You made it," Bryan replied coldly.

"And you continue to hold me responsible? How cruel."

Bryan said nothing as Greg took the last of his belongings to his car and closed the door behind him.

An impasse existed between the men—Bryan's inability to forgive Greg and Greg's inability to build a closer relationship with Bryan.

After a while, Bryan went into the living room and sat in his favorite rocking chair. He looked out the window as he rocked. It was a beautiful sunset, but he felt that there was something symbolic about it that evening. Was it because the friendship that he and Greg had shared was over? He was filled with a strange emptiness. He had never felt like that about anybody and did not understand the unfamiliar emotion. He felt alone for the first time. As he continued to watch the sunset, his vision became blurred. He thought, *I cannot deal with this. I cannot cope with someone whose only goal in life is self-indulgence. I'm not going to be another statistic on his list of gratification.*

With the realization of the reality of the situation, Bryan immediately turned his thoughts and attention to a paper that was due in at the university the next day.

The following month, September, the ship left San Diego to make another tour to Asia, duplicating the previous route. The environment and the routine of ship life inadvertently reestablished the previously unacknowledged bond between the two men.

20

DA NANG, VIETNAM, SATURDAY, JANUARY 27, 1968

B ryan sat at a table in Joe Tran's Bar, waiting for Greg and passing the time by reading up on the history of Tet Nguyen Dan, or Tet. As well as being fascinated by the historical background of the celebration, he wanted to be fully prepared for the New Year festivities that he was going to share with Tuyet and Greg. He already knew that the word *Tet* meant "festival" and that Tet was the first morning of the first day of Vietnamese New Year. Unlike the American New Year, which was only one day of celebration, Vietnamese people celebrated anything from one week to several weeks, depending on where they lived.

An American marine and his Vietnamese wife, who were sitting at the table next to Bryan, saw what he was reading and opened up a conversation with him.

"That book looks interesting," the marine said. "My wife has just been explaining the celebration and what we're going to be doing this week. This will be the first opportunity for us to celebrate Tet together since we were married, due to the present political situation. By the way, I'm Tim, and this is my wife, Nhu An."

"Hi, I'm Bryan. It's good to meet you. I'm waiting for my friend. This is all so fascinating," Bryan said, "but I'm a little confused how the date of Tet is worked out."

"We Vietnamese people go by two calendars," Nhu An said. "One is like your calendar, where the dates are the same, and the other is the lunar calendar. Tet has had its roots in the Chinese lunar calendar since the Shang dynasty in 1300 BC, so now Tet begins on the second new moon following the winter solstice, which occurs anytime between January 21 and February 19. And in some places the celebration lasts until the spring equinox."

"I'm still confused," laughed Bryan. "Does the Vietnamese calendar follow the same twelve zodiac signs as the Chinese?"

"Yes, but we use the zodiac signs when we determine someone's age. The zodiac signs don't represent horoscopes like the astrological signs many Americans believe in."

Nhu An explained that each year was represented by a different animal and that the upcoming year would be the Year of the Monkey.

"I was born in 1947, the Year of the Pig," interjected Tim. "My wife says that some people believe you have the same character traits as the animal of your birth year. Pigs tend to have a very strong need to set difficult goals and carry them out."

"How did the order of the twelve animal signs come about?" Bryan asked.

"According to Chinese legend, the twelve animals quarreled one day over who was to head the cycle of years," Nhu An said. "They asked the gods to decide, and the gods held a contest: whoever was first to reach the opposite bank of the river would be first in the cycle, and the rest of the animals would receive their years according to their finish.

"The twelve animals gathered at the riverbank and jumped in. Unknown to the ox, the rat had jumped on his back. As the ox was about to jump ashore, the rat jumped off the ox's back and won the race. The pig, which was very lazy, ended up last. That is why the rat is the first year of the animal cycle, the ox second, and the pig last."

"What a fantastic story!"

"So when were you born, Bryan?"

"In 1945, but I don't know what animal."

"Hmm … 1945. That was the Year of the Rooster," Nhu An said. "Roosters are hardworking, shrewd, and definite in decision making. Because of this, they tend to seem boastful to others. Born under this sign, you should be happy as a world traveler. Do you know anyone born under the sign of the Rat? They are most compatible with Roosters, being artistic, creative, sensitive, and generous to the people they love."

"That kind of sounds like me," he mused. "Thank you, that was most enlightening. So what are you both doing on New Year's Eve?" Bryan asked.

"Last-minute shopping," Tim said with a smile, "then back to the house for the noon feast to welcome the spirits of the ancestors who return to join us. The best part is that moment between the old year and the new."

"And the most important," his wife said. "At this time, which is called *Giao Thua,* a tremendous barrage of drums, gongs, and firecrackers announce the midnight hour and scare off the evil spirits. Nobody dares to sleep at this hour!"

"I shouldn't think anyone could with all that noise," Bryan said.

"After we have wished everyone a happy New Year—chuc mung nam moi—we shall drink rice wine and champagne," explained the marine.

"Well, *chuc mung nam moi* to you both, and thank you again for enlightening me," Bryan said as Tim and Nhu An prepared to leave. "It has been good to meet you, and I hope you and your family have a wonderful New Year."

Bryan wanted to order a Coke, but the stories of how the VC laced it with acid caused him to substitute a beer. If it was not shredded glass frozen in ice, it was another primitive way the VC chose to fight. *I wonder if the British thought of the colonists in the same way,* he mused. He tried not to think about the real reason for him being there—to meet Greg. If he thought about it, then he would be tempted to leave. He wanted to clear up things with Greg, and this was most likely to be the best time. Also, he felt a thrill at the opportunity to experience Tet, which was enticing.

A French Citroën 2CV car pulled up, and Greg darted out of

the car. He was dressed in a loud madras shirt with white pants and sandals, as if he were in the States. He looked more like a surfer than someone in the military. He noticed Bryan and beckoned to him.

"I'm so glad you changed your mind," he called as Bryan approached him.

"I almost changed my mind again, but I respect your feelings and did not want to disappoint you." He gave Greg a hug. Greg was surprised by the out-of-character physical behavior but happily returned the hug. Bryan blushed. "We'll have a great weekend at Tuyet's. I brought some extra civvies to change into," he said as they settled into the car.

"We will be staying at Tuyet's parents' villa, a great place by the beach and not far from Da Nang. I wish the weather were warmer. It would be a great place to go swimming."

"Where are her parents?"

"They're in Saigon."

Bryan observed the beautiful view as he and Greg made small talk.

"So what is this news that you wanted to share with me?" Bryan asked.

"Well …" He paused for a second. "I'm going to ask Tuyet to marry me. I have never felt this way about any woman in my life."

"Do you think she will?"

"I think so, but sometimes I think her interests are with someone or something else. She tells me to enjoy the time we have together and not to make things difficult, but she's also told me she has never felt this way about anyone. The clear direction that she once had seems clouded with confusion."

"What does she mean by 'difficult'? Marriage?"

"I really don't know. Sometimes I sense a genuine mystery about her."

A few minutes passed. Then Greg turned and smiled at Bryan as he drove. "So tell me—I'm really curious—why did you change your mind and not go to Saigon? You seemed so committed that even I thought I wouldn't change your mind. I'm really surprised. Tell me the truth. No bullshit!"

"No bull—ha! Well, the truth is I'm in love with Tuyet."

Greg suddenly stopped the car. "What!" He sounded shocked and angry. His face white and his torso turned toward Bryan, he was poised to lunge forward like an animal before the strike.

"Relax, for God's sake. I'm joking!" Bryan's voice trembled.

Greg dropped his head back against the seat. "Don't do that! God, I'm nuts about her and out of control. I'm sorry. So answer my question."

"I was missing you both and feeling quite lonely. Going to Saigon by myself just didn't seem like a lot of fun."

Greg looked at him and smiled. "I'm glad you're here," he said.

As they continued their journey, Bryan noticed that workmen were building stalls near the market and giving public and private buildings a new coat of paint. "What are they building?" he asked.

"Stalls to sell holiday items, such as New Year's greeting cards, candied fruit, and decorations. Prices for everything have already begun to rise, and just look at the number of shoppers. They're buying clothes as well as presents for their family and friends."

"Woo! Just take a look at that flower market. It runs the length of the whole street! I've never seen so many different kinds of potted flowers."

"The hoa dao, or peach flower, only grows in North Vietnam, and it is the special flower of the Vietnamese New Year because of its color, which is believed to bring many favorable opportunities throughout the year. In the South the hoa mai, or yellow apricot flower, is the symbol of Tet. It's a forest plant or something. Tuyet told me that the market is the focal point of the city, as many people buy flowers as a symbol of spring. Apparently the ideal is to have the flowers bloom only at Tet, so a lot of care is given in picking just the right ones. I think we shall be coming here tonight to choose a Tet tree."

"What's that?" Bryan asked.

"I'm not really sure. They're similar to our Christmas trees, I guess, except they have miniature oranges on them, which should be ripening right about now. The more fruit on the tree, the luckier the owner will be, so Tuyet wants a twelve-foot tree covered with hundreds of oranges," he jested. "Well, here we are!"

They left the car, and Tuyet came out to greet them. She was wearing Greg's navy denim jeans and a white silk blouse. Her long, slick hair, free and light, moved with her every step.

"Oh, I'm so happy that you joined us this weekend." She embraced Bryan and kissed him on the cheek as she took him by the arm. "We shall surely have a magnificent celebration. Let's go inside, and I'll tell you all about it."

As Bryan entered the villa, he observed that Tuyet had already begun making preparations for the celebrations. Strips of red paper— *cau d'i*—with sayings of wealth, happiness, prosperity, and longevity were pasted up. She had bought flowering branches of mai and dao for good luck and other fruits with names symbolizing her wishes for the coming year. She had also either covered or hidden away brooms and other cleaning equipment, and Bryan recalled that one of the many superstitions was that all cleaning should be done before New Year's Day, so that good fortune would not be swept away.

"Tuyet, what is that wonderful pineapple-type fragrance?" Greg asked.

"Oh yes, you're right. It is a pineapple. We buy them to show that our houses are clean. The word for *pineapple* in Vietnamese is also equivalent to 'it smells good.' Now let's eat, and I will tell you more about our customs if you are really interested."

"While I was waiting for Greg at Joe Tran's, I got talking with a marine and his Vietnamese wife, and they said that Tet begins on the second new moon following the winter solstice. How would you define 'new moon,' Tuyet?"

"Technically, it is when the moon is between the earth and the sun. The new moon reaches its highest altitude at noon—rather like us, as tonight we have reached our highest altitude by being together for this special celebration. The three of us are in between the earth and the sun on life's path at present. We have to find the courage to face the truth and either follow something known that is safe and secure in our hearts or something unfamiliar that is new and exciting that may take each of us in a different direction. While we make our decisions, the truth, like the invisible moon, is elusive."

"What is truth? What is not truth?" Bryan asked.

"The answer is not so simple, because the truth can change. I can change. You can change," Tuyet answered enigmatically.

"Woo! That was thought provoking!" Greg said.

"Now come, and let's enjoy our meal together," Tuyet said, quickly changing the subject.

Before Bryan and Greg sat down at the table, Tuyet prayed to send the Kitchen God, or Ong Tao, to the heavens. "We believe that the Kitchen God watches over our household, and now we send him to the Jade Emperor at the heavenly court to give him a break from watching over the family for the past year. On New Year's Eve, we pray for him again, and this time we ask him to come back and resume his duties. So tonight we shall have a feast!"

The dinner started with *pho*, a delicious noodle soup prepared by quickly boiling noodles and placing them in a bowl along with shallots, parsley, and shredded beef. The broth was made with boiled bones, shrimp, and ginger. Along with the pho, they had a side dish of Vietnamese spring rolls, which were wrapped in rice paper and filled with fried minced pork, crab, onion, mushroom, and eggs. The main dish was *cha ca*—filleted fish slices broiled over charcoal and accompanied by plain rice.

"Please help yourselves to salad. There are also peanuts, noodles, and lemon sauce. Please also try some Vietnamese wine. It is very good and made from rice. Greg, would you prefer a beer? There is Saigon Export in the refrigerator."

"Thanks. Don't get up. I'll get it."

"This is delicious," Bryan said. Greg nodded enthusiastically in agreement.

Before the sweets and dessert, Tuyet burned some sacrificial gold paper and offered a carp skeleton for the Kitchen God to ride on his journey to heaven. "I hope this will influence his report favorably," she said.

She then fetched a large plate with the dessert. "I've prepared the traditional *banh chung* for you both."

"What exactly is that?" Bryan asked curiously.

"It's a sticky rice-and-meat cake filled with beans, onions, and pork and has been boiling in leaves for ten hours. The cake symbolizes the earth and is the start of the process of cooking. Everything must be prepared beforehand, as traditionally, we do not cook during the holiday season. Please, eat, eat!"

"The dinner was wonderful," Bryan said eventually as he stood and placed his napkin on the table. "Thank you too for your erudite explanations of what is a truly wonderful celebration. It is marvelous to be here with you both. Please excuse me; I'm beat! I think I'm ready for sleep." He walked over to Tuyet, took her hand, and softly kissed it. He looked into her dark-brown eyes, which glistened in the reflecting candlelight. Her beauty permeated the room. "This is a dinner I will remember for a lifetime. Thank you again."

He put his hand on Greg's arm, looked into his eyes, and in a soft voice said, "Good night, Greg."

Greg turned and, with a lingering look and a slight tilt of his head, replied, "Good night," momentarily holding Bryan's gaze.

Hours passed, and Bryan was awakened by what sounded like an argument. Loud voices echoed and sounded through the villa. The words were difficult to comprehend in his half-asleep state. As suddenly as the voices had commenced, they ceased, returning the villa to dead quiet. A deep sleep came with ease, for Bryan was still drowsy from the wine and champagne at dinner.

"Bryan! Bryan, I hate like hell to wake you." Greg's heavy voice trembled and quivered. "I don't know what I'll do," he moaned. "She refuses to marry me," he cried into his hands. "Why in hell does she do this to me?"

Bryan reached over and turned the lamp on.

"No, leave it off. I'm so embarrassed, and my eyes are red and puffy from bawling."

"It's okay, buddy. It can't be all that bad. There must be some sort of misunderstanding." He reached over and hugged his friend. "I'm sure that you will work it out."

"She will not leave Vietnam, damn her! Some shit about this is her first love. The world is so fucked up. I don't know what the hell she is talking about. I thought I was everything to her. I don't think I can make it without her."

UNIVERSITY OFFICE, ALEXANDRIA, VIRGINIA, AUGUST 1991

B ryan's thoughts were suddenly interrupted by a knock at the door. "Yes?"

"Dr. Ruocco, forgive me. Mr. Richardson is here. Will you be able to see him?"

"Of course! Show him in," he said, pushing himself from the windowsill and turning quickly. He became filled with butterflies as he started toward the door.

"It's getting close to four thirty, and the office staff and I will be leaving," Amy said. "Is there anything else you need?"

"No, nothing. Thank you, Amy. Have a nice weekend."

Radnor entered the office and scrutinized the room—walls with bookcases, filing cabinets, a large table with textbooks, and tidily placed folders. The office seemed quite commonplace for a university. What drew his attention was a section of the office that seemed to be commemorative. A large photo of the Vietnam Veterans Memorial covered the wall, and newspaper headlines placed in sequence told the story of the Vietnam War. The last paper had a black ribbon and medal hung from it, and the headline read, "Saigon Falls to the Reds."

Radnor had changed so much that he was hardly recognizable. His face, after another twenty-three years of age, now had defined lines. His hair was white and had thinned and receded. Outwardly he looked as though an aged man had taken possession of him. Bryan was overwhelmed with both shock and joy at seeing him.

"Hi, buddy. Long time no see." Radnor's familiar voice validated his physical presence.

Moving toward each other, they embraced and were unable to control their emotions. Bryan could not hold back, and his eyes filled with tears. Radnor started talking in tones that trembled and quivered as if at any moment he would begin sobbing.

"Let me look at you." Bryan gently pushed him backward. "Time has surely been good to you. You look exactly the same," he lied. "I'm really glad to see you. I had no idea you were in town. My God, whatever brings you here? Would you like a drink? Tea or coffee? How's Marian? Did you have any kids? Come and sit down over here. So what's new? What's been happening all these years?" Bryan asked excitedly. "How I wish we had kept in contact."

"A coffee would be good, thanks. Marian and I divorced about seven years ago. We have a girl in elementary and a son in the service—the navy, of course. I remarried about three years ago and have a two-year-old boy from that marriage. Bryan," he said solemnly, "the reason I'm here is that I need your help."

"Sure. What can I do?" Bryan asked, staring in wonder.

"I'm one of Senator Andrew Seaton's congressional aides."

The name Seaton sent icy chills through Bryan. "Greg's dad?"

Radnor removed his suit jacket, took a handkerchief from the pocket, and wiped his forehead clean of perspiration caused by the emotional meeting and the August heat. Bryan's eyes were drawn to the MIA bracelet that he wore.

"That feels better. I'm with Seaton's task force, locating MIAs in Vietnam," Radnor said. "From recent data collected, we have discovered that Greg may not have gone AWOL."

"What? He must have taken off with Tuyet. Where else could he be?" Bryan asked quickly.

"What makes you so sure?"

"He loved her and would do almost anything for her. This I know for sure. Although treason? Never!"

"I wish I could share your certainty about Tuyet." Radnor paused for a few seconds. "Are you prepared for some earth-shattering news? She's a Red and is now a delegate for Vietnam, a diplomat for the Communist government. She's working at the UN in New York."

Bryan was so startled that he trembled. A sudden burst of black images flashed through his mind. He looked with a numbed stare.

"Are you okay?"

"I'm fine. Please, go on."

"Are you sure?"

"Yes, please continue."

"We find it difficult to believe that he went over to the other side. The senator needs to clear up this mess. Our sources also tell us that they have never seen Greg with Tuyet. This information is quite secret and could be compromising for the senator. Can you tell me anything about the last time you saw Greg?"

"I'm sure you know just as much as I do. He never returned to the ship and most likely remained on the beach. We never saw each other after that day. My only concern was to get home to my dad."

"That's all you remember? Did you hear or see anything? Did Greg say anything? You don't remember anything?" Radnor repeated in an agitated tone, as though Bryan was keeping something from him. There was a long silence.

"The only damn thing I remember is wanting to get to my dying dad." Bryan's eyes filled with tears as he continued, "My ultimate concern was my dad, not a man mental over some damn woman. You should remember we were not getting along. He wouldn't listen to reason. It was not working between them. Tuyet did not want to leave Vietnam. She stirred some strange behavior in him, and after a while I didn't know him." Bryan thought for a moment. "So that's why she was not so anxious to leave." He shook his head in distaste.

"So then you didn't see him on the beach the two days you were away?"

"No! A thousand times, no! What the hell gives you the right to question me in this manner? I resent being questioned as if I'm on trial," Bryan said in a cutting and forceful tone.

"I'm sorry." Radnor walked toward Bryan and hugged him. "I didn't expect my visit to make us so angry and hostile toward each other. I, for sure, did not foresee this. Please accept my apologies. I see all this is too painful for you. I just want to get to the bottom of this, but I only seem to run into dead ends. The last thing I want to do is upset you." With hands stretched over Bryan's shoulders, he asked, "May I be honest?"

"Sure, please do," Bryan said, wiping his eyes.

"What keeps puzzling me is that you seem so defensive. Bryan, what's going on?"

"Damn you, Radnor!" Bryan said freely, in a state of total emotion. "Let what has been unknown remain so. The senator is only trying to cover his ass."

"This is not like you. You've only known Greg's view of his father."

"He should have treated his son better when he had the opportunity. It's all too late now."

"What do mean, too late?"

"I don't know. I'm confused."

"You're still a bad liar, with the certainty in your tone and your habit of not looking at people when you're hiding something. I remember you acted the same way the day he disappeared."

"Lying? I'm not lying. I just don't remember. Damn it, I've been experiencing nightmares, flashbacks, and memory loss. I've been diagnosed with PTSD and have been trying to deal with that—not forgetting the sexual trauma I experienced, which resulted in years of therapy in the attempt to try to fill the missing gaps in my memory," he responded angrily.

"Oh, I'm so sorry, Bryan. How could I have forgotten the rape?"

A few moments passed, seeming like an eternity. Both men were emotionally battered, and their strength continued to diminish from the distressing topic.

"We have to try to fill these gaps," Radnor said. "Maybe I can help you?"

"If you know something, spill it."

Radnor turned and stared directly at him. "You're right; I think I may know something. I believe that you may have the answer," he said, pointing at Bryan.

"I wasn't sure about a lead I got a few weeks ago at the VA hospital. That lead was the reason for me coming, but only now do I believe it. I was interviewing a soldier, who was a casualty of Agent Orange, about benefits to which he and his family were entitled. As he was signing the papers I had gone over with him, he paused and placed the papers on his lap and recalled, 'You know, the strangest thing happened to me when my buddy and I were on a search-and-destroy mission. It was just at the start of the Tet Offensive, so it seems to stick in my mind. As our helicopter approached the target area, two men in black VC pajamas and conical hats dashed across an open field. One of them lost his hat, and the thing that drew my attention to them was that he had red hair. As the waves of air blew the grass in circular forms, his hair stood out like flames of fire against the green.'

"I asked what became of the two men, but the soldier did not know, as all hell broke out when they flew over them. The mention of the Tet Offensive sparked my interest in the soldier's story, but when he said red hair, he had my total attention. I put the two together when I realized that the location of the search-and-destroy mission was near Tuyet's parents' villa, close to the Marble Mountains. Bryan, you were the redhead, and Greg was the other man. For God's sake, why can't you say? Was it you? Was it?"

"How could it be me? I was in Saigon, but I can't remember. Did I go?" Bryan hesitated. "Please don't be so quick to make assumptions. You have no idea what hell this is. Wait. Let me think again. Give me some time and space, please!"

He paused, thought for a moment, and took a sip of water. "Yes, now that you mention it, something is coming back. I have a shadowy recollection of images and sounds, but there are still pieces lacking. The picture is not quite complete. Let me think for a moment."

Minutes passed in silence. Then in a soft tone, almost difficult to hear, Bryan said, "Yes. It was me."

"Why in God's name haven't you ever told anyone? Why would you keep this to yourself? What gives you the right?"

"Radnor, I really just cannot recall."

"Bryan, he was my friend as well, so please let me help you in any way I can. We recently managed to get in contact with Carly, and she gave us some of Greg's letters. This letter is the last communication she received. Let me read part of it to you, and perhaps something in the content might trigger some recall." Radnor summarized the letter, which spoke of Greg's intention to terminate his relationship with Carly, marry Tuyet, and either take her back to the States or stay in Vietnam.

"May I see the letter?" asked Bryan.

Radnor handed him the letter. Bryan's hand trembled. He was overwhelmed at seeing the familiar handwriting. As he tried to decipher some of the words, he drew it nearer to him and groaned. Taking a deep breath, he was suddenly conscious of a familiar scent. He held the letter up to his nose and lips and closed his eyes. As he inhaled, a whirlwind of memories flashed in rapid succession through his mind. The faint smell of that familiar cologne, which was unique to Greg, filled him with such joy and pleasure that had been forgotten for so long. "Greg, Greg, Greg," he muttered.

Bryan bit hard on his lip, trying to suppress his emotions. His heart pounded like the recurrent *thwap-thwap* sound of the rotor blades of a helicopter. As he handed the letter back to Radnor, he noticed that blood from his lip had dripped onto it. A tear trickled down his cheek and onto his lip. As he tasted the combination of blood and tears, his head spun, and his knees weakened. He put his hand out in a vain attempt to regain his balance and prevent himself from collapsing on the floor.

"Bryan! Bryan! What's happening? What's going on? Are you okay?" Radnor asked anxiously as he helped Bryan to a chair.

"The straw mat, the straw mat ..." mumbled Bryan.

"What? You're not making any sense."

The familiar feel of the straw mat on the floor of his office had evoked the memory of the conical straw hat that had blown from his head on that ill-fated day. He had attempted to retrieve it just after he had left the villa with Greg.

"Oh my God! Oh my God! It is all coming back, just as the doctor said it would. Now I understand. The pieces fit together. It was seeing the color red, hearing my heart beat like the rhythm of helicopter blades, smelling the scent of his cologne, tasting tears and blood, and, finally, touching the straw mat. The picture is now complete." He hesitated. "Yes, yes, he's dead. My special Greg is dead."

This revelation almost sent Radnor into a state of shock; he was rendered speechless.

Bryan gradually composed himself, organized his thoughts, and, in a calm and controlled manner, began to recall the suppressed memory of Greg's death, which until now had eluded him.

"This was so tragic an affair that it lost its reality. The memory was so lost that even reminders could not revive it. My recollections could not be restored with either tokens or objects. Even the feelings were gone, as though they'd never existed."

"Just take it slowly. I know how difficult this is for you."

"I'll tell you everything, no matter how distasteful it is to you. Are you sure you want to know? I forewarn you, I cannot spare your feelings or personal beliefs. I will leave nothing out. In exchange, a resurrected memory that has been lost for all these years will be unveiled."

Bryan made himself comfortable on the large wing chair. His body seemed to lighten of emotional weight. He stared at the ceiling, tightened his grip on the arms of the chair, and then looked directly into Radnor's eyes. After a long pause he began, "As you recall, Greg left the ship early that Friday morning. I remember he was radiant and excited. His eyes sparkled. His smile was wide and filled with enthusiasm ..."

USS Delaware, *Friday, January 26, 1968*

"Aren't you going to ask where I'm off to so early?" Greg asked Bryan as he made up his rack and packed his duffel bag.

"From the amount of clothes, enough for a week to a lifetime, I know where you're off to! How about you let me sleep? It's five thirty, and there's another half an hour till reveille." He pulled the pillow over his head. "I've made plans to go to Saigon with Special Services and need my rest before the long journey."

"I wish you would reconsider and join Tuyet and me to celebrate Tet. It will be as much fun as our own New Year's. Why don't you reconsider? Tuyet will be expecting you."

Bryan sat up. "You mean you didn't tell her I wasn't coming?"

"Thought I could get you to change your mind," Greg smirked. "No luck, hmm? I'll miss you," he whispered quietly in a message that was intended for Bryan alone.

"Forget it, and watch what you say. There's enough scuttlebutt about you and me. They're already saying I wear my skivvies backward! You'd better get moving before you wake the whole crew. Just go, damn it."

"Anyway, if you change your mind, this is where you'll find me," Greg said as he pushed a note under Bryan's pillow.

Within minutes Bryan heard the sounds of Greg making his way through the compartment; his footsteps moved across the deck and clanged as he made his way up the ladder topside. Silence replaced Greg, and a puzzling void filled Bryan. What was happening to him? He had never experienced such an unusual mood swing. He felt separation and loneliness when only a few moments before he had felt nothing. His thoughts drifted as he glanced across at the empty rack. A strange vacancy filled him. He tried to dismiss the emotional experience and go on with shipboard activities. It was only after he gave serious thought to his feelings and found an acceptable explanation that he could go on. He thought, *These two people are like family to me. I have been with them both so much in the last three years. Greg has helped me through the rough times, and Tuyet is warm and caring and has always included me in everything. They are very important people to me, and I guess it's love I feel for them both.*

Soon after breakfast he returned to the compartment to prepare for his trip.

"That is so neat, going to Saigon," Radnor said as he leaned on the locker next to Bryan.

"I'm sorry. What did you say? I was reading."

"Letter from home?"

"Yeah," he replied as he pushed the letter under a neat set of folded clothes. As Radnor continued talking, the contents of the letter reran through Bryan's thoughts.

Bryan,

I know you said that you didn't want to join us, but I really believe that's not the case. I don't care about the guys on the ship. My only concern in life is Tuyet and you. I wish you would change your mind. I want to share some wonderful news with you. You may not realize it, but you are more than a friend. I hate the way we have been treating each other in the past few months. It makes me miserable and hurts as well. I have never really asked much from you, but I want you to join us for what I believe will be a very special occasion—a time to celebrate, the three of us. Please join us. It would make me extremely happy. I'll be at Joe Tran's Bar and Restaurant at noon, waiting for you. I know you won't disappoint me.

Always,
Greg

"You'll be in Saigon for nine days?"

"Sorry, Rad, I can't talk now. I've got to catch the shuttle to Da Nang airport. I'll tell you about the whole trip when I get back from Saigon," he said.

University Office, Alexandria, Virginia, August 1991

While at the University Office, Bryan began to recall the night at the villa.

Greg had continued to weep. Bryan had pulled him close to comfort him, Greg's head lodged beneath his chin. While Greg cried profusely, Bryan patted and stroked his back and rocked him. Bryan began to shiver with elation at the closeness of Greg and his scent—that familiar cologne—while delighting in this foreign sensation of truth. The realization of Greg's natural essence was overtaking him. He ran his fingertips through Greg's thick hair, and a feeling of incomparable ecstasy erupted. Greg gently lifted his head from Bryan's chest, and, still locked in a half embrace, Bryan reached to light the room. Bryan had succumbed to the emotion that he had borne for so long. The unfamiliar had become the familiar. A tempest of emotional upheaval engulfed him. Unable to subdue, diminish, or control his feelings, he submitted.

"I want to look at the face of the man I have always loved," Bryan said. "I never wanted to admit it, but at this very moment I know my truth."

As Bryan spoke, Greg took his hand and held it in his. Their casually joined hands tightened in a union that was a warm, physical response to an emotional connection.

"This makes me very happy to hear, especially now. I had no intimation. It was hidden so well, even from me."

"But, Greg, I'm so concerned about Tuyet. I can't hurt her. And what about your present state of mind? Do you really think you can pursue these feelings under these conditions? As for me, I'm so frightened."

"Bryan," Greg said, stroking Bryan's arm, "Tuyet has always understood my feelings for you. I have never made them a secret. That may have been her reason for declining my marriage proposal. She has known from the beginning that I'm capable of loving both men and women. I love her more than any woman I have ever known. However, my unfortunate hunger extends to you as well. I hope you can understand or will try to." He stood, kissed Bryan on the forehead, and started to walk away.

Bryan sprang from his bed. "Greg, you can't go now. Not now, when I want to be with you more than ever."

A few minutes of silence passed.

"I love you, Greg. I always have. It's only now that I realize my feelings go back to the first time I met you. Truly, I don't know the reason I distanced myself from you. It may have been social brainwashing or not knowing you felt this way. I do know that you have always been there for me and I could not account for my feelings. I never wanted to admit it, but now, I will no longer live the lie. If Tuyet knows, I feel no guilt in what I'm saying. I care for her dearly. I could never intentionally hurt her. So please, let me be here for you. I want to help make the pain go away like you did so many times for me." He stretched out his hand to Greg. "I want you to stay."

Greg turned, stood for a few minutes, then slowly walked toward Bryan, and took his hand. "I love you," he whispered. Then the room became dark. The words echoed in Bryan's mind, filling him with disbelief. It was incomprehensible that Greg had actually uttered those words to him. The joy and ecstasy that he felt was all foreign to him.

The first light of morning filtered through the closed louvered windows. Bryan glanced over at Greg. He was unrecognizable with the absence of light. Bryan's eyes were fixed on him. Was this all a dream or reality? He lay in bed and watched the room slowly illuminate. Greg's darkened, featureless face slowly gained definition, the light revealing his straight, uncombed hair, bleached blond by the sun; rough, unshaven face; and deep-set, closed eyes. He lay still and breathed heavy within a deep sleep. Bryan felt almost tranquil, remaining motionless so as not to disturb Greg. He felt so alive, and for the first time in his life, he felt in harmony with the world. Things all seemed to fit, and the puzzle was complete. While he thought, he never took his eyes off Greg.

Slowly Greg's eyes flickered open, and he stared at Bryan. He smiled and then stretched. "Good morning, Bryan." He yawned and put his arms round Bryan. "How are you? Have you been up long?"

"Fine. I feel a little different. It's a strange, new feeling. I don't know how to explain it. I feel no guilt," Bryan said and smiled.

"Why should you? It's all inborn and natural. I hate to ask you, but was this the first time that it was consensual?"

"Yes. I have never slept with a man before. I had no idea it would be like this. I feel alive for the first time. If I'd had any idea, I would have let myself go earlier."

Greg admitted, "This was where my conflict was—that I was not the first and that the experience had been poisoned by those animals."

"In my anger, I subconsciously wanted you to be the first, but your weaknesses denied that for me, and I have to forgive you for that. I too am responsible for holding back and being in denial. I blamed you for the event, but I too indirectly caused it."

"Some people spend a lifetime and never let go. They can't be blamed. It is so difficult to come to grips with oneself. I remember, my first time was at the Naval Academy. I really believed he and I had something special, but later I was forced to deal with his guilt. I guess he thought by turning me in he could feel more like a victim and not responsible for his behavior. But that was then, and this is now." He paused for a few moments. "What day is this?"

"Sunday, the twenty-eighth. Two days before Tet."

"Gee, I have a whole week left. I don't know what I will do after Wednesday or Thursday. I guess I will go back to the ship, since my proposal of marriage to Tuyet has been refused. I expect Tuyet will be with her relatives near Da Nang to finish Tet. I thought I would be with her."

"That hurts, hmm?"

"It does, but a little less, thanks to you and last night."

"I've got an idea. I still have that room at the Majestic Hotel in Saigon until Sunday. Come with me to Saigon. I hear that's the place to celebrate Tet. This is a New Year's I want to remember. Also, I think it would be too depressing if you had to return to the ship. Saigon will be a place where you can forget; it'll be a new year and a new start. You need someone and things to do now. What do you think?"

"That sounds great. Saigon would be nice." He thought for a second and mumbled, "Saigon, Saigon—a place to forget?"

"What? I can hardly hear you."

He put his hands on Bryan's shoulders. "I want you to know that I had no idea all this was going to happen, I mean with Tuyet and all. I hope you don't feel second best or used. It really was not my intention. I truly love you."

"I can handle this if I'm the only man in your life. I think I can deal with the love you have for Tuyet."

They hugged. Greg then scurried from the room. "See you at breakfast, and then we'll be off to Saigon."

Tuyet stood with her back slightly bent alongside a table near a window, cutting vegetables for an omelet. Her long, slick hair was tied with a gold ribbon. Greg walked slowly toward her and placed his arms around her waist. He pushed her hair out of the way with his cheek and kissed her neck. The taste of her warm, soft skin excited him even without her turning or making much of a response.

"It has happened. Please look at me," he said, turning her.

"This seals our fate then. I have made a wonderful breakfast for you and Bryan. I hope this will leave us with fond memories."

"Don't try to avoid what I'm saying here. What are you on about?"

"I guess the time has come for me to deal with the other part of you. I missed you very much last night. How I longed for the closeness of you. That absence was so unbearably painful. It made me realize how selfish I had become. My love for my country has almost taken second place to you. My driving force has been lost since I fell in love with you. Now it is time for you and me to deal with my desire to make a difference in my country. I've succumbed to personal pleasure while my people and my country are torn to hell. As I told you last night, I'll never leave Vietnam. I love my country. Just as your needs have surfaced, so have mine. Truly, I understand the passion for something other than you and me, but I do not know whether I can deal with it. I cannot condemn you for the transgression of two loves, for I also share that fault, except my second love is for a country. We have reached the point where it is time to part."

"Because of Bryan?"

"No, not really, although I admit that part of my reason for inviting Bryan was because I was in doubt of where your fidelity lay. However, the realization of what I have become has made me see more clearly. We can't have it both ways any longer."

"Then I'll stay here with you." He dropped to his knees and bawled like a child at her feet. He clasped at her ankles. "Please don't leave me. I love you so much. Don't leave."

She stooped and gently pulled him to his feet and then softly stroked his face with her fingertips. "Please get up, my sweet, so very handsome Greg. Have you heard a single word? It is over. You haven't forgotten last night. What about Bryan? I'm sure he will be hurt if you stay."

"He understands me."

"You don't know that! His life has now changed. He has loved you. I hope you haven't used him in some spoiled way of yours for a selfish purpose."

"What a cruel thing to say."

"I don't mean to be. I just find it so difficult to believe how quickly you have forgotten him. I hope you won't hurt him. Please understand me; it will not work any longer."

"Stop! Please stop talking like this. Your words are so savage. What has come over you? It's not fair. You've known all along. I'm so confused. Damn! I don't want to hurt anyone." He started to weep again.

She held him, her eyes moistening with tears. Her lips kissed his warm ear as she softly said, "It's better this way. We really have no choice. We will all find happiness with our new decisions."

She realized he could not help himself, and the sudden hint of future pain filled her. Feelings of weakness were advancing and becoming overbearing, and she knew that she had to move quickly, as she wanted to give in. "Greg, I'm leaving for town. Please, by the time I return, you and Bryan should have left. I wish to say goodbye to Bryan. Please eat the breakfast I have prepared." She drew his face to hers. The kiss of parting burned within them.

Bryan entered the room. "Have I picked a bad time?"

"No, Bryan, I wanted to say goodbye."

"Goodbye? What's going on? Is it something I did?"

"No, buddy. It's the time for causes," Greg said sardonically. "Causes that kill, destroy, or delude men of exactness. Tuyet hears the call to help her countrymen. What a bunch of shit. We're the little people, always betrayed by politicians for their own ends."

He walked over to Bryan, who was overwhelmed and shocked by Greg's behavior. "You wouldn't walk out on me for a cause that is worthless, would you?"

"No, never."

"Wait until we get home. We're despised by people of our age because of a cause that we thought was just, a cause that you and I now know is a joke. The only hope we have is to find truth in the love of another human being. The world is all lies and is fucked." He darted out of the room.

"Bryan, how sad I am. I love him and have no other choice but to let him go. I want you to take care of him and tell him I truly loved him. Someday he will realize the sacrifice I was forced to make." She hugged him and kissed him on the cheek. "I will think of you always. Goodbye, my dearest friend."

Bryan stood in complete shock. "Tuyet, I can't believe all this. You are a part of me. I'm hurt at the thought of saying goodbye. You are the sister I never had—a family member. This is all impossible. I just cannot believe that I'll never see you again. I'm willing to accept you as part of the relationship with Greg. My love for you makes it easy. What can I do to make you change your mind? I'm so filled with pain and joy."

"Nothing, my dearest Bryan. My friend, you need not sacrifice. It is the beginning for you. Please forgive me, but I must leave now. My departure must come before the New Year. We Vietnamese believe that the events of which we partake in the New Year will follow through the next year."

"Then you're not coming back?" he said, wondering whether he had really heard correctly. He stood paralyzed. The pain of parting caused him numbness. "Goodbye, my dearest madame Tuyet DuMont," he whispered to himself as she left.

He sat at the table and stared at the wonderful food that filled it, wondering how this had all come about. It was not supposed to have happened on this day. All of it was so unexpected.

Hours passed. Greg had not returned to the villa, so Bryan headed toward the beach to look for him. The cloudy, damp, cold weather followed the script of the dreadful day's events. Bryan walked with indecisiveness in his search for Greg. *What if he does something nuts like going AWOL?* he thought. After a short walk he saw Greg crouched down, drawing in the sand with his fingers. Bryan warily walked toward him, bent down, and touched his shoulder. "How are you doing?"

"Just writing in the sand, watching the waves wash away my thoughts, and wondering what the hell to do with this ring I was going to give Tuyet. A circle of so-called eternal love," Greg mused as he fiddled with the ring. "What was it you used to quote from Euripides? Something about a man can find a way to tell counterfeit gold from genuine gold but has no way to recognize a genuine, real person from one who is false. How do you think I am? I feel like hell! I just don't understand life. Why the hell have I been cursed? Now I've made shit out of two people's lives."

As Greg twisted the ring off his finger, Bryan sensed his emotional intent to toss it into the waves, grabbed his arm, and said, "Don't be so impulsive. You'll only regret it. Your decision to ask her to marry you and the care you took in buying the ring was not sudden, so why throw away the symbol of your love and fidelity? You can't throw away what you had or pretend it never happened."

"You take it then, and do what you want with it. I just don't want to see it anymore."

"Okay, calm down. I'll wear it and keep it safe until you want it back. Just hang in there, buddy, and give yourself some time."

"Thanks, buddy."

"This may sound somewhat over-romantic, but I think I could live with whatever decision you make. I would find it so hard to deal with a choice that does not include me, but I understand you. You have given me a new life. I realize now that I was half alive—a walking dead man. You don't know how thankful I am."

"Well, Bryan, whatever I did, it looks as if you're stuck with me," Greg said with that boyish smile. "Someday I may understand her determination and beliefs, but my gut feeling tells me there is more. I just don't get it."

A few minutes of silence passed. "So are you ready for Saigon? It's party time, big party time," Greg said, knowing that pleasure always supplanted pain.

"Sure, I'm ready for the Paris of the Orient. It should not be too difficult to catch a military flight out of Da Nang."

22

SAIGON, VIETNAM, SUNDAY, JANUARY 28, 1968

On their arrival in Saigon Bryan and Greg headed to the famous Majestic Hotel to settle in and orient themselves.

"Nice and warm down here," Greg said. "You were right; there was no problem getting a flight out of Da Nang to Tan Son Nhut."

"There is as much traffic here as at Kennedy airport. Let's wave down a cab."

"Well, I'm ready for my history class on Saigon," Greg joked. "What's the story here?"

"I have the book right here," Bryan said as he began to read. "Saigon was built on the ancient city of Khmer. Here, a small population lived in an area of forests, swamps, and lakes. The origin of the city's name is unsure, probably deriving its meaning from Sai Con—'relating to the forest' or 'kingdom of the forest.' The actual meaning and roots are disputed and unsure. The first area of important trade and commerce was Ben Nghe, which flourished in the eighteenth century. This is the present-day area of Saigon called Cholon. In the nineteenth century, Saigon continued to grow in spite of the constant conflicts between its people and the Cambodians. In 1859, the French subdued Saigon in a European frenzy for Asian colonies. This foothold allowed the French campaign to conquer the whole country and its neighbors. Vietnam lost the struggle to hold back the European conquest, and their six hundred years of self-rule came to an end. In 1883, the French captured Hanoi and established the Cochin China colony with Saigon as its capital. The city was improved, modernized, and beautified to French taste, and Saigon took on the character of a French provincial town.

"With the conclusion of World War II, the Japanese surrendered Saigon to the Vietnamese. Upon the return of the French in 1946, a movement for independence arose. The French were unable to suppress the insurrection in spite of their many battlefield victories. With the defeat at Dien Bien Phu and the growing public discontent and protest over the war, the French agreed to leave Vietnam. In 1954, with the French departure, Vietnam was divided between north and south, and Saigon became the capital of the newly created republic of South Vietnam ..."

Within forty-five minutes they reached the hotel, which overlooked the Saigon River.

"Well, here's the hotel," Greg interrupted, somewhat relieved. "Thanks for the lecture!"

Bryan approached the front desk as Greg took a seat in the lobby.

"Good morning, sir," the receptionist said. "Welcome to the hotel. Can I help you?"

"Yes, I have a reservation. The name is Ruocco."

"Yes, sir. I received your telegram explaining that you would arrive later. Rooms are quite expensive and difficult to find with the New Year. You also have some messages. Key for Mr. Ruocco, please," he said, turning to another receptionist. "Shall I call a porter?"

"Thank you," Bryan replied as he fixed his eyes on Greg, who was sitting in the lobby looking at the passing crowd. He had signaled a waiter and appeared to be ordering something.

"Sir will be staying until Sunday?"

"I shall be here until then," he answered without turning and stretched out his hand to take his messages and a letter. As he walked toward Greg, he leafed through the items in his hand—a letter from home and a call from the Special Services on tour information.

"Sir, your drink—gin and tonic with a twist of lime—and your newspaper. May I get something for you as well?" the waiter asked, turning to Bryan.

"No, thanks." He turned to Greg. "Are you okay? No second thoughts?"

"No. Why?"

"You don't usually drink so early in the afternoon."

"I'm great and am sure glad we're here," he said. Then he read from the newspaper, never lifting his head, "The *Stars and Stripes* reports that President Thieu has granted amnesty to nearly five hundred prisoners, including many political detainees, in honor of Tet, and Saigon's nighttime curfew is lifted."

"Great! Can we go to Cholon this evening for dinner?"

"No! Wait! Let me finish. Khe Sanh is still under siege."

"What?"

"The Third Battalion Twenty-Sixth Marines and a North Vietnamese Army battalion began at Khe Sanh, fourteen miles below the DMZ and six miles from the border of Laos. Thirty thousand NVA troops surrounded six thousand marines. President Johnson is so concerned that he's having hourly reports sent to him. The main ammunition dump was hit, detonating fifteen hundred tons of explosives."

"I hope we're not having another Dien Bien Phu, the battle that ended the French rule in Indochina."

"Maybe that should happen. I'm beginning to wonder if we should be in this damn country."

"My thoughts exactly, Greg." Bryan stood up and said, "Let's get to the room so that I can get cleaned up, and we can get something to eat. I don't know about you, but I could eat a horse."

"Nice, real nice! This must be expensive," Greg said as he walked around and opened the doors to the balcony. The city below the sixth floor gave an impressive view, bustling with typical activities. The boulevard below was lined with trees, and the sound of indistinguishable, muffled conversation from the street could be heard, to say nothing of the persistent drone from the rumble of the traffic.

"Well, I'm going to get cleaned up," Greg said. He started undressing, and as he headed toward the bedroom, he gave Bryan a wink.

Bryan laughed it off, called the desk, and ordered dinner to be brought to the room. After a few minutes, Bryan headed toward the bedroom. As he unpacked, Greg slid his head, dripping wet, through the bathroom door, sending hot steam pouring out. "Hey, sailor." Bryan joined him.

Suddenly the interlude was interrupted by a knock at the door. "Room service."

"Just a minute. I'll be there," Greg called as he wrapped himself in a large terry-cloth robe and headed toward the door.

The waiter rolled in a large, lace-covered table with silver trays of covered food—their own private restaurant.

"Anything else, sir?"

"Yes. A bottle of gin, tonic water, and fresh limes," he replied as he tipped the waiter and paid the bill.

"I'll return with it shortly, sir."

"Bryan, showtime." Greg picked up the tray and returned to the bedroom to finish dressing.

"Let me finish up and join you for dinner."

After the waiter dropped off the gin, tonic water, and limes, Bryan opened the balcony windows and arranged the seating for an evening of intimacy. He then rearranged the table setting and checked to see if all was in place. He had to make this evening and the time in Saigon very special for Greg. The pain of losing Tuyet was evident on Greg's face. Bryan pulled his seat out and occasionally sipped at a glass of wine. The sky darkened as dusk approached. How his world had changed in just twenty-four hours—it was quite unbelievable. His thoughts were neither of home nor of the things or pleasures that had been so much part of his life. His sole thoughts were of Greg and how he felt with him.

He suddenly felt a pair of warm hands gently touching his neck as Greg crouched down behind him. "May I join you for dinner?" Greg asked, his breath warm on Bryan's neck. "Everything looks wonderful."

Bryan turned and smiled. They embraced and kissed. Greg took his hand and said, "I don't know how I would have made it without you. I feel so guilty about today. I don't want you to feel used or second best."

"I only want to know that you love me."

"I do. Why do you need to hear it again? I meant what I said last night at the villa. Everything I said was the truth."

"It's so hard to believe that I could feel this way. It's so unreal. I have never experienced this happiness before. I only think about you, and I become so excited at the thought of you."

"Well, kid, you got it bad." Greg smiled. "You're in love, and I'm happy that it is with me. So let us toast our new relationship."

"I can't help thinking about—"

Greg placed two fingertips on Bryan's lips. "No. This is our time, and I don't want to hear her name again. I want us to enjoy the discovery of each other. It's hard to believe that we've known each other for close to three years and it has finally come to this. It has taken us so long to find the honesty to express our feelings. Boy, how I wanted you. I got so close the summer of '67 when you got that Dear John letter from Michelle. So close, then nothing. I'm cursed! When I looked in on you later, you were gone. Where did you disappear to that evening?"

"God, I had forgotten about that. I walked for hours and cried my eyes out. I thought it was over her, but it was in fact the fear of having feelings for you—feelings I didn't want to admit, feelings I thought I had forgotten. I was reminded of a high school friend whom I felt the same about. As I passed the grocery store on our corner, they were blasting 'Ode to Billy Joe.' That repeated over and over in my mind, and I ended up at the naval hospital, where they filled me with antidepressant pills and sent me on my way. I guess that if I had succumbed, I would not have been able to control myself. How I suppressed those feelings, thinking that they were everything else but love—feelings I have known in my life. I feel so strange and filled with butterflies and excitement."

"Do you know when I thought that I had lost you for good?"

"No. When?" Bryan asked as he brushed away a lock of Greg's hair that had dropped in front of his eyes. "How do you manage to pass inspection with that long hair?"

"You're not listening. I wet it down. The time you were raped by those fuckers."

Bryan pulled back and grunted. "You're right; I hate the thought of any other man touching me!"

"That tore me apart because I wanted to make your first time a beautiful experience, but those bastards took that away from me."

"But you were the one who helped give me my life back with that genuine concern and caring the following morning. You were the reason I didn't commit suicide, although I sure contemplated it enough."

"I knew it was bad, but I had no idea it was that serious. God, that makes me feel good, knowing that I was able to do something. I don't know how I could have dealt with your death."

"When did you realize I was a homosexual? I never had any idea about you. You're not the image I was taught. I never thought a man as masculine as you could be homosexual."

"I was never really sure. I just felt that certain feeling and hoped that you felt that way too. I also spilled the beans."

"When?"

"When we spent the night at Radnor and Marian's, you remember? We talked in the living room."

"Yes … So that's what the hell you were driving at."

"Have you thought about when we get out? It won't be long until June. I'm not going back to Virginia. I think I would like to live in California. Would you like to stay in California?"

"I would, but it's far from my dad."

"Your dad? That's right; you and he are very close. From the way you talk about him, he seems neat."

"You would like him, and I'm sure he'd like you as well. But I don't know how he would handle all this. I can't live a life he wants me to live, and as I don't want to hurt him, I guess he'll never know."

"I think you may underestimate his willingness to accept you and your life's natural choice."

"I guess so, but I think that is something we can deal with later. I do think I could go almost anyplace you go. I just want to go back to school and get my degree."

"Then California is the best place to settle. College is dirt cheap, and cost is something you should consider, besides finding a neat place to live."

The discussion continued throughout the change of dusk to night's darkness. They talked as though they had just recently met, and, to some extent, it was their first genuine interaction. They had passed the junction of veneers and falsehoods and reached the convergence of the highest level of truth and honesty, leaving behind the invisible cover of fraudulent behavior. While they talked, enjoying the city and the view of the city's night events taking place below them, the peaceful night was suddenly broken with an explosion in a far-off city district.

"Wow! Check it out!" Greg said with excitement. The sky unexpectedly filled with a burst of flares, and searchlights were quickly followed by rockets, tracer bullets, and mortars.

"Some VC activity over in the Cu Chi district," Bryan observed.

"Boy, these people seem to go about their business as if nothing is happening," Greg said as he leaned over the balcony, watching the people below. "The news from the *Stars and Stripes* seems to indicate that the tide of war is turning in our favor. The Communists seem to be beaten at last."

"I don't buy that view. You know that paper is one-sided," Bryan said, shaking his head slightly.

"Other than fighting near Khe Sanh, what else is going on? They seem to be reporting the same news in *Newsweek*. The VC has done very little. Maybe we can now get the hell out of this damn place. I sometimes question your loyalties. Now that we're not keeping anything from each other, are you a Communist? Tell me."

"Okay, a Communist, right. No, seriously, I think this may be the calm before the storm. These people are fighting for their homeland."

"You're sounding more like a Communist to me."

"No, listen, I really think this is just a pretext for something big and far more tragic."

As quickly as the noise had begun, it ended.

"I guess I had somewhat of an overreaction. It all seems to be over. So what about hitting a few nightclubs and bars?" Greg asked.

"The only place I know is Cholon, where they never sleep. It's some kind of big market with waterfront bars," Bryan said as he looked at a map and figured the distance. "It looks to be about three or four miles from the hotel."

"Let's go for it."

They collected a few things and excitedly left the hotel.

"Nice and warm," Bryan said. "Shall we take a cab?"

"Let's catch a pedicab," Greg suggested as he waved for one. They hopped in. "How much to Cholon?"

After a little negotiation they were on their way. Cholon was Saigon's Chinatown, where merchants and businesses flourished twenty-four hours a day. The streets were crowded with people in search of merchandise. It was noisy and filled with energy. Chinese architecture of pagodas and temples dominated the landscape.

"We will have to come back during the day. This place is unreal," Greg said as he took in the surroundings.

"I don't know how the Communists could ever suppress these people's desire for profits. This is how to win the war. Show these people how to make even more money."

"Boy, what smells good?" Greg looked at a store displaying meats and poultry hanging in rows. Some were cooked, others raw; others were in the process of being cooked. "That makes me hungry. Shall we get some food?"

"I'm a little hungry. A bowl of pork fried rice and a beer would be nice."

Throughout their late-night meal Greg continued to drink heavily, appearing to have little reaction to the alcohol.

"You sure have mastered those chopsticks," Greg observed.

"Are you okay?"

"Sure, just feeling good. I think we should head back soon. That tour with Special Services starts early."

"I agree."

At the hotel room, Greg wobbled, as if walking a high wire.

"It has finally hit you," said Bryan, grasping at his waist. "We best get you to bed."

"No, I'm fine." With that, his head dropped, and he passed out.

"My God, you are heavy," Bryan said as he struggled to undress him and put him to bed.

MONDAY, JANUARY 29, 1968

"Hey, buddy, let's get up. We only have an hour before they stop serving breakfast," Greg said as he rubbed Bryan's head to awaken him. There was no response. "Let's hit the deck, Carrottop."

"After the binge last night, how are you able to be up? Anyway, don't call me that! It reminds me of a creep I once knew in high school," Bryan said as he sat up and rubbed his eyes and then combed his hair with his fingers. "Enough now!"

"I figured that would get your butt out of bed."

"I can think of better ways to get my butt up and out of bed," he replied with a wink and a smile.

"My God! I've unleashed a sex maniac!"

"Seriously, Greg, how's your head? You've done some heavy drinking in the last few days. I've never seen you drink that way." Bryan was concerned.

"Best one can expect, allowing for my behavior."

"What does that mean? Is there something wrong?"

"Let's talk over breakfast," he said.

Bryan left the bedroom, paused, and observed Greg sitting with his legs crossed on top of the table and a cup of coffee clutched in his hands, looking as though he were having an out-of-body experience. He appeared oblivious to his surroundings, his eyes fixed, staring, focusing intently. It seemed that time had almost stopped.

"Where are you? Where have you gone?"

"I wonder where she would be in Saigon. I wonder what she is doing. Tuyet, my Thien Mu," Greg muttered under his breath.

"What did you say?"

"Nothing. This is nice," Greg said, changing the subject. "We've sat by this window for the last two days. Let's call room service and order breakfast. I'm starved. I want the works—juice, eggs, steak, hash browns, toast, and black coffee."

"I'm full just listening to you," Bryan said. "Coffee, juice, and dried cereal will take care of me."

"I don't know how to say this, Bryan. I want to explain this correctly."

Bryan took a deep breath.

"I want to return to the villa and talk to Tuyet just one more time. I would never forgive myself if I did not try once more. By no means does this indicate that it is over between us. The three of us must come to terms with our situation. I never thought I would be so lucky as to have the love of two people. I'm so very fortunate. I love you, and it hurts me to ask this of you."

"I thought I heard you mention her name." Bryan's voice began to quiver. "I was foolish to believe I could satisfy all your needs. I put aside those other things you require. I know it will be difficult to share you, but the alternative is unthinkable. I agree only if you realize that your position is the most difficult. Juggling the two of us, how will you do it?" Bryan hesitated. "That was a silly question. I already know the answer to that, as you've done it before."

"Don't jump the gun. She has not agreed yet."

"At this point I cannot deal with the thought of losing you. I would agree to almost anything. I'm hopelessly in love with you, and, in this ludicrous state, nothing I do would be correct. Let's either look for her here or go back to Da Nang. My gut feeling is that she is still in Da Nang."

24

TET OFFENSIVE, VIETNAM, 1968

U nknown to Bryan, Greg, and the world, an event was to take place that would cause shock waves so great that the political and social fiber of the United States would unravel. The great Tet Offensive would topple Lyndon B. Johnson and divide the country further. Analogous to the Battles of Gettysburg and Midway, unknown to its contemporaries, this was the turning point in the Vietnam War. The division in the United States would shift to a fervor of antiwar sentiment even among the ranks of the previously supportive. This shifting view would result in the Americans' first encounter with defeat. A guilt of transgression, shame, and shock would stalk the American psyche.

The Tet Offensive was planned by Vo Nguyen Giap, the North Vietnamese minister of defense. His major achievement was his decisive victory at Dien Bien Phu in 1954—the battle at which the French were defeated in Indochina. Both he and Ho Chi Minh planned a general offensive. The Viet Cong, with the support of the North Vietnamese Army, would attack the South at once—an offensive that would affect the political, psychological, and military stability of the American and South Vietnamese governments. The Viet Cong's goal was to attack government offices, police stations, military headquarters, and communication centers. With radio stations secured, they would make propaganda broadcasts, and people would join the liberation armies.

The South Vietnamese and Americans counterattacked with utter ruthlessness, bombing and shelling heavily populated cities. By mid-February, the US casualty rate reached an all-time high—543 killed and 2,547 wounded in action in a single week. According to American estimates, 165,000 civilians died in the three weeks following the start of the Tet Offensive; two million more became refugees.

Tet was a sacred holiday for the Vietnamese. The New Year was the target date. Tet was also a time for truce and an opportunity for a surprise attack. In the hope of diverting American strength from the major towns and cities, Giap launched attacks along the South Vietnamese borders and the demilitarized zone in the fall of 1967, and at the start of 1968 battles erupted at the US outposts of Con Thien, Dak To, and Khe Sanh.

On Tuesday, January 30, in Da Nang, parked in its usual place was that strange and awkwardly designed Citroën 2CV, which was still a welcome sight to Greg. Excitement filled him as he increased his stride. Acknowledged yearning and joy coursed through him, and his heart pounded as he opened the front door.

"Thien Mu!" he called. "Tuyet!" He darted through the villa, but there was no reply. Within a few minutes he returned to Bryan, his face blank and his eyes moist with restrained tears.

"She's not here!" he cried with surprise and extreme disappointment.

"She can't be far. Her car is here," Bryan reassured him, to little effect.

"It's too cool in here. She hasn't been here for a while. I wonder where she is." Greg moved his head from side to side in apparent confusion.

"Still visiting her relatives I guess," Bryan said, continuing to reassure Greg. "This is just the first day of Tet."

"It seems strange to me. This place hasn't changed since we left. Everything is the same." Greg appeared puzzled while surveying the villa. "Maybe you're right and she is still visiting relatives. Sure glad you bought food from the exchange. I'm hungry!"

At 0300 on Wednesday, January 31, the first day of the Tet truce, NVA and Viet Cong forces attacked Saigon with a force of five thousand. Saigon was considered a fortress of security and had been spared the devastation experienced by much of the country. The Viet Cong had infiltrated the city prior to Tet. The large number of visitors in the city for the holiday allowed forces to pass unnoticed. These forces were unarmed; war supplies had been smuggled into the city weeks before by funeral and food vendors. Troops broke into units and then dispersed into suicide squads. They marched to the Independence Palace and forced open the gates for the liberating army. From that point, fighting broke out throughout the city. The Communists unleashed their attack. They attacked Tan Son Nhut with the objective of destroying the Seventh Air Force command center and General Westmoreland's headquarters. After eighteen hours of combat between Viet Cong and US forces, the Communist advance was halted.

The Communist forces attacked the quarters of the national police and those of the US officers and enlisted men. City communications were under attack. One major objective was the South Vietnamese government's radio station. After the Communists blasted their way into the building to announce the "liberation of Saigon," the South Vietnamese shut down the ability to transmit. The Viet Cong, realizing their objective was not possible, detonated explosives, sacrificing themselves and destroying the building.

The Communists took both American and Vietnamese officials from cars, compounds, and off the streets and held summary courts. After being tried and convicted, these officials were shot by firing squads. These trials and executions were staged for the Vietnamese civilians.

The American embassy was attacked by nineteen Viet Cong commandos. At 0300, with intelligence warning of a possible attack, commandos wearing civilian clothes and red armbands attacked the complex and the embassy with mortars. For eight hours, five military police repelled the attackers until they were relieved by two platoons.

Saigon was placed under martial law by orders of President Nguyen Van Thieu. That day the chief of the Saigon police executed a Viet Cong soldier in the street. The execution caused outcry within the United States, as it was televised throughout the nation on the evening news.

By February 1, Saigon was in total upheaval and urban war. The Communists were concentrated in Cholon, a community populated with Chinese and Buddhist agitators and with a history of antigovernment sentiments. The Viet Cong held out in the Buddhist pagoda of An Quang. It was here that Americans and South Vietnamese encountered their fiercest resistance. It was not until February 20 that the offensive lost its momentum. On February 23, the American and South Vietnamese forces subdued Cholon.

Almost simultaneously with the attack on Saigon, the Communists attacked countless other cities and towns throughout South Vietnam during Tet. Viet Cong forces, supported by a large number of NVA troops, launched the largest and best-coordinated offensive of the war, driving into the very center of South Vietnam, and attacked thirty-six provincial capitals, thirty-four district capitals, five major cities, and scores of American and South Vietnamese military bases. The attack reached from as far north as the demilitarized zone to as far south as the Mekong Delta.

The twenty-seven days of the Tet Offensive illustrated and clarified the situation in Vietnam. The government of South Vietnam was ineffective without the confidence and the support of the country's interior. The Communists took control with little or no resistance. Their ability to amass such a military force and strike at will symbolized the loss of any sense of security.

The Tet Offensive was a military victory for the Americans and South Vietnamese, but it was an unknown political victory for the North Vietnamese.

Both military and political leaders in the United States began to reevaluate America's position in Vietnam after the Tet Offensive. The American people began to question their leaders and the war. On March 31, President Johnson told the nation that he would not seek another term as president. The Republicans' victory with the election of Richard Nixon to the White House was the nation's response to the war.

25

UNIVERSITY OFFICE, ALEXANDRIA, VIRGINIA, AUGUST 1991

Suddenly Bryan stopped talking.

"Is there a problem?" Radnor asked.

"No. I'm a little dry and thirsty from all this talking."

"Need a break?"

"It's hard for me at this point. We're almost at the moment of my eternal hell."

"Are you sure you can go on?"

"I think so. I just want to get a drink. Would you like something also?"

"No, thanks."

Bryan returned and continued, "I remember that we spent the day lounging about and eating. I was tense and concerned the entire time there. What would be the outcome of our return to the villa? What was in store for us all? I felt only pain at the thought that he might remain in Vietnam. How could I deal with that? Greg continued to drink heavily, and I was helpless to do anything. Late that night, into the early morning of the thirty-first, Tuyet had still not returned. Greg had passed out earlier that evening from almost twenty-four hours of heavy drinking.

"Sometime late in the night, pounding and firecracker-like sounds woke me up. The noises continued to rumble, and I was frightened ..."

Tet Offensive, Vietnam, 1968

"Greg! Greg! Wake up!" I shook and pulled at him.

"What's going on?" He started to rise. "Damn, what a fucking headache."

"Shut up and listen!"

"It's just fireworks for Tet. Go back to sleep." He pulled the pillow over his head.

"At this hour?" Bryan darted to the window in the hope of making sense of the disturbance. The sky over Da Nang was brilliant with huge flashing yellow-and-orange lights.

"Oh my God! Greg, come here and see your fireworks."

"I hope this is worth getting up for. Damn this head," he mumbled as he made his way to the window, holding his hand over his forehead. "Fireworks, hell! Only a rocket attack could cause an explosion with such intense light at that distance. If my sense of direction is correct, that's Da Nang Air Base. It looks as if all hell is breaking loose over there."

"We need to find out what the hell is going on. Maybe we should leave tomorrow?" Bryan said, his voice vibrating. "I want to get the hell out of here."

"Relax. There's not much we can do at this hour. Outside is most likely crawling with VC," Greg said, gasping for air.

The night seemed endless, as neither of them could sleep. They packed hastily and intended to leave the villa that morning. Greg was preparing a hasty breakfast, his personal problems overshadowed by the present situation.

"It won't take long before we're out of here. I never thought I would look forward to seeing the ship," Greg said as he sloppily made sandwiches.

"I've got to do something. I think I'll get cleaned up." Bryan left the kitchen. Nervously he lathered his face. The mirror reflected the open window across the room, and as he shaved, flutters of black figures silently passed. He quickly dropped to the floor. Fear and disbelief overtook him. *It can't be!* he thought. *VC?* Slowly, he crept like a cat toward the window and rose at a snail's pace. As he slid his head up the wall, his heart pounded. The window corner allowed for a restricted view without possible detection. Vietnamese guerillas, clad in black pajamas and conical straw hats, drifted by. He fell back to the floor and frantically returned to the kitchen.

"Greg! Greg! There are VC just outside. What the hell are we going to do?" Bryan said as he burst into the room.

"Bryan, I'm scared enough. Don't play. Tell me you're joking," Greg said, shaking him and losing all stability. "Tell me you're fucking around!"

"I wish to hell I was. Quit shaking me and get a grip on yourself. They're just outside."

"Shit, we can't leave yet. There is something big going on. I wish I understood what. Not knowing is hell."

They both stood in silence and then decided to try to leave the following day instead. There was no sign of Tuyet, their leave was almost up, and their nerves were shot.

The next morning, Greg and Bryan searched the villa for Vietnamese clothing to wear until they could get to Da Nang. They packed their blue jeans and other navy gear, and then they made a break for it, dressed in black pajamas and conical straw hats. Their goal was to get to the main road, catch a cab for downtown Da Nang, change clothes, and return to the ship. They left the villa, and within a few minutes the hammering sounds of helicopters swarmed over them like locusts. Bryan looked up and saw what appeared to be American UH-1 Hueys. At that point, Bryan's hat flew off, and as he reached to pick it up, the earth rumbled, and the villa exploded in a ball of fire. The whole world seemed to be an inferno.

Bryan ran behind Greg as they dashed and dodged explosives and waves of bullets. Greg was heading toward an area of dense trees and shrubs. The intuitive impulse for survival immersed them; it was not until much later, when the shock and disbelief had subsided, that fear and horror set in. Bryan's actions were totally involuntary, and events were overtaking him. His eyes were fixed on Greg and the direction they were running. When they were within seconds of the dense foliage, a spray of bullets shaved the shrubs and tree branches. Bryan's eyes were drawn to the shearing of vegetation, and as he followed the horizontal destruction, he saw it cut into Greg's lower back. He froze as bullets penetrated Greg, only a few feet away from him. Greg's blood and body segments sprayed Bryan's face and chest. The Armageddon that surrounded the two seemed to freeze and mutate. Greg's head turned, bobbing; his arms flung in a crucified position; and then he fell backward. Bryan caught him as he fell and stared at his face, which he clutched with trembling hands.

"Greg! Greg! Hang on, buddy. You'll be okay."

"God, everything has gone black and white."

"It's okay! It's okay!" Bryan reassured him as the fear and horror caused him to cling to Greg for protection.

"No, buddy ..." Greg began to slip in and out of consciousness. "Pictures. Black and white ... All grainy."

Bryan became oblivious to the sounds around him as he focused on Greg, mentally trying to escape from the revulsion of the inevitable.

Greg's eyes looked up, reflecting the passing of black-and-white clouds against the blue sky. "Bryan, it's the last call."

Moist, warm blood streamed and soaked through Bryan's pants as life emptied from Greg's body. Greg's head, turned slightly, rested limply on Bryan's chest. Bryan's vision became blurred with tears as he realized that death was imminent.

"We'll make it! Oh my God! Greg, we will!"

Greg struggled to speak. "Bryan," he said in an undertone, "my best friend and love." The death rattle had already commenced in his throat. "Tell ... tell Tuyet ... we ... tried."

Bryan continued to hold him close as he began choking. He gasped his last words. "Tuyet, my Thien Mu." It was as if he was trying to atone and make his peace. Then he slowly raised his arm and touched his fingertips to Bryan's forehead. He slowly traced Bryan's face, and then his arm dropped lifelessly upon the ground. His face changed to a ghostly marble white, as if a sheet of snow had covered him.

University Office, Alexandria, Virginia, 1991

"Oh my God, he's dead? You actually witnessed his death? My God, now I can understand why this memory has been suppressed for all these years," cried Radnor, alarmed and dismayed. "The horror of all this must have been unbearable."

Bryan's head fell to the side of the wing chair as he confirmed, "Yes, he died. Now it all comes back. Now I remember. Radnor, I remember!"

Radnor went into shock as the revelation sank in, and the trauma became unbearable for both of them. Bryan went into a state of suspended animation as he relived the horror of Greg's death.

Eventually Radnor asked anxiously, "Are you okay? Shall we stop now? The anguish and agony is becoming insufferable for both of us. Please, let's stop." He put his head in his hands in utter despair.

"No, I have to go on. I don't want to forget. I remember thinking at the time, *No, God! No, God! This can't be happening.* My head dropped to his face, covering him as if to protect him. I hoped that I would join him. While I rocked his lifeless body, hands pulled me from him, and a familiar voice called my name, urging me to let go of him. Realizing that it was Tuyet's voice restored me. All I could think was that those bastards had killed him, one of their own. I wondered what the hell was going on and asked her to take me home, where my dad would explain and make some sense out of all the madness. Then I must have passed out."

26

HUYEN KHONG CAVE, MARBLE MOUNTAINS, VIETNAM, JANUARY 1968

As Bryan's head lay in Tuyet's lap, the strong dampness of the cave and familiar smell of deodorant soap permeated his nostrils, reviving him.

"Good, you're awakening. How are you feeling?" There was no response. She wiped his face and head with a cool, damp cloth as his body started to snap and twitch.

"Be calm. It's okay. You're safe now."

"Where am I? I'm so thirsty. My head …"

She lifted a chipped porcelain cup to his lips. "You're safe now. We're in a cave and protected from the bombing. Bryan, it has been a terrible day. You and Greg—"

On hearing Greg's name, he became agitated. "Greg. Where's Greg?" he interrupted.

"Bryan, our dearest friend didn't make it."

"Didn't make it? Oh no. So it wasn't a bad dream. It really happened. Greg did die in my arms. Oh God." Agonizing pain deformed his features as he looked at her face, which glistened from the naked lightbulb that hung from the roof of the cave.

"Yes, sweet Bryan, it is true. Our dearest friend is dead." As she spoke, her warm tears trickled onto his forehead and slowly mixed with his.

"It's so hard to believe."

Despite his blurred vision, he noticed her dark clothing. Never had he seen her dressed in such colorless attire.

"Why are you dressed this way? What's going on?" he moaned in anguish and pain. "I must be dreaming. All this cannot be happening."

"You're not dreaming. We're in a cave in the Marble Mountains. This is the infirmary for the VC. You have been out of it for the last twenty-four hours. Soon it will be dawn, and I'll escort you down the mountain to where you can catch a cab to your ship."

Bryan suddenly became angry. "Damn you! Answer me: Why the hell are you dressed that way?"

Cautiously she replied, "Because I'm a Vietnam Cong San."

"A Communist! A goddamn Communist?"

He sat up and pushed her hand off his head. "I don't believe any of this. My best friend is dead, and the woman we loved is the enemy. This is all so fucked." He placed his head in his hands and sobbed. "God, why is all this happening? I want to wake from this nightmare."

"Bryan, please be quiet. The others will be offended by your words and behavior. It is difficult enough for me to justify your presence, as well as your rescue and the sympathy I exhibit." As she spoke, her comrades seemed to be discussing her and commenting on Bryan's angry reaction. "Please don't make my position any more compromising than it has already become."

"But why? I don't understand."

"I'm like you, a human being and a nationalist. I'm no different from the person you loved just a few days ago. I was then what you know now. You are experiencing what I have been going through for years—being torn between human love and cruel reality. I have been forced to choose between the greater good and the selfishness of the individual. Communism makes it all possible. It is my blueprint and guide, and I'm here because I have made the choice. I'm committed to my country and its cause."

"Bullshit, all of it. Greg's dead. Don't you care, or did you ever?"

"You're not being fair. I loved him in ways you will never know or understand. I still carry that love."

"So while we were at the villa hoping that you would return, you and your comrades were destroying and killing Americans and Vietnamese. All for the greater good, you say! What kind of good can justify death?"

"I cannot justify death. Conflict in its madness does not allow for the love of enemies. Otherwise there would be no war. That is why it is all such a mad scenario. We follow the insane call only when our enemy has no face."

"If Greg knew any of this, it would have surely destroyed him. Thank goodness he will never know the truth. Or maybe the truth would have saved him. I don't know the answer. I only know that we're both responsible for his death. Americans have killed him, and, vicariously, we assisted. Why didn't you make him understand?" he asked, weeping.

"I tried to explain many times, but he would never listen. His death is not one person's fault. He is a casualty of the insanity of it all. Please try to understand. My pain is so unbearable." She reached out to him. He responded in kind, and they hugged and trembled in each other's arms, mourning Greg's death.

"Tuyet, where exactly are we, and why is there such a strong smell of soap?"

"The infirmary is next to a storage room where we store American bars of soap."

"Why American soap?"

"We bathe with it to confuse the Alsatian dogs. The scent it gives off identifies us as friendly. Please limit your questions. The less you know, the better. I already have a difficult task to persuade them to let you go."

Bryan became agitated. "Oh no! You said I would be free at dawn," he cried anxiously.

"I had to say that to keep you calm. Please don't get upset. I have to leave now and meet with my superiors. I'm sure I'll be able to convince them ... See you later." She hugged him.

"Wonderful! Now I may become a POW." His tone, although sarcastic, also rumbled with fear. "Tuyet, I don't think I can go through much more."

The command post was stark, with the exception of a long wooden table and a long bench. Above the table hung a large red flag with a gold star in its center. Tuyet sat on a box in front of her superiors: three commanding officers, two local villagers, and a North Vietnamese officer.

"Comrade Tuyet, we're here upon your request to discuss the prisoner. As village cell head, I feel your devotion and sacrifice for the revolution is in some way only slightly greater than that of your brothers and sisters. The financial contributions from your bourgeois background are greatly appreciated and, naturally, needed. But as we're all equal, special considerations concern us all."

"Comrades, I have realized my past mistakes, and my deeds have overshadowed my previous acts. Hopefully I have proven myself, and I would surely make no further request of my superiors. This young man is no real asset to the revolution."

"That is a decision to be made by your superiors, not you!" interjected the North Vietnamese officer. "This young man and those like him could serve us well at the end of the war. I believe he should be sent north with other detained prisoners."

"I'm not so sure. I believe we should allow him to leave," the village cell head said. "My reason is this: the treatment he has received here allows for excellent propaganda. He can only speak well of us to his people, considering we saved him from his own. He is like a stone thrown into a pond, with the rippled circle reaching far from its center. I vote to release him."

"Excellent point," agreed a high-level cell member from the district. "I also vote to release him."

"Comrade Tuyet, free the sailor," commanded the village cell leader.

All but the village leader and Tuyet exited the command post.

"Tuyet, let us just say that my debt to you has been paid," the village leader said. "I hope that you will not regret your actions and that our great Tet Offensive awakens the Americans and ends the puppet government in Saigon."

Shortly after, Tuyet eagerly rejoined Bryan. "My superiors have made a decision; you can now be escorted from the cave. You are allowed to leave."

"Thank God. Thank you, Tuyet."

"My comrades and I will escort you to the bottom of the steps. Come!"

She then blindfolded him and, with the assistance of two VC soldiers, led him from the infirmary down the precarious slope of the mountain. He ran his hands along the walls for guidance, feeling the craters in the rock, and fresh air filled his nostrils when, unknown to him, they passed an air vent. Tuyet placed his hands on the slippery marble, which he grabbed tightly as they began their descent. Bryan then heard something that sounded like the rumbling of a gate; he was unaware in the dark that they had reached the entrance to the temple complex. They reached the bottom of the steps, and at this point Tuyet removed his blindfold. As his eyes adjusted to the light, he immediately recognized where they were. It was the same mountain that he had descended less than two years earlier.

"I guess this is where we must say goodbye, but first I will direct you to your cab. I'm sure that you are quite lost!"

"No, I know where I am. Tuyet, I feel that I'm in a deep sleep. I'm so tired and empty inside."

"We have been through a considerable ordeal." She took his hand. "Hopefully, someday we can put this horror behind us or possibly understand it."

He stopped in the road and looked at her. The rising sun brightened and accentuated her beauty. "I will miss the lovely face that captivated Greg and caused him to love you." Then, with his fingertips, he combed her hair, which felt like soft silk. "Hopefully I will leave with a better understanding."

"At least you now know my reason for separating with Greg."

"Yes, and I understand. But leaving you is one of the hardest things I have ever done."

"I'm a reminder of our past. It is best that we leave quickly. The pain is so difficult. Bryan," she said as she touched his face, "you're a reminder of the only man I have ever truly loved. I loved him enough to entertain the thought of leaving my country. I was, then and now, prepared to make sacrifices for him. Fate has decided our lives, and today we both lose two people. I pray that we can live with the loss. I will miss you so. Be strong. *Tam biet.* Goodbye."

"*Tam biet,*" he whispered as she quickly darted across the street and disappeared into a crowd of merchants.

Emptiness filled Bryan, a hollowness he had never experienced before. The awareness that he would never see either Greg or Tuyet again rapidly changed the desolation to pain and anguish. He stood motionless. *I hope that I will see her again,* he thought.

"Where would you like to go?" asked the cabdriver.

"Naval Supply Center."

Within minutes the cab drove off. Bryan quickly turned to the rear window and looked at where he and Tuyet had once stood. The view became obstructed by clouds of dust.

27

UNIVERSITY OFFICE, ALEXANDRIA, VIRGINIA, AUGUST 1991

"I guess you know the rest," Bryan said as he breathed a sigh of relief.

"I think you are a courageous man for having gone through this hell. You will have to come to grips with the past. Believe me, I will do nothing with this revelation that discredits you or Greg; I will repeat only what is relevant to changing his status from AWOL. Everything that may disgrace or dishonor his memory will remain between us. A society with so much prejudice and repulsion could not understand the virtuosity of your past."

"I'm greatly appreciative."

"Now that I know the truth about what happened to Greg, I feel obligated to find out what happened to him."

"I want that too. Let me know if I can assist."

"First of all I will need to verify eligibility for interment at Arlington, so I shall work through Special Services. I shall also need to talk to Senator Seaton as Greg's next of kin and obtain the necessary documentation. This may take some time. Just obtaining his military records from the National Personnel Records Center could take up to a year. Anyway, it is good to know that our friend died while on active duty and that his last period of duty ended honorably. I'm so sorry that I even contemplated that he would have gone AWOL."

"No apology is necessary. How could you have known? I'm just indebted to you for helping me to recall the sequence of events."

"I will try to contact Tuyet in New York. I'm sure that she will furnish us with even more details. I'll be in touch. Will you be okay?" Radnor asked as they headed toward the door.

"I'll make it."

"It's been a long and emotional evening for both of us."

"True, but I feel very composed and tranquil."

USS *DELAWARE*, VIETNAM, FEBRUARY 1968

Bryan could not forget the horror that echoed within him as he returned to the ship. Within a short time of his arrival at the Naval Supply Center, he was filled with a gnawing feeling, which was surreal. He sensed that some important incident or dramatic event had occurred, but it was incomprehensible. His memory was impenetrable.

Finally, the ship had to return to Da Nang Harbor, which afforded daylight protection from nighttime sabotage. Bryan caught the first shuttle back to the ship, reported in, and made his way to his berth.

"Bryan, I see you're back," Radnor called down the long ship's passageway. "It's good to see you." His voice became louder as he approached. Bryan slowed his walk and took a deep breath. He wanted to act as normal as possible.

"You've got to tell me all about the excitement in Saigon. I was wondering about you and Greg—"

"Greg and I? What do you mean?" Bryan interrupted in a defensive tone, misinterpreting the question. He turned his head quickly as he stopped speaking.

"I guess with all the confusion you and Greg did not get the leave-cancellation orders?"

"No, I never did. I don't know about Greg."

"I guess he'll be back today. You know we're getting ready to get under way for Okinawa—going back for those heavy supplies and then returning. I know how you hate those supply trips."

"Going without sleep for twenty-four hours is what I'm not looking forward to!" Bryan said.

"So was Saigon fun?"

"Saigon was wonderful. It was a return to civilization. Good food, good hotel, and lots to see. Only the French could turn the city into a miniature Paris."

"I guess the VC attack messed everything up?"

"Sure did. It was hell getting out. I waited for hours to return to the base." Momentarily he confused his escape from the villa with his departure from Saigon, and he began to question where in fact he had been waiting. "Now I've got to get below and get squared away. I'll talk to you at lunch," Bryan said as he darted down the passageway.

"What's the big rush?" Radnor asked, but Bryan was gone.

The ship got under way, and with the passing of hours, Bryan could not accept that Greg was not returning. He filled his mind with work and found anything that would distract him from reality. At lunch he acted normally, and after lunch it was a shipboard practice to take a nap before returning to work. His head resting on his soft pillow, he fell asleep. Before long, the boatswain's whistle blew, and it was time to return to work. He made his way to his stock area in number one hole and descended several flights of steps deep beneath the waterline. It felt as if he were in the belly of a whale. This was his sanctum from the others—a peaceful and private place. He made his way to the bales of unused rags and threw himself on them; his eyes blurred as he thought about Greg.

"Oh God, I don't think I can do this. I hurt so much." He sobbed to the point of complete weakness, and his fatigued body slipped into a deep sleep.

"Hey, Carrottop! Are you going to dinner or sleeping till morning?" Shocked at the sound of Greg's voice, he awakened. His friend's voice filled him with delight and a physical contentedness as he looked up at him. What a joy to see him! So it had all been a bad dream!

"God, what a dreadful dream I had about you," Bryan said as he rose from the bale of rags. "I'm so glad to see you. You don't know how happy I am."

"Same here," Greg said as he put his arm around Bryan. "Tell me about it at dinner. I've been starving since I left the cave."

"Cave? What are you talking about?" Bryan felt a strange twitch within.

"Tuyet saved me as well. I was in the infirmary in a cave in the Marble Mountains. They were attending to my wounds, but, as you can see, I'm much better now."

"Strange that Tuyet never mentioned you. I was sure that you were dead." Bryan paused. "God, I'm just so relieved that you are okay. I want to hold you."

"Sure, but I don't understand why you're acting this way. I'm here, and everything is fine."

Bryan felt good in Greg's embrace.

"Everything is fine, Bryan."

"Bryan … Bryan … Bryan!" Someone was calling his name, and as the voice grew louder, his eyes sprang open. He had been dreaming, but why had it seemed so real? He felt a warm joy mixed with a tingle of pain and a sense of Greg's presence. As he became more awake, he recognized the voice still calling him.

"Bryan, Bryan, are you down there?" his first-class supervisor called, his footsteps jangling as he made his way down the ladder.

"Yes, Tag. I'm just checking stock."

"I've been looking all over the ship for you," Tag said, looking out of breath and unsettled. "I'm afraid I have some very bad news for you. Sit down for a moment, Bryan."

"What's the matter?"

"Your father had a severe heart attack and is in intensive care."

"What? My dad? When? Where? Oh no! No!" Bryan fell to his

knees in shock, and Tag reached down to pull him to his feet. "I've got to get to him. I've got to get there."

"The ship's office has already completed your leave papers. You can catch the first flight out of Da Nang. I'm sure everything will be okay. Is there anything I can do?"

"No thanks," Bryan said in a trembling voice. "Thanks for taking care of things."

RETURN TO PHILADELPHIA, PENNSYLVANIA, FEBRUARY 28, 1968

Bryan fastened his safety belt for the descent into Philadelphia International Airport.

"The temperature is thirty-two; clear with the threat of light snow by the morning," informed the stewardess.

Bryan had been traveling for more than twenty-four hours, and he was in a state of unrelieved mental and physical fatigue with the accumulation of his unaccounted-for loss of memory and time as well as his father's potential imminent death. Events of the last few days seemed almost illusory and fantasized. The lost pieces from his past few days were not returning to him no matter how hard he tried, and the return home made them feel even more dreamlike and unreal.

He felt so helpless and alone. His world was without control or reason. He felt like an autumn leaf blown and tossed without direction while simultaneously bound and imprisoned, solitarily confined in the space of a blackened box from which there was no escape. He now understood the threshold and boundaries of madness and the point of insanity. Would he see his father before he got worse? The thought caused him horrendous pain.

He looked out the plane's window to ease his thoughts. The outside world was becoming dark. A lightened horizon traced the sun's slow exit, and the evening sky was painted in gradations of streaked charcoal and dusky-blue lines. He looked at his watch; it was almost five o'clock. The plane touched down, and objects flashed past the window. Finally the plane came to a halt.

Thank God I'm home, he thought as he quickly released his seat belt.

Within a short time he reached his mother, who was waiting at the terminal. She looked thin and tired, and he could see that she was under a great deal of strain.

"Oh, Bryan. Thank God you have come home. It is so wonderful to see you. I need you so much," his mother sobbed as she hugged him tightly.

"Mom, how is he, and how are you holding up?"

"He seems to have stabilized and may have a limited recovery," she said as she continued to clasp him. "His heart is weak, and now the recent stroke may result in him losing the use of his left side. Oh, Bryan, I am so frightened."

"I want to see him," he said anxiously.

"Of course, as soon as we get your luggage." She placed her hand on his cheek. "You've lost weight. How I wish you were coming home under better circumstances."

As they made their way through the airport terminal, he could hear chanting and what seemed to be a vocal disturbance. "Hell no, we won't go! Hell no, we won't go!" The sounds became louder and more distinct, and then he saw a group of antiwar protestors greeting servicemen and servicewomen as they entered or departed the airport.

"This is why I suggested you change into civilian clothing," his mother said. "The war situation has split America, and vets are not welcomed home. Not like in your father's time, when they were hailed as heroes."

"There are two sides to this war story," Bryan said. "If I knew three years ago what I know now, I might be doing the same thing."

"Boy, you have changed your view. You are growing up in a world that is not so black and white."

Bryan's first indication of the change during the last three years was the physical appearance of the young men, with their long hair, beards, and untidy attire. What had become of the cordovan penny loafers and V-neck sweaters? How much of the world he had left was now gone? He was in a time warp, like waking from a coma. The world had changed and left him behind. He had become so isolated and insulated from the real world while he was in the navy and in Vietnam. Now he had to return to an unfamiliar present and find his lost past. As these thoughts filled his head, he scanned the group of protestors, his eyes drawn to one protestor behaving in a confrontational manner with a marine. They were calling names at each other, and it was becoming violent.

"You hippie bitch, get the hell out of my way!" The marine pushed her, but she stood fast.

"Who are you calling bitch, you baby killer?" She spat at him.

"Oh my God!" Bryan exclaimed. "That sounds just like Michelle. Mom, I think that's Michelle!"

"No, it couldn't be," said his mother compassionately.

"Michelle, Michelle, is that you?"

The woman turned and stopped her altercation with the marine. "Bryan? Bryan Ruocco?" They both looked shocked to see each other. They stood motionless and stared at each other, giving themselves time to adjust to the physical changes that had taken place since 1965. They drew close but somehow could not embrace. Michelle now represented the unfamiliar present, and he, the past. In a frozen moment, a snapshot of time, without an exchange of a word, they recognized that they no longer held any common ground. Too much had passed between them.

"Is this what has become of you? How could you?" Bryan asked in total disbelief.

"Bryan, this is me, and my behavior is justified, so don't be so quick to judge."

"Oh, I understand far more than you realize. You hold only half the picture. I hold both halves. I would like to see you again, but at present my sole priority is to be with my dying father. I'll be in touch."

"Oh, Bryan, I'm so sorry that you had to come home to this."

"I'm sorry that I had to come home to a lot of things," Bryan mumbled, shaking his head as the words of her harsh letter of severance ran through his mind.

Several Hours Later

Bryan walked quickly through the hospital halls. When he reached his father's room, he paused, took a breath, and pushed the door open. He was filled with anguish at the sight of the life-sustaining equipment.

"Dad, I'm home. Please get well," he pleaded as he reached for his father's hand. "I need you now more than ever." He placed his head next to his father's shoulder, crying with anguish. "Dad, oh, Dad, life seems to have dealt me a bad hand. Please don't leave me."

Bryan's voice awakened his father to his presence. "Bryan, leave you?" his father said in a soft, hoarse voice, placing his hand on Bryan's head. The touch was reassuring, dispelling and easing the pain just as his father had done so many times when Bryan was a small boy. "Where do you think I'm going?"

"Dad, you're awake!" Bryan straightened up quickly.

"My boy! Am I dreaming? Are you really here?" He took Bryan's hand and held it between his.

"I'm here, Dad. Thank God we're together." Bryan embraced him and kissed him. When he pulled back, his father smiled. "How do you feel?"

"Under the circumstances, okay."

"Dad, we have so much to talk about. I need you to get better so that we can plan the future. I also need your understanding and help with some real concerns. I've never needed you as I do now."

"What is it, Son? What troubles you?"

"Not now, Dad. When you're better." Bryan tried to change the subject. "It seems the *Wall Street Journal* is saying that the war in Vietnam is doomed. Even Walter Cronkite said that the war is to end in a stalemate."

"You are home, and how happy I am. Bryan, step back and let me see you. It's been almost three years. You have grown into a fine young man, and how proud I am of you. My work as a father is complete, and you have become a wonderful person. Through your letters I have not missed the wonder of your transition. With each letter I have grown with you and shared your travels and learned of your friendships. In learning so many new things about you and all those people who have played such an important part in your life, I feel a particular closeness to Tuyet and Greg, as if they were my own friends."

Bryan's eyes tightened, and he bit down on his lower lip. Chills ran through his body. At the mention of Greg and Tuyet, something inexplicable flashed through his mind, but he could not decipher it.

"Those people were important to you and will continue to be throughout your life. I'm just overjoyed that you are home." His father's voice slowly softened, and it became difficult to hear him. He drifted off to sleep.

"Bryan, let your father rest, and we will return later," his mother said.

A Few Weeks Later

As Bryan helped his father into a wheelchair on one of his regular visits, he said, "Dad, a few weeks ago we talked about my friends. I would really like to talk about them now that you are feeling a little better."

He pushed the wheelchair toward the window and stood behind his father, tightly grasping the rubber chair handles.

"What is it about your friends?" his father asked.

Bryan thought for a moment. "Maybe this is not the time."

Bryan's father turned his head and looked up. "There is never a right time. Tell me, Son, what is on your mind?"

He dropped his head onto his father's shoulder and began to cry. "You don't know the hell I have gone through. I still can't believe it all happened. How I need to tell someone ..."

"What do you mean, 'tell someone'? Why can't you tell anyone? What is going on? Is there some kind of problem?"

"Dad, please don't get upset. It's hard to explain. Something terrible happened, and I just can't seem to remember the events, however hard I try."

"Try!" his father said compassionately.

"I can't tell a soul."

"For heaven's sake, why not?"

"I don't know how to deal with it all. Where do I start? What hell I have gone through, and now you. What kind of God does this? Tell me."

"My poor, poor, dear son." His eyes glistened. "You can tell me anything, and I will try to help you get through this. Come round." Bryan crouched down, and his father put his arms around him as he wept.

"What a terrible thing I have done. I'm so ashamed."

"There's no need for shame. Try, Son; please try. It's not your fault."

"I'll try. I'll try."

"We must learn from those whom we have loved and lost. The love that we humans so infrequently share must be kept alive for those times when we're without it. It's a dead heart that can never renew love."

"Dad, please don't get philosophical!" Bryan pulled away from him. "Damn it! Talk directly. What are you trying to say?"

"What I'm trying to say is that I have read between the lines of your letters. I believe I know and can understand the type of relationship you had with Greg."

"You're right. We were the best of friends."

"Bryan, please. We have always been truthful with each other. This is not the time to change course. I love you and can understand the hunger for love."

"Love? My God, how did you know when I just so recently realized it myself?" He jumped to his feet and turned from his father. "For the longest time I thought it was everything else but love. How did you figure it out? I'm so embarrassed and ashamed. That is one of the truths that I have been trying to hide."

"Son, there is no need to feel ashamed. It is not something you chose. I've always hoped for the best for you. You are a devoted son, and I love you in spite of life's twist. Please don't turn away. It's nothing to be embarrassed about."

"Then tell me, why do I feel less of a man? Why is it I feel that I have failed you?"

"Son, never say that. You have never failed me. The ability to admit your true feelings is the ultimate test of a real man."

"Then why has all this happened? Do you have the answer?"

"I wish I did."

"So much has happened in three years. How unfair of me. This is not the time."

"Bryan, there is never a right time, only the realization of the opportunity. I don't have the answers. Come; sit by me and let me look at you. Our time together is not endless."

"Dad, please don't talk like that."

"I want you to feel free to tell me whatever you feel you can. I'm not going to judge you. Do you believe me?"

"I do, but I don't know where to start. I still can't remember." His eyes filled with tears, and his voice quivered. "You must rest now. Let's talk about it tomorrow, and maybe something will trigger my memory."

The following day, Bryan entered the room and approached the bed closest to the window. Lying on the bed was a thin, pathetic human figure with a masked face. The once-vibrant and energetic man was now reduced to a pitiful figure clinging to life, struggling to breathe. Bryan could not look anymore.

As he sat in the chair next to the bed, the black clouds and the patter of raindrops drew his eyes toward the window. The raindrops descended one after another like tears.

His thoughts were interrupted, as he was unable to disregard the sound of his father's breathing, his desperate will to cling to life. He could no longer be selfish and keep him here. He had to tell him to let go, fight no more, and succumb to peace. It was painful, and he felt himself holding back. The words weren't coming out right—they seemed slurred and garbled. He hurt and could not release the pain.

His father was bleached white and motionless, his eyes closed. Bryan's pain became unbearable, and his eyes filled with tears.

He touched his father's forehead, forced an eyelid open, and said, "Look at me. You may go now."

God, what more can I go through? he thought. Bryan sat beside his father and took his hand. His father's grasp tightened and then weakened.

"Dad, what is it? … Doctor! … Someone please help! Dad! Dad! Not now!" Bryan jumped to his feet. "No! God, no! Not that presence of death again!"

Slowly he dropped to his knees, pounding the floor with his fist. "Such a cruel God you are. What have I done to deserve such vengeance? How much more do I have to take?"

The doctor bent over and placed his arm around Bryan.

"Goddamn you. Don't touch me," Bryan screamed as he pulled away. "This is all a fucking dream. Was it yesterday I was in Vietnam? Today I'm at home. Where the hell am I? I've got to be dreaming. This is all an illusion. It's unreal. It's unreal!"

"Nurse, get help quickly," said the doctor. "Calm down, son. Just relax."

Within a few minutes the horror of three men surrounding Bryan caused him to unleash a beastly strength in an attempt to repel his suppressors. Flashbacks of that all-too-familiar, unspeakable event intensified his resistance.

"Not again, no, not again!" He was injected with a sedative to subdue him. As the drug began to take effect, Bryan relived those black shadows that had once dominated him, the shredding of branches, the spray of blood across his chest.

Bryan yelled, "Dad! Dad! You never told me what to do. What do I do?" He felt as if he were drowning. He could hear voices, but he could not reach the surface. His movements and struggles were futile. He continued to sink, an immense weight drawing him deeper into the abyss. Things became darker, then black, until he could see only a pinhole of light. With the diminishing light he felt nothing. Suddenly everything stopped, as though someone had turned off a switch.

"He'll be all right now, Doctor. The sedative is working," one of the orderlies said as they took him into another room to rest.

"These poor boys. They send them back without any kind of transitional treatment or rehabilitation to civilian life. What a damn pity!" the doctor muttered as he left the room.

Bryan's eyes gradually opened. He felt an empty void and a loss within him, but strangely, he could not quite remember what had transpired. As he surveyed his surroundings, he began to recognize the familiarity of his own room and became more oriented. He closed his eyes again, trying to recall events.

"Bryan, Bryan, how are you feeling? Oh God!" his mother said in a trembling voice.

He had not realized that his mother was sitting by his bed. He turned to look at her. "It's all really happening, isn't it, Mother? Dad's dead, isn't he?"

"Oh, Bryan, I don't know how to comfort you. I can hardly deal with it myself." She cried into her hands. "I need you to be strong. I can't deal with another crisis. We have to be brave so that we can get through this."

Bryan tried to reassure her and stroked her head. "Of course, Mom. We will get through this together," he said in his drowsy state. But inside he felt as if at any moment he would explode.

SAINTS PETER AND PAUL CEMETERY, SPRINGFIELD, PENNSYLVANIA, MARCH 1968

A s with so many March days, a breath of spring had broken the winter routine. It was a bright and warm day, with that sense that nature's renaissance was not far off. The past few days of warmth had turned the brown grass to green. Purple, white, and yellow crocuses had broken from the once-frozen earth. Bryan walked arm in arm with his mother as they followed the pallbearers, the cortege of mourners trailing behind. With the last words of respect given, Bryan became distracted by his surroundings and heard only the sound of last summer's oak leaves rustling above. He filled his lungs with the warm, fresh air and slowly walked over to the coffin. He positioned a yellow rose on it and then reverently touched the brass plate bearing the name "Joseph D. Ruocco."

"Goodbye, Dad. Thank you for your lifetime of understanding. I'll always love you." The nameplate became blurred through his tears.

Bryan was unaware of the people around him and was overcome by emptiness and loneliness. This agonizing grief, which should have been alien to him, was all too familiar. Why? He could not comprehend this inexplicable feeling of an additional loss.

After the coffin had been lowered into the grave, Bryan and his mother looked at the many floral tributes. His mother's strength had dissipated, and she seemed ready to collapse. Exhaustion and the emotion of the day had depleted her. Bryan quickly put his arms around her to support her and gently helped her into the waiting car to return home. As he closed the door, he took a deep breath to try to regain his own strength. Suddenly he felt a hand on his shoulder. He turned with his hand still clasping the door handle. He was unprepared for the sight of Michelle standing by his side.

"Bryan, my deepest sympathy."

"Thank you for coming. I apologize for the unfortunate way in which we met again after all this time."

"You mentioned that you wanted to meet, but unfortunately this is not possible, as I have prior obligations."

"Obligations? What obligations?" Bryan asked.

"You see, I'm committed to the antiwar movement, and we're preparing for a massive demonstration at the Democratic Party Convention in Chicago later in the summer."

"Michelle, this is neither the time nor the place to discuss this, but since you mention it, I can understand why we can't meet. I've become the symbol of everything you now detest. We have become strangers, and what else can be said from one stranger to another?" Without waiting for a response, Bryan joined his mother in the car and returned home. Relatives and friends made their way to waiting cars to follow them.

As they entered the house, Bryan gave his mother a reassuring hug.

"Mom, I need to be alone for a while," he said as he removed his jacket and tie.

"The relatives and friends will be arriving soon. I don't think you should leave."

"To hell with protocol. I'm going to my room. Please leave me alone to grieve. I'm serious, Mom; I want to be left alone."

The room was too bright for him, so he dropped the blinds and cut the daylight with a pull of a string. Then, the room was almost completely dark, illuminated only by the light that escaped through the base of the door. He stripped and tossed his clothes at the light source. As he rested on the bed and pulled the down comforter over himself, he hoped the obscurity of darkness would diminish the pain. If he could neither see nor hear anyone or anything, perhaps the pain could be bearable, but in spite of his attempts, his mind created a vista of scenes upon his closed eyelids—a vivid encore of the day's events. He was able to see and hear those activities so clearly. Music filled his ears, from classical to rock. The funeral reran over and over. The pain would not stop. It only ate at him. Just as he felt that he could bear it no longer, he succumbed to a deep sleep.

"Bryan! Bryan!" called his mother.

"Yes, Mom?"

"May I come in? I'm worried. You have been in your room for almost forty-eight hours. It frightens me. Is there something I can do or get you? Are you hungry? Let me come in."

"Please, Mom, I'm not ready. I'll be okay." He sat up in bed, his arms wrapped around his legs. "I'll be down shortly."

"If there is something I can do, please tell me."

"Sure!"

"Oh, you've gotten a letter from the admissions office at Swarthmore College. Can we talk about the future?"

College! College! With this hint of excitement, light suddenly seemed to fill him. *Maybe this will help me through,* he thought. He opened the door just enough to peek through. "Mom, I'm fine." He kissed her on the cheek and took the letter from her hand. "I think I could go for a really big breakfast. I'll be down in about twenty minutes. I think it is time that I rejoined the world."

She smiled and ran her hand along his face. Then he gently closed the door, immersed in the content of the letter:

ADMISSIONS AND RECORDS OFFICE
SWARTHMORE COLLEGE, SWARTHMORE, PA

NOTICE OF ACCEPTANCE FOR ADMISSION

Bryan Joseph Ruocco

**This acceptance for admission is valid only
for the term beginning 9-14-68.**

He walked toward the window, and as he opened the drapes, the room was filled with the golden light of the morning and the promise of a brighter future. He looked up into the cloudless sky and whispered, *Dad, this is what you wanted me to do. I'll make you proud.*

UNIVERSITY OFFICE, ALEXANDRIA, VIRGINIA, AUGUST 1991

The phone interrupted Bryan's thoughts. "Sandy, hi! Welcome home. The time? Oh yes, I'll see you in a few minutes. God, I need to talk to you, I have some great news," he said excitedly. "I'll meet you in the parking lot. I'm on my way."

Sandford was of Irish Italian extraction, almost six feet tall, and was slenderly built with straight black hair and deep-violet-blue eyes.

The hot, humid night went unnoticed as Bryan made his way to his car. Sandy was patiently waiting, leaning against the car, his hands on his violin case, which was resting on the roof. He was still dressed in his tuxedo from the afternoon's concert. "My God, what has happened?" asked Sandy, withdrawing from a kiss on Bryan's forehead. "You're trembling!"

"God, you won't believe what has happened tonight. I have spent the last several hours talking to Radnor Richardson."

"Radnor. Your old navy buddy? What a surprise! How wonderful to meet up again after all these years."

"That's right." Bryan paused. "But the momentous consequence is that as we talked and revisited the past, Radnor invoked familiar circumstances and pictures that, when pieced together, gradually unlocked my memory, and the truth about Greg emerged."

"Really? You finally remembered? It's all come back? You were able to tell somebody? I can't believe it!" Sandy was so excited and overwhelmed that he hugged Bryan. "That is wonderful! God, I wish I could have been the first to know what you've rediscovered, but I don't care—as long as you've told someone. This could mean that you'll be free from that Vietnam hell and the nightmares and shrinks. Maybe there could be a future for us now."

"I sure hope so. But I think that this is just the calm before the storm, as I now have to come to terms with not only his death but also the loss of a newly discovered love." Turning to Sandy, he said sensitively, "After all these years I haven't been fair to you, have I? I mean, I haven't even given you the consideration to include you into my past."

"I'm not in your past. You do not have to feel guilty about that. I'm in your present. Now! The only time someone is important in your past is when they are gone, and I'm not gone!" Sandy gently grasped his chin. "Look at me. I love you. I've always loved you, since we first met at Swarthmore College. You know that I understood the hell you've kept within you, and yet I always believed this day would come. I'm so happy that I'm here to witness your return to life."

"And you've always accepted and stood by me. I think you're nuts for sticking with me all these years. I don't deserve you."

"Yes, you do—you've always been fair and honest. We deserve each other. Let's go home, and you can tell me the whole story. The kids are probably starving."

"Yeah, right! Kids! Two dogs and a neurotic cat!"

32

NEW YORK CITY, NEW YORK, FALL 1991

Bryan had arranged to meet Tuyet at the Russian Tea Room on West Fifty-Seventh Street in Manhattan. In 1927 former members of the Russian Imperial Ballet had opened the Russian Tea Room, described as a Russo-continental restaurant, as a meeting place for Russian expatriates. The large, red awning over the entrance made it an easy location at which to meet.

Bryan paced the restaurant entrance, eagerly awaiting Tuyet's arrival and also curious about why she needed to talk to him before meeting Radnor. He was in knots and feeling nauseous as flashbacks of Greg, Tuyet, and Da Nang played within his thoughts. It all seemed unreal and almost fictional; at the same time it excited and frightened him. Perspiration rolled from his forehead, and the cool, late-October evening felt refreshing. A rhythmic clinking and flapping sound temporarily distracted him, and his eyes were drawn to rows of large, red banners with gold, cursive letters attached to the capitals at the entrance to Carnegie Hall, which was adjacent to the restaurant.

"Bryan! Bryan!" called a familiar voice.

"Oh my God! Tuyet, it's really you! Let me look at you. I can't believe that I'm really here with you. How little time has changed you!"

"I appreciate your flattery," she said. They embraced for a few moments, and he kissed her forehead.

"I want to know everything. The smallest detail of the last years." His voice gushed with excitement as they proceeded arm in arm into the restaurant.

"Before we catch up on the past, I believe we should discuss the reasons for our meeting," she said in her genteel voice.

"Excuse me," interrupted the waiter. "Would you like a drink before dinner?"

"Yes, that would be nice to celebrate our reunion. A bottle of Dom Pérignon, please."

"Yes, of course, sir." The waiter withdrew.

"Tuyet, first of all I'm somewhat bewildered as to why you want to meet with me before talking to Radnor about what became of Greg."

"And I'm wondering why I suddenly became a contact regarding Greg after all these years."

"Let's get our table, and we can talk during dinner. We have so much to share."

"Yes, I should like that."

Once seated, Bryan began, "In August I received an unexpected call from Radnor, whose search for Greg had led him to me. He had no idea that I was suffering from memory loss and PTSD and had been receiving therapy from various counselors for all these years. Tuyet, it was dreadful. I experienced flashbacks, nightmares. I knew that there was something I needed to remember, but I just could not recall the events of that sad day in Da Nang. The events had been completely eliminated from my memory."

"Bryan, I'm so sorry. I had no idea. Please continue."

"Over the years certain colors, sounds, voices, smells, situations, and emotions seemed to evoke some sort of familiarity, but I didn't know why. I could not make any connection. Radnor and I talked for hours, and gradually the pieces came together and unraveled my memory concerning Greg's death. Radnor's search is now complete, and he feels obligated to bring Greg home. I want that too, but I wanted to talk to you first, to ask for your help in returning his remains to his family."

"Has the moon a crescent?"

"Still talking in riddles and parables! God, I forgot! This reminds me of one of the happiest times of my life, when we were all together just before Tet and you explained the Lunar New Year."

"I'm happy to say that it is better than that; the moon will soon be full."

He took her hand. "I feel like a cross has been lifted from my shoulders," he said intensely. "My nightmares have ended, and this experience has given me a new outlook on life. I just want to put it all behind me—and I can with your help."

"My dearest Bryan, I will do whatever is in my power."

"Thank you," he said as he kissed her hand. "Consequently, with the unexpected visit from Radnor, once again we've come together, still trying to put closure to twenty-three years of pain and mystery. Now tell me everything that has happened to you since that day."

Tuyet locked her hands and pulled them to her chest. "I was not sure, but I had hopes that when President Ngo Dinh Diem was toppled, the government's discrimination toward Buddhists would end. As a Buddhist, I was outraged by Diem's policies, and with the election of President Nguyen Van Thieu in 1967 and his continued policies of Catholic favoritism, I was forced to make the decision to always consider myself a Vietnamese nationalist first.

"I was always overcompensating for my social position and abuse of people like me and my parents and foreigners. I joined a student protest group in Hue opposed to the discrimination against Buddhists. The Communists were the only group taking a stand against the South Vietnamese government, so my dilemma was to either join them or continue to support inept political organizations. Therefore I aligned myself with them, as they were being proactive. I thought that being involved with the Viet Cong would prove my veracity, but in November 1968 my crusade was interrupted."

Tuyet paused, took a deep breath, and continued, "I had a child."

"A child? Whose child?"

She paused and looked away and then said soulfully, "Greg's child.

When I realized I was pregnant, I knew the knowledge would cause Greg to do something quite rash."

"Greg's child?" There was silence. "Did he know?"

"No, of course not. I never told him I was pregnant. So much was going on those last few days before the Tet Offensive. He became a madman that night he proposed, and we fought horribly all night. How he tried to convince me to marry him and return to the United States. He cried, and it tore me apart. Outwardly my feelings appeared cold and uncaring, but inside my thoughts were of the great deception that I had carried out and continued to display. How impossible it was all becoming. How little he knew about me and our relationship, which had started as part of a cover. I had been instructed to pursue the relationship as a decoy. Who would suspect a Viet Cong dating an American? How unfair and guilty I was to keep so much from him. In the beginning I had no idea this would happen. I never thought that I would fall in love with Greg. The Americans may have killed him, but I was the VC's objective. How I was torn between my love for him and what I believed in. He was the enemy, and the whole situation was becoming impossible. Imagine if he had known about the baby—he would have gone AWOL or something.

"When I continued to refuse to marry him, he began punching walls and breaking things, yelling a thousand things that I could not understand, such as, 'Why is love always taken from me?' I was so frightened by his behavior that I cried and could not stop trembling. I had never seen him like that. At some point he noticed my fear; he raised his arms in retreat, cried, and left the room."

"So that was what the fighting was all about that night."

"Yes, that is what it was. And that is what my conflict was. I can't imagine how he would have been behaved if he had known that I was pregnant and was having thoughts about terminating it, which grieved me, as it was so against my religious beliefs."

Bryan was in shock.

"Yes, I seriously thought of taking this course of action. It was not the time for a husband and a baby, but the pain and my desire to have Greg, against my philosophical convictions, caused conflict. I had a revolution to help carry out. Foolishly I had forgotten my goal, and self-interest had taken hold. I seriously believe that had Greg lived, I would have done it, but fate intervened and made my decision for me. When I went back to get his severed body, the pain was so great that I only remember the horrific sounds I made, moaning and groaning. I sounded like an animal in pain, just before death, crying while I labored with his lifeless body. Had we never met at all, none of this would have happened. All these thoughts ran through my head, but I carried out the task and realized that enough death had transpired. With Greg's body in front of me, I had no right to sacrifice the child as well. I placed my hands at my stomach, knelt before his coffin, slowly dropped my head, and promised this child life—again, torn between my human needs and my purpose. My natural maternal instinct, my religious beliefs, and my love for Greg won.

"I'm sure that he would not have left Vietnam if he'd had any inkling of my situation. The relationship had to end. Time was running out. We both know how he was. After I had the baby, my parents took the child, Gabriel, to France in 1969. I kept the promise I had made at Greg's coffin that I would give our child life, and I resumed my place with the Viet Cong. With the secret peace talks in 1970 between Kissinger and Le Duc Tho, I was assigned to Paris as part of the peace conference, under the pretense that I was North Vietnamese, to ensure the interest of the Viet Cong. I returned to Vietnam in January 1973 but then went back to Paris and stayed there until January 1975 with Gabriel. I then had to decide whether to return to Vietnam or remain in Paris. I was told that I could best serve the revolution by remaining in Paris, but it soon became apparent that after the fall of Saigon, they wanted me out of the picture. I was a half-breed, and so was my son. Amerasians—*con lai*—were often scorned by the Vietnamese and subjected to discrimination and hardship. The pseudo-classless society was in its early stages, and my son would never fit in. The system was already beginning to corrupt itself. It was then I made my decision to leave Gabriel with my parents and to return to Vietnam to continue the fight to bring about the true Communist, classless society they purported to advocate. I felt that I had to be the conscience of the revolution and wanted to ensure my place and Gabriel's in the new order. Another sacrifice had to be made, and I left my son behind. No sooner had I returned to Hanoi than the government sent me to the United Nations in New York."

"You still burn with the fervor of youthful idealism. I admire that. Like so many others, I have sold out to the status quo."

"Bryan, who knows what is the right path? I believe we must all follow what we truly believe. Idealism has no room for human frailties. I'm convinced that if humankind can entertain the thought, then we should be able to attain the ideal." Tuyet took his hand and looked into his eyes. "This brings me to my request."

"Tuyet, you know I will always do whatever I possibly can for you, for Greg, for us."

"I would like you to intervene for me. I would like you to contact Greg's family. They should know that they have a grandson. When Gabriel left Vietnam, he was only a few months old, and he knows very little of his father's birth country. He has been raised in France and has gone to Catholic schools throughout his life. It was the compromise I had to make with my parents. I'm not such a fool as to think that he would have any kind of life in Vietnam. Even I have fallen victim to the prejudice of my comrades. That was a major reason for my returning and ascribing to the doctrine. I have made compromises time and time again. I have no excuses anymore," she said, clenching her fists. "If Senator Seaton agrees to recognize Greg's son, I will agree to return Greg's remains to his family to be repatriated. I dislike using this as a bargaining chip, but I owe this to my son."

"I understand," Bryan said. "But where are his remains? What do you know about all this? What have you known all these years? I have been going through a living hell trying to remember that hideous, horrific, unspeakable day. Tell me. Tell me." Bryan's voice became urgent.

"Bryan, you sound so angry. Please consider my feelings and what I went through. Try to understand my situation at the time. I did what I thought was in the best interests of my son. After Greg died, I always put Gabriel first in my life."

"Forgive me, Tuyet. I'm so sorry. Please be patient with me. All this is so very difficult for me. So many ghosts are appearing. I'm so very sorry."

"Bryan, just try to calm down, and let me tell you the full catalog of events that day. Do you think you can face it?"

"Yes, with your support. Please, just tell me the truth. I really need to know after all these years."

"I was helping in the infirmary in Huyen Khong Cave on New Year's Eve, and as I looked down from the mountain, I noticed that the lights were on in the villa; I knew that you had both returned. In the morning American helicopters swooped down and started firing indiscriminately all around the area and at the mountain, and I knew that the cease-fire was broken. I saw two VCs running away from the villa, and naturally, I was concerned for your safety, knowing that you were inside. As soon as the firing ceased, our first priority was to move the injured from the infirmary, which now had a gaping hole in the roof, to safer caves in case of another attack. It was then that one of the doctors noticed the villa was a blazing inferno and that there were two people lying in front of some dense foliage. He called for assistance, and we hurried down the mountain path. Bryan, nothing had prepared me for what I saw that day. You were the first one I recognized, as you'd lost your hat, exposing your red hair. Your face and clothing were covered in blood, but you were breathing, drifting in and out of consciousness. My colleague took care of you while I went over to Greg. His features were barely recognizable. To identify him for sure, I had to look at his dog tags. When I read the name …"

Tuyet paused, holding back the tears in a dignified manner. "I'm sorry, Bryan." After a moment, she composed herself and continued, "After Greg died, I had to call upon the help of my acquaintances within the Viet Cong to assist me. It was important to me that his body be treated gently and with respect. When it was safe, a Buddhist priest helped his spirit to continue its journey to higher states. We continued with the ritual bathing ceremony, repeatedly pouring water over his hands to cleanse away impurities and negative energy before his body was placed in a coffin and taken to the chapter of monks. Cremation took place within three days, as is our custom.

In Mahayana Buddhism, especially in my Vietnamese tradition, we pray for the dead for forty-nine days, which gives the spirit time to be reborn again into a new life." Tuyet paused. "Are you all right, Bryan?" she asked.

"Yes, yes," he stuttered. "Please continue."

"During the service at the cemetery, the monks sat facing the coffin, which was then placed on a pyre made of brick. We lit torches, incense, and fragrant wood and tossed them beneath the coffin so that the actual cremation took place at once. Later his ashes were put into a casket. Since that day the monks have kept the casket in a small temple in the cool Huyen Khong Cave, in the same chamber that you were taken to on that dreadful day, Bryan."

"Oh my God! You mean that we were both in the same cave and I didn't know? And Greg's remains are still there?"

"Bryan, you were in and out of consciousness. You did not know anything or anybody. You did not even recognize me at first. Yes, Greg's remains are still there."

Bryan was traumatized for a few moments and then consumed by relief. "This is all so overwhelming. I'm so relieved that you were there to take care of everything. I cannot thank you enough."

"Bryan, he was our dearest friend, and we both loved him. You would have done the same in my position. I often recall the quotation by Charles Colton that 'friendship often ends in love'—that is what happened to both of us."

"Tuyet, I don't know what to say except that I will talk to the senator personally and let you know."

"But, Bryan, I will not send Greg home alone. You must return with me to Vietnam so that we can both make the arrangements for returning him home. I believe it is the only way for me to let him go. I somehow feel that he is with me while he rests in Vietnam, and I still pull my strength from him. To let his remains go is to let his spirit leave me as well. Regrettably, within a short time I will be letting go of my son and the man I once loved, and I shall be free to accomplish my life's goals."

"Return with you? I don't understand. Why? Is it really necessary?" His eyes moistened, and his face twitched with hurt. "I don't want to relive that day he died. That terrible feeling. That pain and anguish. Please don't ask me to do this."

"I must ask this of you. I have never loved any man as I did Greg. You were his friend and lover; I know that you can do this for him. I cannot release him to anyone other than you. If you don't, the hurt you will cause will exceed beyond both of us. I have made my sacrifices and done my part. It is time for both of us to put this behind us. Bryan, recovery demands closure. I'm convinced that this is the only way."

"I really don't know if I can do this. It is all so sudden."

"Even from the grave he continues to control you." Tuyet took his hand. "I will give you time to decide. But now I think you must prepare yourself, as Gabriel will be meeting us for coffee and dessert shortly," she said, changing the subject and looking at her watch.

"Here? Tonight?" Bryan asked in amazement.

"Yes, almost any minute. It is ten o'clock already. Bryan, thank you for dinner. I hope that we have a better understanding now that we have talked and that what we do will free us both from the past." As she spoke, her face changed from rigid and unemotional to soft and radiant. She placed her hands on the table and lifted herself up. "He's here," she said as she alerted Gabriel to their location.

Bryan turned and saw a young man making his way through the crowded restaurant. For a few moments he was spellbound. The young man's handsome facial structure and build mirrored Greg's. He stood about six feet with straight sandy-colored hair and hazel eyes. Bryan was astounded by how similar his walk was to Greg's, with that shifting movement of confidence, that slight gentle motion of the head, and that smile. He had inherited his father's wonderful smile—a smile that caused a reaction in even the most unconscious beholder. "The resemblance is uncanny," Bryan said.

Gabriel greeted his mother and kissed her on the forehead, and they all sat.

"Gabriel," she said, "I should like to introduce you to Bryan."

"Hello, Bryan," he said, shaking Bryan's hand with both of his own. Bryan was speechless. "Wonderful to meet you." He paused and then said, "Forgive my staring at you, but I cannot get over the striking likeness to your father."

"Mom often says that. I'm used to it. Pleased to meet you, Bryan. For years you've been a silent black-and-white photograph with my dad. It's unreal. It's as though I shall soon meet him as well."

"I'm sure I've changed some since that photo was taken!"

"Just a little," Gabriel said with a smile. "Mom tells me that you are going to help me reunite with my dad's family?"

"Yes, I hope so."

"This is all so exciting to me. I have a thousand questions. Is it true that my father has an older sister and two younger brothers?"

"Yes, that's true. Greg was closest to his sister."

Gabriel's voice was full of uncontrollable excitement. "When will I get to meet my other family? I really am anxious to do so."

Bryan looked at Tuyet. Her face reflected the sorrow of a son deprived of his father's family.

"Gabriel," Bryan began tentatively, "your grandparents have only recently found out the details about your father's death. They do not yet know of you, and before tonight, I had no idea of you either. Your mother and I haven't seen or heard from each other since 1968. As for your grandparents, they are presently dealing with the news about your father. They will be extremely cautious, which is understandable, given their past experiences that led to false hopes."

"Why is that? Why have they only just found out?" asked Gabriel, looking at both of them in turn. "You and my mother have known for years. I'm confused." His eyes flickered, and his forehead tightened. "Something seems very strange. Are you keeping something from me?"

Tuyet and Bryan both stiffened, and there was silence. Bryan took a deep breath. "Gabriel, I do not want to begin this new relationship with any misunderstanding or inaccuracies, but I think that this is not the time for further explanations."

Tuyet said, "Gabriel, can we tell you what is a very delicate story later? I would like you and Bryan to get acquainted."

"I think I should know."

"I agree that you should know, and you *will* know everything,"

Bryan said. "But I feel with the limited time we have, right now is not really best. I beg you to take into account the feelings and situations of your mother and me and others. Gabriel, it is really in everyone's best interest to explain later."

"As I said, I'm confused and don't understand what all the mystery is about, but I guess I have no choice. I'll just have to wait—but I want to know the entire story."

"We promise that you will know everything," Bryan assured him. "Now, please tell me about you."

"There's really little to say. I'm a pre-law student at Columbia."

If only Greg were here, Bryan thought. Gabriel was bright and had inherited his parents' good looks and brains, and Bryan fell into an almost hypnotic trance as he spoke. It was eerie that Gabriel projected similar mannerisms to Greg—his eye and head movements; his strong, confident voice; and the endearing smile that had enthralled Bryan.

"Bryan, Mom, hey, look at the time. I really can't believe that we've talked for over an hour. I think I'll skip dessert. I need to get back. Lots to do in the morning! More research!"

He rose from his chair, kissed his mother, and shook Bryan's hand warmly. "Really great meeting you, and I would like to get together again and talk more about my father. Would that be okay?"

"Of course! I would like that. I'll call you and suggest some dates. Maybe you would like to visit Washington?"

"That sounds great. A weekend could work for me. I could fly or take the train. I must go now. Thank you for your help, Bryan. I look forward to talking with you later. Mom, I'll call you tomorrow."

Bryan stared as Gabriel left, shaking his head and weeping. "From that hell came a wonder. A wonder!"

Tuyet moved close and embraced him. "It will be fine. Greg continues to be with us."

He gently withdrew from her and gripped her shoulders. "I will go with you and bring Greg home."

WASHINGTON, DC,
MAY 1992

"So how was the flight down from New York?" Bryan asked when he picked Gabriel up from Washington National Airport.

"Okay, I guess. How far is the senator's home?"

"Not far—about twenty minutes. They live in Georgetown. Please relax; the family is very warm. I remember back in '67 when your—"

"I thought they lived in Charlottesville," interrupted Gabriel.

"That's correct. They reside in Georgetown while the Senate is in session."

"Sorry, I interrupted. What were you saying?"

"That I first met them in 1967 at your aunt Laurice's wedding. But things were different then."

"What do you mean?"

"Your grandfather was quite outraged by your dad's behavior— getting kicked out of Annapolis, joining the navy, and leaving home."

"Mother talked some about Annapolis, but she always held back. I'm under the impression that this weekend will end these years of mystery."

"I hope to do just that. Here we are."

Bryan and Gabriel made their way up the flight of steps to the three-story, white town house built circa 1850. The high-gloss door with a large brass door knocker opened.

"They're here. Good, they're here!" the senator announced. "Welcome, Bryan. It is good to see you again," he said, shaking Bryan's hand.

"Good afternoon, Senator. It is good to see you too. Senator, I want to introduce your grandson. This is Gabriel."

"Come in! Come in! Oh my!" he said as he shook Gabriel's hand. He led them into the pale-peach Victorian parlor trimmed with a red satin ceiling border. A large brass converted gas chandelier hung in the center of the room.

"Please sit down," he said as he directed them to the ornate, black mahogany couch with red tuft fabric next to the heavy marble fireplace.

"Wonderful to see you again, Bryan," the senator repeated.

"Thanks for having us," Bryan and Gabriel both responded.

"Ellen! Ellen! Bryan and Gabriel are here. My, this is wonderful. I finally get to meet you," the senator said to his grandson.

"It's good to meet you, although I feel a little strange."

As Ellen entered the room, Bryan and Gabriel sprang to their feet.

"Oh my God, Bryan, you never alluded to the resemblance."

"How wonderful to meet you. My Gregory's son!" she cried in amazement. "I'm your grandmother, Ellen." She reached out, took his hands, and then touched his cheek, and Gabriel gave her a hug.

"Please, let's all sit down." As she spoke, the senator took her hand. "It is so wonderful that you have come to meet us. You cannot imagine how happy this has made your grandfather and me. Gregory left us under very unpleasant circumstances. As I'm sure you know, his whereabouts were unknown for more than twenty-three years. We had no idea about you or your mother. The news of you and the answers to previously unanswered questions concerning Gregory have brought us peace and joy. What are your future plans?"

"I would like to remain here in the States and become acquainted with my father's family."

"That makes us both very happy. We will do all we can to make your transition into the family as smooth as possible."

GEORGETOWN, DC,
JUNE 1992

Months had passed since the restoration of the blank pages of Bryan's life and his new acquaintance with Gabriel, Greg's son.

"I hope you'll like this French restaurant. It's like a typical establishment you would find on the Left Bank in Paris. It's real popular with the locals," Bryan said to Gabriel as they reached Chez Odette.

"It looks great. I just hope that they cook the steaks well!"

"Good evening, sir. Do you have a reservation?"

"Yes. The name is Dr. Ruocco, a table for two at eight o'clock."

"Yes, sir. Come this way. Your table is ready."

During dinner they talked about their respective pasts. Suddenly Gabriel took out a creased black-and-white photograph from his wallet. "I'd like to ask you about this picture," he said.

"Picture? What picture?"

Gabriel handed him the photo, which was of Greg and Bryan. "Oh my God! I don't believe this! Where in the world did you get this?" Bryan asked as a smile came over his face. "I'd forgotten all about this occasion. How much has been lost from my memory."

"Yes, but can you tell me about it?" Gabriel asked.

"I don't think I'll ever forget the day that was taken." Bryan paused and took a deep breath. For a moment, he seemed to be lost in time.

"It's a silly picture," Gabriel said. "Dad looks happy, and you look enraptured."

"It was taken on the ship on our first trip to Asia in 1966, right before we met your mother. Where did you find it?"

"Mother gave it to me," Gabriel said disconsolately as he stared at the corner of the picture. "My father had it on him the day he died." After a silence Gabriel said, "My mother took his personal belongings, and among them was this picture and one of her. This picture seemed to be important to him, don't you think?"

"I haven't seen it in years. It reminds me of happier times."

"It also says a lot," Gabriel said, changing the tone slightly. "I want to hear it from you. I've had my suspicions, but Mother said that I would find out in time. I think this is the time. I don't have a problem with it. I just want to know."

Bryan began, "I think at this point in his life your mother and I were the two people he loved the most. He had a thirst for love that could not be satisfied. Although he was in love with both of us to a certain extent, he really loved your mother more. But when she refused his love, he turned to me. That's pretty much it. I've carried my love for him all these years. Are you upset by my honesty?"

"No, no problem. You were his best friend, and I can see how he could care for you because, in the short time that I have known you, I feel that I have grown close to you, like a son to a father."

Bryan was taken back by Gabriel's words and for a moment was speechless. "I don't know what to say. I'd like to get to know you better, maybe as the son I never had—nor am likely to have. It would fill a great void in my life. You know, it's strange that you are the one good thing that has come from this whole tragedy."

"Thank you for your honesty, Bryan. And, by the way, thank you for your earlier invitation. Yes, I would like to go to the beach for the Fourth of July weekend."

35

REHOBOTH BEACH, DELAWARE, JULY 1992

Rehoboth Beach was a city along the Delaware beaches often described as "the Nation's Summer Capital," as it was a popular vacation destination for visitors from Washington, DC, and Philadelphia as well as Maryland and Virginia. It was most famous for its beaches, wooden boardwalk, eclectic shops, and tax-free shopping.

It was rather warm for seven in the morning. A heavy humidity thickened the air, and the ground was still moist from the thunderstorm the previous evening. There was a strong allusion to the impending heat of the day. As Bryan put his luggage in the trunk of his car, the birds were concluding their morning song. He looked up, wondering what the day would bring.

As he reversed out of the drive, Sandy waved from the front door. Bryan stopped the car and called, "Hi, Sandy. I didn't want to wake you."

"That's okay. I just wanted to see you before you left and let you know that as soon as my orchestra rehearsal has finished, I'll drive down and see you on the Fourth. I have managed to find a substitute for the Fourth of July concert at Wolf Trap. Take care, Nutkin, and have a good time."

"Great! Thank you," Bryan said. He gave Sandy a smile and a thumbs-up and drove off. He took the route across the Parkway to Georgetown, where he was due to meet Gabriel. When he arrived at the senator's house, Gabriel was already standing in the driveway with his luggage in his hand, looking anxious.

"Hi, Gabriel."

As they exchanged greetings, Andrew and Ellen Seaton came out of the front door. "We thought that we heard voices. Good morning, Bryan. How are you?" Ellen said, giving him a hug.

"Good morning, Senator and Mrs. Seaton."

"Would you like to come in for some coffee before you leave?"

"No, thanks. I want to get moving so that we can avoid the traffic. We'll stop off somewhere for brunch."

"Enjoy your weekend. Drive carefully and have a safe Fourth," the senator called as Bryan and Gabriel made their way to the car. Bryan noticed the senator's warmth and recognized that something had changed since he'd met the senator at Laurice's wedding.

They headed east down US Route 50. On seeing the signs for Annapolis, Gabriel exclaimed, "Ah, Annapolis! Mother told me about the Naval Academy there and said that it was where my father did his freshman year."

"Would you like to stop and visit? We could also get brunch."

"Yes, I'd like that. Is there anything else of interest there?"

"Not really. It's the capital of Maryland and is said to be the sailing capital of the world. Lovely little town. The chapel is interesting. Look, you can see the high dome already. It is visible throughout Annapolis."

"I wonder why they built the academy here," Gabriel said.

"Its predecessor was the Philadelphia Naval Asylum, but in 1845 the secretary to the navy, George Bancroft, decided the naval school should be moved to 'the healthy and secluded location of Annapolis in order to rescue midshipmen from the temptations and distractions that are necessarily connected with a large and populous city!'"

They entered the grounds and saw the large motto emblazoned

on the wall: *Ex scientia tridens*—"From knowledge, sea power." Bryan pointed out the crypt where John Paul Jones, the first well-known naval hero in the American Revolution, was buried. "He originally came from Scotland but fled to his brother in Fredericksburg to avoid the hangman's noose in Tobago for murdering a sailor," Bryan said. "Look, this is the Tecumseh statue, one of the most famous relics on the campus. It's a bronze replica of the figurehead of the USS *Delaware*, given to the academy in 1891. Coincidentally, the ship that your father and I served on was named the *Delaware*, and I come from Delaware County in Pennsylvania. You must look at this too! This is the Herndon Monument. At the end of the academic year it's covered in lard, and the plebes attempt to climb it and remove the Dixie-cup hat, which is the headwear of a plebe, symbolizing the successful completion of their first year."

"I guess my father never made it. By the way, why did he get kicked out of here? Mother never really told me."

"According to your father it was his gender selection for a night's sexual gratification," Bryan said.

"The way I hopped around with women until I met Lois, I guess I understand. I suppose it is a male thing!"

They returned to the car and continued their drive across the Chesapeake Bay Bridge. "Wow, this is awesome. I've never seen anything like this. This must be among the world's largest and most scenic overhead structures," Gabriel said.

"Right. It is the direct connection between the recreational and oceanic regions of Maryland's Eastern Shore and the metropolitan areas of Baltimore, Annapolis, and Washington, DC. Before the bridge was built, there were just two vehicular ferries that ran from Annapolis."

After a few moments, Bryan said hesitantly, "Gabriel, regarding our earlier conversation ... I was wondering whether you felt a need for any further clarification or whether you want to tie up any loose ends, so that we can put this behind us and move on."

"Well, yes, there is something that I've been wondering about. I think I can understand how my mother dealt with the impossibility of my father's commitment, but how did you deal with it? I can deal with it because of my French upbringing, which enables me to accept my father's sexual behavior. Although, now that I've lived in America for a while, I think if I were an American, I might have some issues with my father's behavior."

"I subconsciously hid this truth from myself, but I believed I would be enough to sustain and keep him always—overlooking the fact that the void to be filled was infinite. He loved me, and we both thought that we wanted an exclusive relationship. But your mother was heir to his heart, and I was the spare, as were so many others. In the naivety of our youth your mother and I both thought that we could make a commitment to him, but she was committed to her cause, which was paramount. Her natural need to connect with another human being brought about conflict for her. As for me, I had an identity conflict, which was unveiled by your father. Discovering physical and emotional gratification like never before caused me to be unsure of my direction in life. My whole social fabric was shredded in one night with him, and then my internal conflict began. I was unable to shake the religious and social morality that had been instilled in me, so subconsciously I began to punish myself for having experienced that natural joy. I could only ever love what your father had given me and, therefore, could never move on to love anyone else. So you see, my sentence was that exclusive love that no one else could ever provide. He was the scapegoat for the guilt I felt about my true life, which I couldn't accept. I believed that God took him to punish me for my perceived indiscretions. His death was my nemesis and torment for the stolen joy he'd brought to me. I hope that this has answered your question."

"Have you spoken to anyone else about this? Who else knows?"

"No one. It was only when the photograph you showed me triggered another memory and another trace of understanding that I was able to comprehend it myself."

"Thank you for sharing that with me. I think we now have a real understanding of one another, and I look forward to our future." Changing the subject, Gabriel said, "Look, there's the sign for Rehoboth."

They arrived at the beach house, which overlooked the ocean on one side and the lake on the other.

"This looks great," Gabriel said. "How did you come to find this place?"

"Well, Sandy and I have the town house in Alexandria, but he wanted something more traditional at the beach where he could relax and unwind between concert tours, so we had this built here."

Bryan and Gabriel spent the next few days getting to know one another and soaking up the sun and the atmosphere. On July 3, they had dinner at the Adriatico, a popular Italian restaurant with marvelous pasta that reminded Bryan of home.

"What a wonderful restaurant. What's the story here?" Gabriel asked.

"Silvana Butiaro and Nikola Lenici grew up on the coast of the Adriatic Sea but on opposite shores. Silvana grew up in Potenza, Italy, and Nikola in Dubrovnik, Yugoslavia. Nikola left his hometown in 1950 and moved to Alexandria, and in 1962 Silvana and her family left their home in Italy to make a new life for themselves in Alexandria. They rented vacation homes next door to each other on Rehoboth Beach. They fell in love with the coastal community and each other, married in 1976, and opened the Adriatico Restaurante, dedicated to the sea that separated their young lives. The restaurant represents their love of the cuisine of Silvana's Italian heritage, their love of the Adriatic Sea, and the love they shared for one another."

"What a wonderful story. Bryan, it's been a delightful few days. Thank you."

"What are you doing after the Fourth?" Bryan asked.

"I'll be in Washington with my American family, and then I'm going to Charlottesville to see my extended family. What about you?"

"I'm going to Europe with Sandy for a month. He is going on tour with the orchestra, visiting London, Paris, Milan, Munich, and Salzburg, and I have decided to accompany him this time. While he is rehearsing, I can see the sights and visit the museums and galleries, and I'll also get to hear him play."

"How long have you known Sandy? Where did you meet?" Gabriel asked.

"He and I go back to when we were both Swatties at Swarthmore College. I remember very well the day we met. I was coming across the campus on a chilly fall day. I'd just got my books for my history class and noticed him sitting on a bench, reading some sheet music, which I thought was odd. I paused and commented that it didn't look very interesting, to which he remarked that it was exciting and added that we perceive little when we don't understand—sarcastically correcting me! I liked his tenacity, and we began talking, eventually became friends, and found that we had a great deal in common and shared cultural similarities. I had an appreciation of music, and we bounced ideas off one another and connected. He lived in Philadelphia and in due time passed an audition for the violin section of the Philadelphia Orchestra. When he was appointed as principal violinist in the Washington National Orchestra, I offered him a room at my house as a base for when the orchestra was not on tour. He's stayed with me ever since. We're very close––but for Sandy, I think, not close enough. Right, it's ten thirty. Shall we get the check and take a walk?"

"Good idea," Gabriel said.

They left the restaurant, climbed a few steps, and walked onto the boardwalk, which had an array of shops, restaurants, pizza parlors, candy stands, and funnel cake stands. It was buzzing with families and teenagers. They reached the amusement park, where they played a round of miniature golf and went on the Ferris wheel and the roller coaster. They stopped at the ice-cream parlor and continued walking in a northerly direction until the restaurants and stores thinned out and there were only the beach homes on one side of the boardwalk and the ocean on the other.

"Let's sit for a minute," Bryan said. "Just look at the moon and how beautiful it is, reflected in the water. Every time I see the moon I think of your mother and her explanation about the new moon and how truth, like the invisible moon, can sometimes be elusive. Again, the truth concealed from me for so long has finally been revealed, so I guess she was right. It's only recently that I've been able to recall what happened to your father. It was a turn of fate that when you asked questions about your father, Tuyet, your mother, decided that it was time to reconnect with me. Anyway, that's enough reminiscing for one evening! I don't know about you, but I'm ready to turn in."

"Good idea. Me too. It's been a nice day, and I have enjoyed myself. You don't know what it's been like to have grown up without a father. My grandfather is remarkable, but there has been a void, and I have felt a pain for a man I never knew. You have helped me to understand." With those words he embraced Bryan.

Bryan returned the hug as a father to a son, gazed up at the moon, and, alluding to Greg's presence, said, "You're watching us, aren't you? Don't worry; I'll look after him."

"If you look at the barge over there, you'll see a flicker of an orange light. That is where the fireworks will be set off."

"Where's Sandy? How will he find us in this crowd?" Gabriel asked.

"Don't worry. We're always by the grandstand. Anyway, he should have been here earlier. I won't say anything, as he'll be agitated enough. Maybe it's the traffic, or maybe the rehearsal didn't go well and he had to take a sectional rehearsal. It often happens. His music takes priority over everything and everyone!"

The band began playing Sousa marches, signaling the start of the fireworks.

"Every time I see fireworks it reminds me of the same thing: youth, love, and beauty—gone in an instant," Bryan said reflectively.

"Bryan, you have to see it another way. It's not gone in an instant. It's gone to make room for the next thing."

"Did I miss much?" a voice said from behind them.

"There, I told you he'd find us," Bryan said, turning to Gabriel.

"Hi, Nutkin!"

"Nutkin? Where did that name come from?" Gabriel asked, expressing amusement.

"His terra-cotta-colored hair!" Sandy replied. "When I was young, my mother used to read me a story about a red squirrel called Nutkin by Beatrix Potter, an English writer. It was very popular and endeared generations of Brits to the impossibly cute reddish rodents."

"I hated the name 'Carrottop,' so he called me Nutkin, and it has sort of stuck with me. How do you think he found us in this crowd?" Bryan laughed.

Sandy put himself between them and put his arms around them both. The three of them blended in with the crowd, enthralled by the colors, the sound of the fireworks, the atmosphere, and the conviviality. Bryan looked at Sandy, and caught up in the emotion of the event, he seemed to see him in a different light. "I'm so glad you're here," he whispered.

"How could I possibly celebrate the Fourth without you? This is our special time."

36

FIRST ATTEMPT
TO LEAVE FOR VIETNAM,
NOVEMBER 1992

The flight from Washington, DC, to San Diego was painless for Bryan. It so reminded him of the trips he had made in the past: the first time in 1965, the second time in 1966 for Christmas, and then the fateful year of 1968. That was the year he'd lost Greg, his dad, and a segment of his past. Even America had seemed like a foreign country that year. Within a few short years the world seemed to have been turned upside down. *Was it easier,* he thought, *because I left from Washington rather than Philadelphia? It was different. But why?*

As the plane approached the city, his mind was occupied with the arid landscape. Lindbergh Field was unrecognizable. He couldn't help but recall the day he and Radnor had gone to pick up Greg from his Christmas visit home in 1966.

Bryan soon retrieved his luggage and picked up his rental car. The city had changed since he'd left. He wanted to find some link to his past, so he headed for downtown, someplace that he could recognize. He headed toward the old apartment at the top of

Broadway. It was the place where he and Greg had begun to unravel their relationship. He felt a rush of emptiness, and an old pain took hold. The pain was becoming unbearable, so he quickly returned to the car and headed to La Jolla, where he had a hotel reservation. While driving on the freeway, he noticed a familiar white stucco mission church up on a hill. This was Mission Valley, where Radnor and his wife had rented an apartment. He, Greg, and Radnor had had to pass through here on their way back to the ship. All those old memories filled his mind.

At last he made his way to his hotel room in La Jolla, which at least held no memories. The pain and past anxieties subsided. Bryan walked to the balcony and gazed at the view. The beach was filled with people, mostly couples, and sculptured rocks from centuries of ocean tides. The city's terra-cotta roofs rose like steps upon a hill dotted with fan and date palms. He was drawn to the ocean waves and to the multitude of dark-blue hues that met the horizon. In a few days he would cross that ocean once again. This time by air, not by ship. Instead of three weeks, it would be a matter of only twelve hours now. As he reclined on a lounge chair, he watched the sun set over the ocean. The ocean breeze seemed to embrace him, while the sun represented a beacon that directed him to the west. His eyes became heavy, and fatigue took him into a world of peaceful sleep.

It was not quite dusk when the ringing of the phone awakened Bryan. "Hello!" he answered. "What a pleasant surprise! It's good to hear from you."

"So how are doing?" Sandy asked. "I thought I would see if you were okay. Well, you're on your way. I'm quite proud of you, as I know how difficult this is for you."

"So far so good. It was a little tough earlier when I took a short visit downtown to check out the old apartment."

"I'm sure that it will be easier when you connect with Radnor."

"I sure hope so. I should be hearing from him real soon. We have a full day tomorrow, and I will be meeting him for dinner soon."

"Let me know how it goes—I'm just a phone call away."

"Sure, Sandy, I will. Thanks for the call."

Bryan took a shower and prepared to meet Radnor for dinner. As he came out of the shower, the phone was ringing again, and he reached for it while drying his hair.

"Hey, buddy, I'm in the lobby. I just got in from Washington. Shall I come up or meet you down here?"

"Hi, Rad. I will finish up my shower and be down shortly. Have a beer on me."

Within twenty minutes Bryan met Radnor at the hotel bar. "Great seeing you again," Radnor said as they embraced.

"Well, here's to old times." They both raised their beer mugs.

"God, this reminds me of that time you, Greg, and I got together to meet Marian and you drank draft beer for the first time."

"I sure do remember that day," Bryan replied, expressionless.

"So how about we take off to downtown and get some Italian?" Radnor said.

"Good idea. Let's get the concierge to call us a cab."

"Let's get off here and walk up Broadway and see what looks recognizable," Bryan suggested.

As both men left the cab, quietness filled them. Bryan looked for any familiar landmarks.

"There's the YMCA!" Radnor said excitedly. "That sure hasn't changed. The Hotel Shaw is there too, but it's all boarded up."

"No locker clubs, tattoo shops, or go-go bars. All gone. Even the waves of sailors in whites moving up and down Broadway are absent," Bryan said.

They made their way to Horton Plaza. Trendy shops and boutiques had replaced the adult movie houses. All that remained was the circular Roman Corinthian–style temple in the center of the square.

Suddenly Bryan stopped, put his hand to his head, and sat down on a nearby bench. Emptiness and loneliness filled him again, a familiar pain that he recalled from when he was younger; a somber, sleeping pain of vacancy and isolation was revisiting him. This place seemed to awaken the internal volcano of hell within him. It was as if someone were pulling a shroud over him. A jumble of sounds went through his head—"California Dreamin'," "Cherish," and a repertoire of popular music from the sixties played over and over in his mind. He automatically reached for the POW bracelet he used to wear on his wrist and habitually began twisting and turning his hand around his wrist as if the bracelet were still there, as he had done on numerous occasions before when he was under duress. His insides seemed to eat at him. He began to rub his hands as if washing something away. Then flashbacks of hands red with blood on that day he had held Greg in his embrace filled his head. The previous sounds dissipated, and the orchestral introduction to the aria in Verdi's opera *Macbeth* where Lady Macbeth sings, "Here's the smell of human blood still," permeated his mind. The thought of returning to Vietnam was causing a rebirth of the true horror of that day, so well suppressed for all these years. The mourning process had begun. Bryan's absence of grief over Greg's death in 1968 was manifesting itself. How could he handle what was about to come? Fear consumed him, and his eyes moistened.

"Are you okay?" Radnor asked.

"No! God, no! I cannot go through with this. The pain is too much. I must return home."

"You can't let this fear weaken you. I'm here to help you."

"No, I must go." He drifted into the street and waved for a cab. "Take me to La Jolla, please."

"You can't do this! Everything is in place. People are depending on you, Bryan. Tuyet is relying on you. This selfishness is so unlike you. Let me come with you to alleviate your insecurity."

"I hate what you have awakened in me. I have to go home. I must go home," he mumbled as he got into the cab. "Please forgive me; I cannot go through with this. I cannot revisit that hell now. Rad, please, contact Tuyet in New York and ask her to cancel her flight to Hanoi and explain that I need more time. The thought of talking to her adds to my torture and my anguish."

"When will it ever be the right time? There is no such thing. Don't run away again." Radnor reached for Bryan's shoulder, but Bryan flinched from him. "Look at me, Bryan." Bryan would not turn.

"Possibly never," Bryan said in a voice filled with turmoil, tears running down his cheeks. "I can't. I can't. I feel such remorse."

Bryan continued to ignore Radnor's pleas to return, and the cab pulled away.

Bryan was oblivious to the journey back to the hotel, but as he closed the door behind him, he felt a degree of peace. He went to the desk and thought, *I must write to Sandy. He is the only person who can see me through this hell.* The flashing lights on the phone indicating a message did not distract him, as he knew that the voice mail was from Radnor, who would try to change his mind. Not having the courage to talk to Sandy, he wrote instead:

Dearest Sandy,

I feel that I should write to you and try to give you some sort of explanation of what has happened to me in the hope that you will understand. At this point I'm unable to continue my journey.

When my memory of Greg's death was restored, an epiphany began to take hold of me, though I was quite unaware of it at the time. The awakening of my memory resurrected his behavior and attitude as well. The joy of love that consumed me concealed Greg's true essence for all those years. With each year his love became more perfect and flawless in my mind. Unsuspectingly, I have found his hold on me disassembling.

With each new, detailed recollection, his true conduct has surfaced, and other traits have begun to fester. How much I had forgotten. In New York Tuyet told me, "Greg controls you from the grave." It was those words that began to dismantle the memory that I had so falsely created. With the horror of that day his love became consecrated and canonized.

Between my counseling for post-traumatic stress disorder and my unconscious desire to preserve only the beauty of that glorious love, the great myth of Greg was conceived and the real truth concealed. He professed to love me, and I interpreted this as a love exclusive for me. However, I believe he only truly loved me in the flawed, dysfunctional manner that he understood, and that is why that love was never made clear to me. He himself did not comprehend the love he so avowed. I believed then, and continued to believe until now, that only I would and could satisfy and fill the void that so many others could not.

Here in San Diego, I have come to the realization that there is something festering within me. I cannot know or tell what is going on. After all these years, I only feel the same. An emptiness and loneliness fills me, a sort of Greg time warp. Even within the presence of those dear to me, the incubus surfaces. I feel myself anxious to leave. I'm surrounded and summoned by ghosts that eat at me as I wait for them to return, but they never do. So I wait. It's hell, and I hunger and burn for the forgotten time. I cannot shake them off—they do not let me go. The only thing left is an empty abyss.

With my return to the final place he lived, I began to realize that I'm no longer in love with him alone. I'm only in love with a period of time, a past filled with extraordinary people and unique events.

In my mental recovery I've realized a painful and bitter truth: that it would have been only a matter of time before he had tired and moved to another, as he had done on so many occasions during our short time together. What was he in search of? I do not know, but it was a search from which only death could release him. His was an appetite that would always be unsatisfied and could never know fulfillment.

My eyes are filled with tears, as it is all ending, and the past is running through my mind like reruns of old movies on late-night TV. Now I can see the beauty and the ugliness. Sandy, dear Sandy, my fear, my real fear is what will take the place of this void in me. What will fill the void? The present, the unknown, the unwritten? Do I go through life looking over my shoulder or looking to the future and never living in the present moment of now? I cannot continue my journey. I cannot do it alone. I need you.

The love that I harbored for Greg was an abundance of mutated elements of my past—my youth, my innocence, and my first true love. How was I going to keep and preserve it? By keeping past tokens and things that could be touched or seen that would restore that moment in time. Those things took hold of me and held me in bondage for all those years. I have come to the realization that the only sanctuary, the one place where I don't have to deal with this and that never fails me, is that fortress of the present, which I share with you.

Why you have stood by me for all these years I will never know. Your loyalty and encouragement have never wavered. How were you able to sustain all this, in spite of living in the shadow of another? I'm so very thankful. How I look forward to my return and especially to you.

Always yours,
Bryan

He read through the letter and then automatically folded and sealed it and prepared to return home.

As the cab pulled up to the town house, the severe thunderstorm made the drive to the house almost impossible to locate. Bryan searched his wallet to pay the driver. He became anxious as he surveyed the house for any indication of Sandy's presence. The driver helped him put his luggage on the steps to the town house as waves of rain fell upon both of them. When Bryan took the key in his hand, he trembled and held back, his hand frozen. Why was he hesitating? Introspectively, he knew he would have to answer for his unexpected presence. If he answered that question, he would have to answer to himself as well—the reason he had not gone to Vietnam.

Bryan retreated from the door with the key still held tightly in his hand. He started walking up the street without direction. He walked for several blocks, oblivious to the weather and the fact that his clothing was thoroughly soaked. He began to shiver from the cold.

Standing once again at the door, Bryan shuddered, weighed down by his wet clothing. The rain camouflaged his tears, and dropping his head against the door, he rapped the door knocker and rang the doorbell.

Sandy thought he heard a noise at the door and turned the faucet off. The faint sound was muffled by the rumbling of the thunder and the torrential rain pounding at the house. He started down the steps and quickly opened the front door. There stood Bryan.

"My God, why are you here?" he asked, amazed. "What's going on? Come in! Come in!"

"I couldn't go. I just couldn't go back, and I couldn't come home right away, so when the cab let me off, I just walked. Maybe I was hoping that the rain would hide my tears."

"You poor, poor man. Let me get you out of those wet clothes before you catch a cold."

"I'm so sorry that I couldn't go. I'm so ashamed."

Sandy reached out to him, pulled his head close, and hugged him. "It's okay, Nutkin. It's okay. You're home now, and I'm here," he said as he stroked Bryan's soaking head. "Let's get you to bed, and I'll get you some warm milk."

Within a short time Bryan was resting in his room, shaking from the cold and the emotional trauma. As he put his head on his pillow, he said to Sandy, "Play for me. Play and soothe the pain, please? There is a letter in my jacket. It's for you. It is from my heart. Please read it when you are alone."

Sitting across from him in his chair, Sandy started playing "Méditation" from *Thaïs*, which he had played so many times to comfort Bryan in the past. Feeling Bryan's anguish and his own, Sandy played, and they seemed to share the pain. Within half an hour Bryan was sleeping peacefully, and Sandy lowered his violin. He took the soaked letter that Bryan had given him and began to read. After finishing the letter, he gazed at Bryan and said quietly, "I'll figure out a way for you to return to Vietnam, and I'll go with you. I'll see you through this anguish." Then he raised his violin again and began to play once more. *I also play to appease my own ghosts and the pain of wanting you and knowing that Greg managed to deplete you emotionally. Perhaps if fate had allowed him to live, this would never have happened.* He bent over, kissed Bryan on the forehead, and whispered, "I will do whatever it takes to see you through all this and help you to complete your journey. I love you." Quietly he left the room.

NEW YEAR'S CELEBRATION, SOUTH AMERICA, DECEMBER 1992–JANUARY 1993

B ryan and Sandy's trip to South America to celebrate New Year's was a continual, unbelievable enrichment of their lives. South America had no memories for Bryan, and the trip was a wonderful diversion.

Santiago was a touch of Europe on the west coast of the Pacific. Both of them were taken with Puerto Varas, where the moon reflected its image upon Lake Llanquihue, and the towering Orsono Volcano with an icing of snow on its dormant summit.

Then there was Buenos Aires, with its passionate, seductive tango and its exterior of Parisian delights. They visited the rivers of tears of the Iguazu Falls, and then it was on to Brazil and the magnetism of Rio's samba and bossa nova that permeated the Copacabana and Ipanema beaches. Bryan was particularly drawn to the naturally sculpted mountains covered in emerald vegetation.

"Sandy, just look at that summit. The deity seems to be embracing his physical and human creation."

Sandy seemed distracted, his mind elsewhere.

"Sandy, where are you? Is something wrong? You haven't heard a word I've said."

"Sorry, Bryan. I've just been thinking, and I need to talk to you."

"What is it, Sandy? Go ahead. What's wrong?"

"I have an idea, and I know it is short notice, but I'd like to suggest that we return to Vietnam together next month. I have a concert engagement at the Royal Festival Hall in London, and, apart from the fact that it would be so good to have your support at such a prestigious venue, I feel that it would be less painful for you if you made your return to Vietnam in a completely different direction. You can join me in London, and we can get a flight to Bangkok from there. We can spend a couple of days there and then connect to Hanoi. We could see something of the north of the country, travel south, and then arrange to meet Tuyet, Radnor, and the Special Services envoy and collect Greg's remains together. We could also revisit your past together. Hopefully, this might alleviate some of the pain. It will also give you the opportunity to appreciate your past with Greg and possibly acknowledge your present with me. And another thing, we would be in Saigon to celebrate Tet, which I know is important to you. It is the Year of the Rooster, the sign under which you were born. Some coincidence. Did you know that Catherine the Great was born under the sign of the Rooster? All the signs are there for you, Bryan … 1968 was the Year of the Monkey. Julius Caesar, Eleanor Roosevelt, Harry S. Truman, and Leonardo da Vinci were all born under the sign of the Monkey, and during Monkey years you are advised to be aware of the insincerity of other people."

Bryan was about to respond to Sandy's enthusiastic plan when Sandy continued talking without pause—something he normally reserved for the early morning.

"While we're in the Far East, I'd like to fulfill a lifetime ambition and visit Angkor Wat in Cambodia, if you are agreeable. It is only a short flight from Saigon. It would also give you the opportunity to recharge after your inevitable ordeal in Vietnam before returning to the States and undergoing the further pain of the burial at Arlington and the ceremony at the Memorial Wall. So what do you think?"

"You seem to have thought of everything! It's a wonderful idea. Would it be an imposition to leave all the arrangements to you? I really cannot deal with mundane matters at present. Just don't give me any excuse to postpone the return this time!"

"No problem. Leave it to me."

"I wonder if my postponement is in fact a subconscious way not to achieve closure. The past is safe, predictable, and commitment-free." Changing the subject, he said, "Sandy, what can I say? I now know that you are the only person I need to be with on this trip. You are my rock, Sandy. You know that, don't you?" Bryan clasped Sandy's hand. "I'll call Radnor and Tuyet once you have finalized dates."

"I'll get on it immediately."

FINAL RETURN TO VIETNAM, FEBRUARY 1993

When Bryan arrived at Washington Dulles Airport, he was too fatigued to feel a great deal. He was taking a flight to London to meet with Sandy before returning to Vietnam. The thought of returning to the place of Greg's death had not entered him.

The plane to London was only half filled with people. *I wonder if spirits fill the other seats,* he thought. *It is strange that no one is sitting next to me, as if the seat had been reserved for Greg.* He glanced to the right and sensed Greg's spirit next to him. He pictured Greg's face and remembered their past times together.

He felt a strange emptiness, somewhat like when he used to return home after months away—butterflies and a trembling inside. His eyes moistened, and a pain surfaced, but at the same time he felt a peculiar excitement.

A voice from the loudspeaker interrupted his thoughts. "We shall shortly begin our descent into London's Heathrow Airport. Please return to your seats, fasten your seat belts, and put your seats in the upright position. The current temperature is fifty degrees, and the forecast is for rain."

The plane touched down, and after going through passport control, Bryan espied Sandy in the crowd in the arrivals hall. His mood was instantly lifted. It was good to see a familiar face and know that Sandy was there to take him through his imminent ordeal.

"Welcome to London and the British weather," Sandy joked. "It's good to see you. How was your flight?"

"Hi, Sandy. It's so good to see you too. The flight was good." Bryan gave him a hug.

They made their way to the car park and followed the route into central London, past the famous Harrods store in Knightsbridge, around Marble Arch and Buckingham Palace, across Westminster Bridge to the south of the river, and on to Greenwich, where Sandy's friends from the London Symphony Orchestra had a town house.

"There are no plans for tomorrow, so you can just relax. I have to leave after lunch for the final rehearsal at the Royal Festival Hall for tomorrow night's concert."

"What's on the program?" asked Bryan.

"Nothing to challenge the ear—a Rossini overture, Tchaikovsky's Serenade for Strings, and of course the Brahms Violin Concerto. The concert starts at seven thirty, so you won't have to leave here until five thirty. You will have plenty of time to take a walk and a nap before the concert."

"That sounds good. I didn't get much rest on the plane."

They spent the evening at the famous Spread Eagle restaurant in Greenwich and talked about their upcoming itinerary to Asia.

The following day they had a leisurely brunch. Sandy left for his rehearsal, and Bryan spent the afternoon sightseeing. He walked in Greenwich Park and visited Greenwich Palace overlooking the River Thames. He also visited the Royal Naval College, a World Heritage Site, and the famous neoclassical painted hall in the Saints Peter and Paul Chapel. The hall was the finest eighteenth-century interior in the United Kingdom and was often referred to as the "Sistine Chapel of England."

As Bryan watched Sandy perform with the orchestra that evening, he could not help thinking how fortunate he was to know someone with unlimited, bountiful support that still, after all these years, showed no signs of diminishing. He could not believe that he was the sole inspiration behind Sandy's music. Bryan felt very proud. He also appreciated and acknowledged just how much they had in common and realized that he could not consider life without Sandy. He suddenly became conscious that he had finally met someone who selflessly had only his own best interests at heart.

Early the next morning they took a cab to Heathrow to board their flight to Hanoi via Bangkok.

As they found their seats, Bryan said, "Well, at least you have plenty of leg room this time, and there are no screaming children near us, so you will have no excuse to be irritable."

The eleven-hour flight was quite uneventful, and after two meals, three movies, and a couple of catnaps, they arrived in Bangkok totally wiped out.

Fortunately they had a forty-eight-hour layover before their flight to Hanoi, and after a few hours' sleep they were both more congenial.

"How about taking the city tour while we're here?" suggested Bryan. "After all, I doubt that we will ever come back."

"Good idea. I've always wanted to see the three main temples here, especially the famous Temple of the Reclining Buddha."

"A reclining Buddha?" Bryan asked.

"Yes. It's a Buddha covered in gold leaf lying majestically on its side with intricate mother-of-pearl designs on the soles of its feet."

"Right, let's go!"

"I was just reading that there is a limousine trip to the famous Floating Market at Damnoen Saduak and also to the River Kwai. It is a full day. Would you be interested?"

"Yes, sure. I think I've had my fill of temples and pagodas for now," Bryan said.

The limousine dropped them off by the river, where they boarded a narrow long-tail speedboat called a *hang yao* that provided an exhilarating ride through the marshes, passing old stilt houses and riverside villages.

When Bryan saw diminutive boats piled high with coconuts,

bananas, and durians, he commented, "This is a delight to the eyes—a mosaic of colors from a painter's palette."

"And a vibrant profusion of sounds!" Sandy added quickly, not wishing to be outdone in the artistic verbal Ping-Pong game they often played.

The driver met them at the market, and they proceeded northwest to the Kanchanaburi Province and the site of the world-famous River Kwai Bridge.

Both of them were in touch with the horror and pain at the JEATH War Museum, which was dedicated to the memory of those involved in the construction of the Death Railway, who were primarily from Japan, England, Australia, Thailand, and Holland. It was built in the form of an Allied prisoner of war camp with a thatched detention hut and cramped, elevated bamboo bunks. Both Bryan and Sandy were moved to silence at the two Allied soldiers' cemeteries, which contained eight thousand graves of prisoners who died during the railway's construction, along with one hundred thousand Asian civilians.

On the return journey, they stopped off at Phra Pathom Chedi, the tallest pagoda in the world, built in the middle of the nineteenth century.

"This looks like an upside-down ice-cream cone," Sandy said.

"Ice-cream cone," Bryan muttered under his breath. "You're missing the point! The history of this place goes back over a thousand years."

"It still looks like an ice-cream cone!" Sandy mumbled.

After the tour they returned to the hotel to change for the evening. Sandy had arranged a dinner cruise on the Chao Phraya River.

"You seem upset and depressed. Does the thought of this trip bother you?" Bryan asked.

"No, I'm just concerned about you—that's all."

"I'm okay. I'm a little anxious and apprehensive about tomorrow in Vietnam, but it is pleasant to be here in a place with no past for me, spending time at peace. There is no emotion. It subdues me."

They sat silently as the boat slowly cruised past the illuminated temples and palaces. The entertainer on board sang two songs that stimulated some reflection for both of them: "The Shadow of Your Smile" and "You've Got a Friend."

My past and my present, Bryan thought.

Sandy interrupted his thoughts. "Is it another early departure tomorrow?" he asked.

"Sorry, what did you say? I was miles away."

"The flight tomorrow, is it early?"

"Yes, five thirty, and we get to Hanoi at nine forty-five."

Hanoi, Vietnam, February 1993

As the plane came to a halt, Bryan took a deep breath. *After all these years I'm now forced to relive this part of my dreaded past—that horrid day. This day of reckoning has only been postponed, and I'm now somewhat prepared.*

After clearing customs and immigration they hailed a cab to their hotel. After a light lunch Bryan said, "I'd like to visit the Hanoi Hilton."

"What! A hotel?" Sandy questioned incredulously.

"Not a hotel!" Bryan retorted. "It's the nickname given to the prison in which US prisoners of war—mostly airmen—were held during the Vietnam War. Many people wore bracelets with the names of prisoners engraved on them in order to remember them and to promote consciousness. I may have worn mine subconsciously, because someone I knew and loved was missing."

"Whose bracelet did you wear?"

"I wore US Navy Lieutenant Commander John McCain's bracelet. He was shot down and captured over Hanoi and spent the rest of the Vietnam War as a prisoner in the Hanoi Hilton."

"You're looking tired," Sandy observed.

"I just want to rest so that I can deal with what is to come. A lot of memories are returning."

The following day they took a short tour of the city through Ba Dinh Square, where Ho Chi Minh read his Declaration of Independence speech in 1945. They saw Minh's mausoleum, where his embalmed body lay in a glass casket, and continued on through to the center of the city.

"You can tell that this was colonized by the French in the nineteenth century with these elegant, tree-lined avenues and lush parks alongside the lakes," Bryan said.

"I'm intrigued by all these preparations for Tet. Look at those people carrying orange trees on bicycles and even an entire peach tree in blossom! *Chuc mung nam moi* to you all!" Sandy called out.

"I never thought I would be here for the New Year preparations twice." Bryan's mind flashed back. "I remember when I was waiting for Greg in Joe Tran's Bar just before Tet. I had a conversation with a marine and his wife about what they were doing for the festival. Then there was the drive to Tuyet's house where we passed flower markets similar to these. I'm looking forward to returning to Hue tomorrow. Hue and Tuyet are interconnected in my mind."

"Do you think that you might have been in love with Tuyet too?"

"I think I may have been in my own way. We were so young then."

They took lunch in a little restaurant, where Bryan was captivated by the waitress.

"Just look at her. Isn't she beautiful, dressed in her *ao dai*? Look at her delicate serving manners. She reminds me so much of Tuyet and the time she served us our wonderful meal during the preparation for Tet."

After lunch they left Hanoi behind them and traveled by coach through the sprawling Red River Delta to Haiphong. Bryan thought that the rice fields were like blocks of broken emerald mosaic in various symmetrical shapes. Sandy was more absorbed with the people working in the fields, wearing conical straw hats and leading water buffalo.

"I'm glad that we will be able to see Haiphong, as it still retains a distinct French colonial flavor in its buildings, notably the rose-colored Haiphong Museum," Bryan said. "It's certainly an eclectic mix with modern utilitarian buildings and a busy port alongside traditional Vietnamese temples and markets. It was heavily bombed during the war. How I'm constantly reminded of the bloodstains of atrocities at the hands of both sides."

Hue, Vietnam, February 1993

It was a beautiful morning in Hue, and the sun's rays streamed through the open window.

"*Wherever I go, I will always miss Hue,*" Bryan sang softly. "*I miss the cool breeze on the River of Perfumes. I miss the clear moon over the Imperial Screen Mountain.*"

Bryan stopped singing and said, "I wonder if the city of that folk song still exists."

"I'm looking forward to seeing this city. You have told me so much about it. Where are we going first?" Sandy asked excitedly.

"We'll take a dragon boat on the Song Huong—the Perfume River—to the Thien Mu Pagoda."

"Thien Mu," Sandy repeated.

"You sound like Greg! That was his pet name for Tuyet. I can hear him saying the words over and over again. It reminded me of rote learning. He just wanted to get it perfect and kept asking if he was pronouncing it correctly."

Slowly the thread of the reddish dawn was drawn across the horizon, and the bells of Thien Mu tolled.

"Is that the pagoda over there on that little hill?"

"Yes." They climbed the steps and walked around the perimeter, which afforded breathtaking views of the river.

"Let's take a look inside that pavilion," Sandy said.

"You go. I just want to sit for a few minutes to revisit and reflect on that time."

After a while Sandy returned. "That was ironic," he said.

"What was?"

"In the main sanctuary behind the bronze laughing Buddha there were three statues—the Buddha of the Past, the Historical Buddha, and the Buddha of the Future. The nature of this return trip just came to my mind on seeing them."

After lunch they made their way to the citadel, crossing over the Phu Xuan Bridge, and stopped at the four cannons. This was the hard part for Bryan.

"These are four of the nine cannons that are symbolic protectors of the palace. They represent the four seasons. This is where we first saw Tuyet. What a beautiful sight she was, dressed in her pale-yellow *ao dai*. She took us through the Ngo Mon Gate—Noon Gate—to begin our tour. Greg was enraptured ..."

Bryan was distracted for a moment, gazing up at the Cot Co Flag Tower. Sandy followed his line of vision and said, "Wow! Look at the size of that flagpole."

Bryan smiled, as Sandy's comment reiterated Greg's comment on first seeing the flagpole; he was restored to the present.

"It seems strange, seeing a red flag with a central gold star waving from the flagpole. The significance is explained in '*Tien Quan Ca*'— the national anthem. The red stands for the blood of victory, and the gold star in the wind is leading their people, their native land, out of misery and suffering. The last time I was here there was a gold flag with three red stripes flying—the flag of South Vietnam. Come on; let's visit the Imperial Enclosure."

Physically and emotionally drained, they returned to the hotel and decided to have an early dinner so that they could attend a performance of ancient music and dances from imperial Hue. Bryan seemed to be relaxed, and to conclude the evening, they took a ride in a three-wheeled *xich lo*, a pedicab in which the driver sat behind them and pedaled. They crossed the Trang Tien Bridge, or French Bridge, which was lit up with changing colors, returning to the citadel, and then crossed Pho Xuan Bridge—now called the American Bridge.

"This bridge wasn't here the last time I was here," Bryan said.

"That was a great way to see the sights. I'm glad you suggested it. Thank you."

"I enjoyed it too," Bryan said. "But I found it heartbreaking how much was destroyed in the Tet Offensive. This used to be a place of sublime beauty at the very heart of Vietnamese tradition, but a strong force of NVA regulars fortified themselves within the walls of the citadel. Regardless of our differences and despite the regrettable wounds of war, our two countries can live in peace. All things seem possible in Hue. Optimism is a tradition here."

Da Nang, Vietnam, February 1993

Upon arriving in Da Nang, Bryan was unable to find any kind of orientation. "The city is totally unrecognizable," he said. "But already I can sense that the shroud of death and fear that permeated the city in 1966 has been lifted. The only recognizable features are the mountains and the bay."

"We'd better hurry if we're to get to Hoi An by noon," Sandy said.

"I'm sorry we can't stay here in Da Nang, but I know that you understand I can't stay in a place that holds so many memories," Bryan said soulfully. "I can't believe that the day is almost here after all these years. Tomorrow I have to meet Tuyet and return to the haunting place of Greg's death."

The Hotel Hoa Binh (Peace Hotel) with its annex Huu Nghi (Friendship) was set on the bank of the Do River in Hoi An.

"This reminds me of Tuyet's parents' villa, which overlooked China Beach," Bryan said.

Sandy took a walk while Bryan sat and watched the flow of the river, which reminded him of calm ocean waves. He put his head down and watched the peach-and-orange sunset with streaks of blue. His eyes became heavy, and he fell into a peaceful sleep. It all seemed like a conclusion—a finality.

At five in the morning their driver awakened them. The dreaded day had arrived. Dawn had not yet broken, and the land was shrouded in a heavy mist. They followed the coastal road to Da Nang and spent a few moments where the villa had once stood.

"The only remainder from all those years is this wooded area that backs onto the highway from China Beach."

"Is all this China Beach?" Sandy asked.

"Yes. It stretches for many miles north and south of the Marble Mountains. The beachfront is divided into two sections, each with its own local name. Non Nuoc Beach is where we had ship barbecues and played volleyball."

"Not much has changed then. Look at those Vietnamese youths over there playing volleyball."

Slowly, Bryan walked toward the ocean. "I remember the day so clearly. Greg was in a crouched position, drawing a circle in the sand." Bryan duplicated the action as Sandy stood by him. "Then he tried to throw the ring that he had bought for Tuyet into the ocean, and I intervened. He told me to hold on to it. That, as you know, I have done since that day."

They continued their journey to Thuy Son Mountain and arrived at the foot of the steps at the end of the village. This was where Bryan was to meet Tuyet. The moment was imminent, and the earlier absence of emotional pain was commuted into sorrow and trepidation. He was having constant flashbacks of the first time he had been at the mountain with Greg and Radnor, and his eyes moistened. As Tuyet approached, her image restored him to the present, and as they silently embraced, he could feel their mutual pain.

They proceeded along the rocky path up to Huyen Khong Cave. This cool, gothic, cathedral-like cave where rays of light streamed from the open hole in the top was the small Buddhist temple where the monks had kept Greg's remains in a tiny casket. The scent of incense sticks permeated the cave.

Tuyet paid homage to Buddha and disappeared within the temple. She reappeared moments later with a small porcelain container. At that point Sandy sensed the pain that Bryan was now feeling and put his arms around him, tightening his grip. Nothing was said. Sandy knew only too well the grief of handling a small casket filled with the remains of a human being who one had loved—the memory of a strong, vibrant, handsome person with whom one had shared so much, now reduced to ashes.

As Tuyet carried the casket, she kept her head bowed. She could not look at anyone. Bryan opened his hands as if he were about to receive Holy Communion. Tuyet placed Greg's dog tags in his palm and the porcelain casket on top of them and closed her hands around his. They held him in their hands together.

It was almost too much for Bryan to bear. After all these years Greg had been returned to him. He handed the casket to Sandy as Tuyet continued to stand silently with her head bowed.

Bryan reached over to her, lifted her head, and kissed her forehead. He slowly took off the gold band that he had been wearing since Greg had hastily given it to him on the beach. He slowly slid the ring onto her left ring finger and said quietly, "This was intended for you. I know that it was you he really loved. His circle is now complete."

"Thank you, Bryan. Now you must take the gift he gave you—the gift of love—and give it to another. You are now free. Complete recovery demands closure."

As they descended the mountain, Bryan shivered and trembled. He knew that when he reached the bottom, he would have to give Greg up once more.

Tuyet handed over the casket to the representative from the President's Special Services who was waiting at the base of the mountain. It was of some consolation to Bryan that Greg would soon be home in his final resting place. Their task was accomplished. They all departed in silence.

It was Sandy's idea to take a couple of days of rest and relaxation before their flight to Saigon for the Tet celebrations that weekend. He so wanted Bryan to be able to enjoy Tet and wanted to make sure that the occasion would be special for him.

The train journey from Da Nang to Nha Trang took just over ten hours and followed the coastal route, providing spectacular views of beaches, cliffs, rice paddies, and coconut palms, which diverted their attention from the day's events between catnaps. The pretty seaside resort of Nha Trang, with its palm-lined avenues, had a definite touch of the French Riviera. It had been used as a naval base between 1965 and 1968.

They arrived at the Vinpearl resort hotel at midnight, both emotionally and physically drained, and went straight to their room, which was decorated in traditional style with wooden and rattan furniture and Vietnamese paintings.

The next day started off well, but at some point it all became too much for them both. Sandy continued to feel that he was sharing Bryan with a ghost, and Bryan knew that he was still connected to Greg's spirit. A most unpleasant argument ensued, and hurtful things were said. Bryan was filled with remorse and sobbed profusely in the bathroom. He knew that he was destroying his present with the pain he had inflicted on Sandy. It was a difficult day for both of them but probably more so for Bryan, as it was the first time he had shed tears over Sandy. Also the security of the past and thoughts of an unknown and uncertain future caused him to be apprehensive. The combination of the three factors was inexorable.

On New Year's Eve of Tet, they departed Vinpearl resort in the late afternoon for their flight to Saigon.

When they arrived at Tan Son Nhat International Airport, seeing the name of the airport written in large letters brought back memories of Bryan's first trip. Now called Ho Chi Minh City after the founder of Communism in Vietnam, the city was exuberant and noisy with hectic commercial activity. Red flags with gold stars flew from nearly every building. The traffic was frantic with cars, vans, and pickup trucks everywhere and motorbikes and *tuk-tuks* weaving in and out of it all.

"It is strange that I've returned here during the Year of the Rooster and will really get to celebrate Tet in Saigon," Bryan said.

They enjoyed a wonderful dinner and then went up to the roof of the hotel to watch the fireworks.

"Vietnamese tradition holds that the turning of the lunar year should bring auspicious signs of gladness of heart," Bryan said.

As the reflection of fireworks glistened in their eyes, Sandy put his arm around Bryan's shoulders and said quietly, "I'm hopeful for us and our future."

"You know, Tuyet told Greg and me that Tet personifies the whole spectrum of human relationships, both with the living and the dead. She said that everyone should use the occasion to meditate on the past, to enjoy the present, and to contemplate the future. I now understand what she meant."

The next day was New Year's Day—Tet—everyone's birthday, the holiday of holidays. There were festivities at the hotel with everyone wishing each other happy Lunar New Year—*chuc mung nam moi*—and prosperity, wealth, or longevity coupled with the success of the rising phoenix. Sandy was so proud of his well-rehearsed New Year greetings in Vietnamese.

After delighting in the colorful display of lion-dance performances, accompanied by beating drums and gongs, Bryan said, "Let's make a pilgrimage back to the Majestic Hotel. We can have a drink in the bar, which has marvelous views of the Saigon River."

"That would be good. I have acquired a taste for Tiger beer."

As they sat in the bar, Bryan suddenly said, "Listen! It seems like yesterday that Greg and I were here. Nothing has changed. The whistles from the ferryboats; indistinguishable, muffled conversations rising from the street; the rumble of traffic along the boulevard. I remember it so well. We were on the roof, and a few miles down the river a tanker was burning and exploding. In the opposite direction, planes dropped flares on the VC. I could hear mortars, and here we were, drinking pink champagne, while down in Tu Do Street people went about their business as if it were Saturday night back home. That was typical Saigon. And look how fast-moving the river is with all the debris. Do you notice anything else about the river?"

"Not really. Why?"

"Most rivers flow south, but this one flows north."

"Oh yes. Interesting. Shall we try to see your old room?" Sandy suggested, changing the subject.

"Good idea," Bryan replied apprehensively.

They made up some story that they were thinking of staying at the hotel, and the concierge agreed to show them the same room Bryan and Greg had shared. As the door opened, Bryan stood as if paralyzed.

"What is it?" Sandy asked.

After a moment, Bryan said, "I recall him sitting there, his legs propped up, clasping a drink, and he seemed to turn and smile."

He sighed, drew a breath, and gently closed the door. Neither of them could go into the room.

They made their way across Lam Son Square—once a bastion of French high society—toward the Hotel Continental. The grandly carpeted staircases, marble floors, and dark wood doors conveyed a colonial splendor.

"I don't remember seeing so many women driving motor scooters," Bryan said. "I've also noticed that the *ao dai,* the once-ubiquitous national dress, is conspicuous by its absence here and has been replaced by sleeveless blouses and T-shirts. At least the local paper still calls itself *Saigon,* and the beer is still Saigon Export."

Returning to their hotel, they passed Notre Dame Cathedral; Mass was about to begin. All around them people knelt in prayer, and the air was full of incense. It was incredibly peaceful.

They lit candles and sat down. Bryan took Sandy's hand, looked at him, and said, "There seems to be a lifting of something that I can't quite describe. A sense of freedom. A letting go. It seems so painless now. I feel that I'm awakening from a deep sleep."

Sandy squeezed his hand in silent response.

They both concurred that it had been a good day—the first of the Lunar New Year—and according to Vietnamese tradition, if good things happened on the first day, then the entire following year would be good. Such a contrast to 1968 when Greg was killed and Bryan lost his memory and left Tuyet, not to see her again for many years.

It was a bright, sunny day, and they joined a tour to the Cu Chi tunnels that took them past the rubber plantations and surprisingly few forests. Originally the whole of Vietnam had been covered with dense forests. Now the forest edges were receding largely due to firewood collection exceeding regeneration and forest fires, which were more savage because of all the deadwood of trees killed by Agent Orange.

"Seeing this rubber plantation with the trees in perfect rows reminds me of how Tuyet described her parents' plantation outside Saigon. I often wonder what happened to it after they returned to Paris."

The Cu Chi tunnels were an amazing network of over 150 miles, constructed by the Communist resistance. The complex included kitchens, meeting rooms, field hospitals, weapon factories, booby traps, and escape routes.

Suddenly there was a sound of rifle fire as they made their way through overgrown vegetation. Bryan felt the same fear as he had that night at the villa when the VC were outside. It was only the local rifle club practicing, but he and Sandy were both glad to leave and return to the city.

At dinner, Bryan sat in quiet contemplation.

"Where are you, Bryan?"

Bryan didn't respond, and Sandy left him alone with his thoughts. It was their last night in Vietnam, and he understood.

When they awoke early the next day, Bryan was quite chirpy. "I'm looking forward to Cambodia. It will be a pristine place with no memories. I think of it as a blank page, a place to create memories."

"Well, you know that I have always wanted to go there, but I also hope that the visit might diminish the trauma of your return to Vietnam."

"I feel a peculiar sadness at leaving, but I'm not sure why. Seeing the sign at Tan Son Nhat International Airport again reminded me of the time Greg and I left to return to Tuyet. I feel that an attachment is being broken."

Sandy could see that a real agony was beginning to fester in Bryan and knew that a great depression would come over him. The pattern was now familiar to him: Bryan drifted in and out of time, and the moments became more repetitive and proximal—sure signs that an inconsolable despondency was imminent.

Once in Cambodia they rose at five thirty to see the sunrise over Angkor Wat—the largest religious structure ever built and one of the most important temples in Angkor. This was Sandy's dream come true.

Bryan was enamored with the temple's majestic spires and unique bas-reliefs, which created a fusion of magnificence. Angkor Wat was the only temple in Angkor to face westward, and its main entrance was resplendent—the setting sun and death. Their visit to Ta Prohm was awe inspiring. It was a formidable monument to the lost city of Angkor, left as it had been found, with dense, all-consuming jungle vegetation creeping jealously over its walls and its floors torn apart by the roots of huge trees that towered overhead, their leaves filtering the sunlight.

Only birdsong and the chirping of crickets broke the silence. The experience of man's own magnificent creation in stark juxtaposition with the power of nature was tremendous.

"It has been a wonderful day, sharing an architectural marvel with you, Sandy. I have been totally absorbed in Cambodia's national treasure. I'm actually living in today. Thank you. Now I have the strength to return to Washington and put closure to my past and look forward to a future with you."

39

ARLINGTON CEMETERY, VIRGINIA, AUGUST 1993

Bryan was awakened by the telephone. "Hi, Radnor. How are you? Any news?"

"Hi, Bryan. Sorry it has taken so long to get back to you. It took a while to obtain a certificate of cremation and to determine Greg's eligibility before I could schedule the interment, but all the arrangements have been made now for the burial at Arlington. The grave site will be assigned the afternoon before the interment service, and the final farewell at the wall will be on August 13 at eleven o'clock. A military chaplain will be arranged by the cemetery staff, and I have applied for a burial flag. I have also notified the senator, and we will all meet one half hour prior to the scheduled service time. We'll be required to drive from the administration building to the grave site. All documentation of Greg's military service has been submitted."

"Thank you, Radnor. I cannot believe that after all these years the finality is so imminent. You have been a good friend, and I cannot thank you enough for making all this possible—for me, Tuyet, Gabriel, and Greg's family. For me personally, I can now move on and start living my life to the full in the secure knowledge that I have the love and support of my family and friends, which I had not really appreciated until now. I hope that I'm not too late."

"Bryan, real friends are always there for you."

"I know. Thanks again, Rad. I'll see you on the twelfth. Take care."

Greg's last trip home had begun at Hanoi airport, where a C-141 transporter had stood ready. The porcelain casket containing his remains had been placed in an orange box, which had then been placed in a metal container and saluted by American military officers.

Now the day of Greg's interment had arrived. The morning was overcast with heavy humidity and sporadic rain, which seemed to epitomize both the emotion and the forthcoming ceremony. This was just where Greg's family, Bryan, and Radnor had wanted him to go, borne to his appointed place in Arlington National Cemetery by an honor guard amid the salutes and solemn ritual reserved for fallen servicemen.

Military officials gave Greg's medals to Senator Seaton in a ceremony before the burial. Senator and Mrs. Seaton; Greg's sister, Laurice, and Anthony, her husband; Gabriel and his fiancée, Lois; Radnor; Bryan and Sandy; and other family members and friends gathered in the cemetery's main administration building before returning to their cars for the funeral procession to the grave site. At the appointed hour, the hearse drew up in front of the building, and the convoy of cars resolutely followed, passing symmetrical rows of headstones. Life seemed to drain out of them as they left their cars and trudged across a field of arid grass. They followed the quick tramp of the six honor guards who carried the casket from the hearse to the grave site, led by the chaplain.

The casket was set down, and the flag was meticulously stretched, centered, and leveled over it. The chaplain said the words of commendation and benediction, thereby concluding the interment service. The honor guard rapped out three salvos. Bryan's head was bowed, his eyes shut tight. At the ethereal sound of taps from the bugler, many began to weep. The honor guard folded the flag on top of the casket into a neat triangle, displaying only the stars. A soldier presented the flag to his sergeant, the sergeant to the chaplain, and the chaplain to Ellen Seaton, who accepted it with a stifled cry, at which the senator embraced her to ease her and his own regretted pain. In turn, Greg's parents, Gabriel, Radnor, and then Bryan rose from their seats to touch the casket. With that acknowledgment, Gregory Taylor Seaton joined the serried ranks of the dead, and liberation began for them all.

For the senator, he had made his peace. For Ellen, her son had been returned to his mother. Gabriel's unanswered mystery had been expunged. Radnor's pursuit of the truth had been resolved, and Bryan had been liberated from his past.

VIETNAM VETERANS MEMORIAL, WASHINGTON, DC, AUGUST 1993

Even the heat of the summer's sweltering day could not distract Bryan and Radnor from the personal pain that filled them as they made their way to the facade of the memorial.

Bryan thought how strange that this memorial, hidden from view with its curious location and design, seemed to endure as a symbol of shame for America's involvement in the Vietnam War. This dishonor, once held in the past, had made its way to the present. A discredited event all shared, each side contributing to this great tragedy, from the brave warriors to those who had been genuine and pseudo consciences of the nation.

Two worlds, in conflict over the war's morality, collided. Their individual beliefs had been sacrificed for a hollow triumph. With their fervor and determination they'd undermined each other in turn, thereby attributing architects to the wall of the dead—all in search of a truth that was in reality invisible, or visible only through the eyes of the believer. Bryan recalled the agony of Tuyet and the new moon and her profound comment "Truth, like the invisible moon, is elusive." The memorial had grown out of a need to heal the nation's wounds as

America struggled to reconcile different moral and political points of view. In fact, the memorial had been conceived and designed to make no political statement whatsoever about the war. Maya Ying Lin, the designer of the memorial, had said, "This memorial is for those who have died, and for us to remember them."

"It's hard to believe that I haven't visited the wall. You'd think I would have with all the time I've spent in this city," Radnor said as he walked to the book of names encased in a bronze pedestal. "I must admit it's been very hard."

"I can understand. I've been here many times and have to avoid the panel with Greg's name. It's really hard for me too."

"But it's time to do this for us and for Gabriel," Radnor said while he turned the pages of names. "Here it is." He paused, took a deep breath, and, quoting from the page, whispered, "Gregory T. Seaton. Rank: PO3. Petty Officer 3rd class; SVC: NA. Service Navy; Date of birth: January 29, 1945. Date of casualty: January 31, 1968. City: Charlottesville. State: Virginia. Panel Number: 40E, line 30."

"I see it," Bryan said softly, looking at the book. The name seemed to become so magnified that all the pain he had associated with Greg for all these years was reawakened within him.

"Here's the senator," Radnor said as he placed his arm around Bryan, lightly punching him on the shoulder in a gesture to be strong.

"Senator Seaton."

"Radnor, it's good to see you again." They shook hands. "Bryan, how are you? I'm glad to have this opportunity to thank you both for bringing our son home and for putting him to rest."

"Senator and Mrs. Seaton, believe me—it was not so difficult in the end. He was my friend, and I loved him. With your warm acceptance of Gabriel you have already thanked me. I'm sorry that Tuyet was not able to be here, but it might have been somewhat awkward for her in this political climate. Talking about political, how are you able to deal with the circumstances revolving around Gabriel? The press and your opponents will have a field day once this is made public."

"Bryan, I have always put my political career first. It cost me a son and caused me a pain that continually haunts me. If my constituency cannot accept my son's past, then my willingness to accept a crushing defeat at the polls will prove to me that I truly want to make things right with Gregory. I have been given something that many people never get—a second chance."

"You're right about that second chance. I have also been able to put this behind me."

Solemnly, they began the walk toward the eastern side of the wall: Bryan first, followed by Radnor, the senator, and then Ellen Seaton, supported by Gabriel. They made the descent in silence as they passed the first eight-inch panel of five names. The wall progressively soared until it was six feet of reflective black granite, submerging them in the inscriptions of these unsung combatants. Bryan turned to Radnor, whose eyes glistened, showing he was close to tears. Bryan placed an arm around his shoulders. As they cautiously proceeded, they passed people along the path who were touching the wall, tracing names, or placing tokens of remembrance along the wall of sable. Bryan stopped as he reached panel 40E. He scanned the rows of names until he located Greg's. He reached out and touched the stone, tracing the concave letters of Greg's name. The warm marble felt like the touch of living flesh—here was life. Bryan recalled their short life together in his heart and his thoughts as he glided his finger along each letter. He thought of 1968—that cataclysmic year with such far-reaching power that the present was now forced to relive it.

A newly carved diamond now replaced the cross of the missing and concluded Greg's name like a beacon. Bryan's eyes filled with tears, and his heart stung. Peace filled him at the realization that this tragedy was going to end at last. He watched his reflection retreat, and Greg's name rejoined the others on the wall. At his withdrawal, the others proceeded to conduct similar rituals of reverence.

As Bryan stepped back and turned to the left, his eyes rose to the vertex of the black granite wall. This was the meeting of the beginning and the ending, marking a significant epoch not only in American history but also in his life. Suddenly, in the distance, he noticed a slender figure. The distinct outline of the familiar physical features could only be that of Tuyet. She too had come to pay her last respects.

As she drew nearer, their eyes met. She continued walking toward him, pausing a few feet away from the top of the panel. As she stood there, motionless, a light breeze blew her hair. Once all black, her hair was now streaked with silver, but time could neither erase nor alter her beauty. Cascading to her waist, her hair reminded him of black silk embroidered with silver strands. They were all changing, but in their minds they replayed their youth, pristine in its perfection. Bryan realized her fight was not over. She had to make good the promise of the revolution. Tuyet and the revolution were synonymous.

For one brief moment, they were all reunited. Then, once again, she was forced to part from her beloved Greg and Gabriel.

Bryan couldn't help but recall the last time they'd all parted in Da Nang, when Greg had first acknowledged his love for her and shared his feelings about her for the first time. "I shall always think about her standing on the sand-covered pier, waving at us, my eyes fixed on her. That will remain with me forever," he had said. "Our lives go on while she remains untouched by the movement of time." A transformation seemed to take place as he reflected on Greg's words, and Tuyet's image seemed to be immobilized as he returned to the present. Then she withdrew from view, stepping back into the trees.

Bryan suddenly recollected the moment of Greg's death, which caused him to slowly kneel on one knee and drop his head into his hands.

Softly he said to himself, "Special, special Greg. It's finally over." He paused and then slowly concluded, "And you're home."